# THE BIG EYE

BY MAX EHRLICH

THE YEAR is 1960!

Russia and the United States are jockeying for position to plant the first atomic bomb.

New York airports are jam-packed with people fleeing the city.

The brilliant lights of Times Square are dimmed to an eerie glow.

Then Dr. David Hughes, young astronomer, is suddenly called away from a top-secret military conference to return to Palomar Observatory, where he and the rest of the world hear the terrifying announcement:

*Earth will be completely destroyed by collision with another planet in exactly two years!*

David finds some happiness with Carol Kenny, the girl he loves; and, ironically enough, the world is able, in the face of certain extinction, to solve the age-old problems of war, pestilence, and hunger.

The last day arrives. David and Carol go out to meet doom. And then—something happens! Not a miracle, but a wonderful and believable double-barreled surprise finish for this fast-paced yarn that is strictly edge-of-the-chair reading.

# MAX EHRLICH

is one of the top radio dramatists in New York. Born in Springfield, Massachusetts, he studied chemical engineering at Rensselaer Polytechnic Institute. When most of his papers and reports tended to become masterpieces of creative imagination but somewhat dubious contributions to scientific thought, Ehrlich promptly decided to become a writer—a decision in which his instructors apparently heartily concurred—and he transferred to the University of Michigan. He has never regretted the switch. Ehrlich has a record to date of more than 700 radio dramas and several television shows, all produced over national networks. He lives with his wife and two children in Oceanside, New York.

THE SCENE—Idlewild Airport

THE TIME—1960—on the eve of world atomic war!

*"I'm sorry. . . . We're sold out solid. . . . Every flight booked. . . . All booked up. . . . I'm sorry, I know you've got a priority, but we won't be able to accommodate you for weeks. . . . Yes, sir, if we get a cancellation we'll try to call you. . . . I'm sorry, madam, we're all booked up. . . ."*

The voices of the crowd were taut and tense and shrill. They rose and fell in a frightened, unnatural babel. They were urgent, they demanded, they wouldn't take no for an answer.

But the answer was always no.

No one was in the terminal to meet a plane. The airliners coming in from the North, the West, and South were all empty. Only those that were leaving the city were gorged with human freight. The Fear was upon the city and the people of the city. Every face in the terminal was stamped with it, branded with it, so that each was a carbon copy of every other face. The Fear was a kind of Personality, omnipotent, overshadowing all other personalities, making them neutral. It was written in the eyes of the people there, it quavered in their voices, it motivated their restless and agitated movements. It walked with them, stood with them, sat with them, like their own shadows.

It wasn't just a state of mind. It was a Presence. You could almost smell the Fear. It had feel and texture, like a stifling shroud. It had movement, too, like a slow, creeping paralysis, reaching clammy fingers into every nook and crevice of the building, permeating the place.

It was there, and it was inescapable. David felt it seep into his flesh and bones. His skin prickled a little; his mouth suddenly felt dry. He carried his bag to a phone booth and dialed a number.

"David! DAVID!"

MAX EHRLICH

GARDEN CITY, NEW YORK

DOUBLEDAY & COMPANY, INC.

*The characters and the incidents in this book
are entirely the product
of the author's imagination
and have no relation
to any person or event in real life.*

*To Doris, Amy, and Jane*

THE BIG EYE

**1.** It was eleven o'clock at night, in the month of November, in the year 1960.

The great stratocruiser, eastbound from California, slowly began to lose altitude. David Hughes shivered a little as he stared at the empty seats yawning ahead of him along the lower deck. His shiver was one of relief as much as anything else. Outside of the stewardess, he was the only passenger in the huge, luxurious belly of the plane, built to accommodate seventy. It had been an eerie experience to ride alone that way for almost three thousand miles.

In a few minutes the plane would dip and settle into a long glide for Idlewild Airport. And then he would be in New York—and with Carol again.

New York.

People spoke of the city in hushed tones these days. David remembered the startled look on the reservation clerk's face, back at Lindbergh Field in San Diego, some five hours ago.

"New York?"

The man had echoed the word, as if in a dream, as though he couldn't believe what he heard. When David turned toward the ramp leading through the gate, he had felt the man's curious eyes on his back. And when he had entered the plane, even the stewardess, a pert little redhead, had stared at him as though he were a little mad.

She had not expected any passengers. Not on the non-stop flight to New York. Not these days.

He had almost felt impelled to explain: "Look, I'm not out of my mind. I didn't expect to be on this plane myself a few hours ago. No one in his right mind would. But it's orders. Something big."

He clutched the bulging brief case close to him and thought of Carol. This was his chance. This was his chance to get her out of New York before it was too late.

The trouble was that it might be too late almost any hour now.

But all that was back on the Coast, five hours ago. Now he pressed his face against the window and looked down at the earth sliding by below. It was drowned in darkness, but this time it wasn't an ordinary kind of darkness. It was blacker, more suffocating. It was a darkness of Fear, of agonizing suspense, of anxious waiting for God knew what.

This was November, in the year 1960.

The stratocruiser's motors changed pitch, became a little louder. David glanced at his wrist watch—the watch his father had given him just before he had entered Harvard University for his Ph.D. in astronomy.

Eleven-three.

That would be eight-three, Coast time. And just about now, back home on the flat top of isolated Palomar Mountain, six thousand feet above the Pacific, things would be humming. The curved observatory dome would be down, and the great electric driving clock motors would be droning as they set the Big Eye and pointed it up into the thin, clear California air.

The Big Eye was the 200-inch reflector telescope, the biggest in the world, a gigantic marvel of steel and glass, encased in a building fifteen stories high. Working with it was part of David's nightly routine, and he was the envy of every other young research astronomer in the country. Yet he could never get used to the Big Eye; he could never get over his awe of it. Its great mirror alone weighed twenty tons. It could trap and hold the light of a candle sixteen thousand miles away in space. It was a million times sharper than the human eye, and ten thousand times more powerful that the little lens with which Galileo Galilei discovered the moons of Jupiter back in the seventeenth century. It reached twice as far into the hungry vault of the universe as its nearest competitor, far beyond the sun and the planets, into the outer boundaries of space itself.

This was the Big Eye, and it took a big man to run it.

David could almost see Dr. Dawson now, standing on the aerial platform, a pygmy on a dizzy flight, moving upward and outward on curving rails toward the mouth of the giant telescope.

Or perhaps he had already gone down the pipe-rail ladder leading into the top of the yawning tube and was not at his instrument desk in the cisternlike observer's cage. Huddled in his fur coat, heavy gloves, and pull-over wool hat, he would look like some futuristic gnome crouched at the tiny revolving desk up in the top of the Big Eye. It was cold up there in the dome when the roof was down, and the sharp night air blasted downward and in.

David could almost hear the Old Man's gentle, detached voice over the telephone coming to him as he stood at the control switch-boards on the lower tier.

"All right, David. All short settings tonight. Give me the first star."

This was his boss, the man who had taken him out of the Harvard Observatory three years ago and brought him to Palomar. This was the man they called the Wizard of Palomar, a world-famous celebrity in his own right, whose personal arena stretched two billion light years into the outer limits of the universe. This was Dr. Charles Dawson, the astronomers' astronomer, who spoke the language of Einstein, Eddington, Bohr, Thompson, Chadwick, Zwicky, and De Broglie; who did magic tricks with the mathematics of quantum mechanics; whose contributions to the theory of the expanding universe had won recognition and backing in the great observatories of the world.

Most people thought the Old Man never took the trouble to step off his airy eyrie at the top of the telescope and survey his own planet. They believed that to him the earth was a kind of globular platform, conveniently located so that, like an acrobat, he could plant his feet upon it and swing in an arc through space and stare at the heavens. The newspapers played him up as a cold fish, an ascetic with a special and remote kingdom of his own, a kind of sky giant to whom the interplay of earthy peoples seemed to be a disorderly and rather messy Lilliputian game.

But, reflected David, they didn't know the Old Man as he did.

In the past month something had happened to Dr. Dawson. He'd been absorbed about something he had caught in the Big Eye, something big, spending every night at the telescope and locking himself in his study almost every day. He hadn't told David what his research line was, but he would, all in good time. It was characteristic of the Old Man never to break anything, no matter how important it was, till he had it all down on photoplates and charts, signed, sealed, and delivered.

But there was no doubt about it. Something was in the wind back at Palomar—something big.

"Better fasten your safety belt, sir. We're coming in."

The voice of the stewardess, coming from the shadow in the rear of the cabin, startled him, pulled him abruptly out of his reverie. As if in response to her voice, the sign over the pilot's compartment flashed red: "Fasten Safety Belts—No Smoking." He fumbled with the clasp and felt the belt draw tight just as the stratocruiser hung in space for a moment and then dipped for the descent.

He looked down at the city of New York and drew in his breath at what he saw. He suddenly felt cold; a kind of dread possessed him. No wonder he hadn't been aware that they had reached their destination.

It was unbelievable, unbelievable. . . .

New York, at night, had always been a brilliant sight, man's best imitation of the galaxy of stars. It had always been a bejeweled riot, like a reclining dowager wearing a million diamond tiaras.

Now it was a great eerie blanket of darkness, with only a few illuminated islands breaking through the forbidding expanse.

Mechanically David picked out the islands. The Telecast Building way downtown, a hundred and twenty stories high and the biggest of them all, was still a cluster of light. So was Radio City. But the Empire State Building had only a red cylindrical glow on its top-mast to identify it. Some of the main thoroughfares were dimly lit, crisscrossing through the darkness like chains of old gold. As for the rest of the city, there was a solitary light here, another there, and the occasional flicker of automobile headlights crawling along.

That was all.

The stewardess came down from the lounge on the upper deck and moved forward up the aisle. She watched her only passenger covertly as she did so, trying to figure him out. She was a woman, and curious, and she was wondering why he was going to New York now, of all times. She had tried to draw him out in the rather desultory conversation they had exchanged on the way in, but he had been very vague. Perhaps it was something in the brief case he guarded so jealously. She had offered to take it from him when he had boarded the plane back in Dago. But he had refused to let go of it, despite the fact that there were no other passengers.

Something Very Important, she decided.

Still, he didn't look important. The name on his baggage tag had read simply: "David Hughes. Palomar Observatory." If he *was* an astronomer, he certainly didn't look it, not the way she'd pictured the type. He was young, for one thing, about thirty, and good-looking in a quiet sort of way. There was nothing tweedy about him, he didn't wear a Vandyke beard, he didn't need a haircut, and he didn't wear glasses, as you might expect of a scientist. Or at least what you had been taught to expect from the television screen or the movies. He was tall, with a pair of good, broad shoulders, and his clothes were as well cut as those of any of the young men of Hollywood-to-New-York-and-return, who used to ride her flight.

Now the stewardess leaned over and looked out of the window in front of him and said: "The lights get fewer every trip."

"Many people left in the city, Stewardess?"

"Very few, outside of the soldiers. Most New Yorkers, especially those with somewhere to go out in the country, have left. They really started to evacuate about a month ago." She straightened, and now David Hughes saw that there was a flicker of fear in her eyes. "We're canceling all New York-bound flights in a couple of weeks. I hope nothing happens—before then."

He stared back through the window again. "Funny. About the lights, I mean. They used to warn you that you were coming into the city long before you got there. Now—it just jumps right up at you all of a sudden. This is worse than the brownout."

"Brownout?"

"Oh." He glanced at the stewardess. "You wouldn't remember. It was during the last war. I was just a kid then, and my dad and I flew to Chicago from the old field—La Guardia. They had the curtains drawn, and we weren't supposed to look out, but, well—being a youngster, I peeked. They'd dimmed the lights—afraid of air raids—and the city looked pretty dull. But this?"

Idlewild Airport came up suddenly, a huge white wash of light directly ahead and below. A minute or two later, David, unable to find a porter, was carrying his bag up the wind-swept ramp and into the terminal.

Coming out of the night and into the building was like walking into a frightened beehive. The place was jammed with an excited, nervous crowd. Nobody seemed to be sitting down; everyone was milling about. People were crowded around the reservation counters, their faces strained and eager, trying to get passage out of the city. And always the refrain of the weary ticket clerks:

*"I'm sorry. . . . We're sold out solid. . . . Every flight booked. . . . All booked up. . . . I'm sorry, I know you've got a priority, but we won't be able to accommodate you for weeks. . . . Yes, sir, if we get a cancellation we'll try to call you. . . . I'm sorry, madam, we're all booked up. . . ."*

The voices of the crowd were taut and tense and shrill. They rose and fell in a frightened, unnatural babel. They were urgent, they demanded, they wouldn't take no for an answer.

But the answer was always no.

No one was in the terminal to meet a plane. The airliners coming in from the North, the West, and South were all empty. Only those that were leaving the city were gorged with human freight. The Fear was upon the city and the people of the city. Every face in the terminal was stamped with it, branded with it, so that each was a carbon copy of every other face. The Fear was a kind of Personality, omnipotent, overshadowing all other personalities, making them neutral. It was written in the eyes of the people there, it quavered in their voices, it motivated their restless and agitated movements. It walked with them, stood with them, sat with them, like their own shadows.

It wasn't just a state of mind. It was a Presence. You could almost smell the Fear. It had feel and texture, like a stifling shroud. It had movement, too, like a slow, creeping paralysis, reaching clammy fingers into every nook and crevice of the building, permeating the place.

It was there, and it was inescapable. David felt it seep into his flesh and bones. His skin prickled a little; his mouth suddenly felt dry. He carried his bag to a phone booth and dialed a number.

"David! DAVID!"

It was good, hearing her voice again. He felt a surge of quick hunger. It had been lonely at the observatory, damned lonely. Three months straight, working nights and sleeping days, without a woman. Three months straight—without Carol.

"Where are you?" She was breathless, almost incoherent. "David, what on earth are you doing in New York? Where are you?"

"At Idlewild Airport. Just got off the plane. I was afraid you'd be down at the studios, broadcasting."

"I just got in, darling. This very minute. The phone rang—and there *you* were. But what are you doing in New York, of all places, *now?*"

David hesitated. His free hand tightened on his brief case in a kind of muscular reflex brought about by Carol's question. He couldn't tell her, he couldn't tell anyone. He had strict orders. Security. He was there for a reason, a reason so big that it frightened him when he even thought about it. He evaded Carol's question. But she was insistent.

"Darling, what are you so mysterious about?"

"I can't tell you."

There was a pause at the other end of the wire. "Oh," she said finally. "It's hush-hush."

"Something like that. But that's only one reason I'm in town. The other is you, Carol. I've been writing and writing you to come to the Coast. Now I'm going to take you back with me."

"But, David, I told you why I can't go. You know why I've got to stay——"

"Yes, I know," he interrupted. "But enough's enough. When I fly back I'm taking you with me, and that's final!"

She was silent for a moment. Then: "We'll talk about it when you get here, darling. And, David, David, don't stop anywhere, for anything. Come right up to the apartment."

"Okay. But what about a hotel?"

"I'll make reservations for you at the Rutherford. You can check in there later."

"The Rutherford? Never heard of it."

"It's a small hotel—one of the few still open in town. All the big ones are closed and boarded up—the Waldorf, the Park Central, the Ambassador. They've been closing in droves for the last month, ever since the trouble began. And, David——"

"Yes?"

"Try to get a cab up here. There's no other way to get around, unless you walk. The subways and busses stopped running a week ago. And oh—you'll have to walk up ten flights."

"I will? Why?"

"Our elevator man quit on Wednesday. He's visiting a second cousin somewhere out in Kansas." She tried hard to be light. "Everybody's digging up distant relatives out in the country these days."

He laughed and said he was only thirty and he thought he could make the ten flights in slow stages, and hung up. Then he walked through the terminal and out of the gate. A big black air-line limousine waited for him, to take him to the Forty-second Street terminal. The other limousines, coming from the city, were loaded with passengers. But he was the only passenger in his car, headed for New York.

The driver, a big, beefy, red-faced man, raised the telephone receiver on the dashboard and spoke briefly to the terminal in town. Then he swung the big black car onto the Van Wyck Expressway and gave it the gas. Theirs was the only car in the right-hand lane, and they raced along at high speed. But the other lane, moving away from the city, was clogged with cars, bumper to bumper. Horns honked continuously, and the drivers cut in and out of traffic.

They're all going in the same direction, away from town, thought David, and they're all in a hell of a hurry.

He stared at the long line of headlights hugging the curves of the parkway like a great illuminated snake.

"They've been heading out on Long Island like this for days," said the driver. "Anywhere, so long as it's away from the city. Babylon, Sayville, Southampton, Montauk Point—the further, the better. You'll find the same kind of traffic moving into Jersey, up into New England and New York State. And I don't blame 'em."

"Still, you seem to be sticking it out," said David.

"Yeah." The driver lit a cigarette, and his fingers trembled a little. "But don't get me wrong, mister. I'm just as scared as they are. The company's giving me triple pay for staying on the job, and they flew my wife and three kids out of town, but I'm going to quit in a couple of days anyway. I don't like money enough to stick my neck out like this."

David glanced at the driver's face. It had that same taut, tense look, the same haunted look he had seen at the airport. He felt a little queasy. He knew that the same look had settled on his own face now, like a cold gray mask.

You couldn't be here and not be afraid. Not now. . . .

He tried hard to be casual. "Where are they going to find room for all these people?"

The driver shrugged. "I don't know. You take the island here now, mister. It's jammed with extra people, all from the city. Must be half a million of 'em anyway. They're living in shacks, out in the open, anywhere. It's sure a hell of a situation. They declared martial law out here yesterday."

"That bad, eh?"

"Yeah. And worse in the city. They've got a couple of Army divisions in there now. Just to keep order. But as soon as everybody's out, I figure they'll move the soldiers out. As it is, they're sitting ducks right now." The driver shook his head. "You know about all the rumors flying around these days, the funny things happening that nobody can explain. You know who's behind it as well as I do, and what they're leading up to."

Yes, thought David, I know. That's why I'm here now. And that's why I won't be here tomorrow morning. His fingers seemed to perspire damply on the leather of his brief case as he caught the eye of the driver in the reflector mirror.

*If you knew what I knew, driver, you'd turn this big black limousine around and follow those other cars to wherever they were going, away from the city.*

The man at the wheel continued to talk. He was almost garrulous; he seemed grateful for someone to talk to. It was easy to guess that he had driven an empty car back to the main terminal time after time, that David's presence was a surprise.

"You take those GIs now," he said sympathetically. "Those poor bastards up ahead in town. A lot of 'em couldn't take it—went over the hill—deserted. They shot a couple of 'em last night." He shook his head. "I don't blame 'em for cracking up. It's the waiting that drives you nuts. It's beginning to get me too."

They continued down Van Wyck Expressway and into Queens Boulevard, racing by the slowly moving line of traffic on their left. David stared at the residential sections of Queens on each side of the main artery. They presented an eerie sight, a kind of macabre fantasy. They were like vast stone-and-wooden graveyards, dark and empty.

But the houses were not really empty. The Fear was there, living in every one of them. The only sign of movement was on the highway itself, the solid line of cars crawling along, bumper to bumper, impatient of delay, heading east—east and away.

The limousine sped across the Fifty-ninth Street bridge, into the silent and dark and dying city, and swung over to East River Drive. David looked hard at the black buildings and towers etched against the moon-washed sky. The few illuminated windows he could see were isolated, far apart, conspicuous in their loneliness.

And the Fear was the only tenant in these darkened office buildings too.

And then, at last, they passed the great area between Forty-eighth and Forty-second streets—the permanent headquarters of the United Nations.

With a kind of morbid fascination, David watched it slip by. There it was, the great international city within a city, the terraces, the auxiliary buildings and apartments, and finally, the main UN skyscraper itself.

The building towered there now, dark and empty and silent, a great massive mausoleum. It seemed to glower at them balefully as they went by. David fancied that the grass on the terraces now grew rank, and the hedges and foliage, once trim and clipped, would now be ragged and unkempt.

It was a symbol of failure now, a great empty House of the Dead, a house of shattered hopes, of the blighted dreams of mankind.

Back in 1946, when David had been a boy of sixteen, the delegates of the nations had first met on the site of the World's Fair and at Lake Success to bring about the salvation of humanity and the security of the world. There the giants of a decade and a half ago, Molotov, Byrnes, and Bevin, as well as the Greats and the near Greats of the other countries, had met to resolve what hitherto had been considered insoluble problems.

They had begun with fine words, and noble phrases, and good

intentions. But Byrnes and Molotov and Bevin had haggled and fought to begin with, and so had their successors, down through the years, here in this magnificent new setting on East River Drive. Marshall and Acheson, Stalin and Vishinsky, Truman, and now the President and *his* aides and advisers. They had all seen a vision in the beginning, but as time went on the vision had grown blurred and finally died, and at last it was gone. The cold war had grown colder with every passing day, and now it was ready to burst through the bottom of the thermometer.

And finally, a month ago, they had closed the magnificent buildings. The delegates had broken, pointing fingers at each other in recrimination, accusing each other of greed, of imperialism, of stubbornness, of bad faith. And they had broken irrevocably, and for good. The representatives had melted away and gone home, and they had closed the buildings and bolted the doors, and taken down the flags of the nations which had once flown proudly in the great courtyard, and abandoned it.

Now the UN stood there, a series of stone ghosts on East River Drive, seedy and unkempt, the symbol of a Great Failure.

And it had been the Great Failure that had brought about the Great Fear.

Now—*everyone* had the bomb.

Yes, thought David, *they* have it, and *we* have it. And where do we go from here? What now?

The driver turned and saw David staring back at the buildings. "Yeah, look at the joint," he said. "Many's the time I hauled these striped-pants diplomats from Idlewild to the UN. Big shots from all over the world. And where are they now? Hiding in caves, maybe, I dunno. All I know is we've got millions of dollars' worth of real estate back there, but it's not worth a nickel now."

"Maybe they'll open it again some day," suggested David hopefully. "Maybe they'll still be able to get together."

"You mean that conference the Secretary of State's having over in Russia right now?"

"Yes."

"Nuts," the driver snorted. "Not a chance. It's too late. People have gone crazy. They're set on blowing themselves up, and nobody's going to stop them. It's like watching a car without brakes rolling down a hill toward a cliff. Everybody's standing around, hollering 'Stop, stop,' but nobody's doing anything to stop it. The only question is, who's going to blow up who?" The beefy man lowered his voice. "And between you and me, mister, the Russians have already started it. They've already started to give us the business right now."

"What do you mean?"

"You know what I mean. The stories that are going around. The Reds are supposed to have something extra, something that we haven't been able to figure out yet, and they're using it right now. Look at all the funny things that are happening all of a sudden. The earthquake in Dallas and another in Montreal. The way the television and radio has been blacking out all of a sudden."

David was silent for a moment. "And you think the Russians are responsible?"

"Who else?" The driver looked at him, a little incredulous. "Things like this don't happen all of a sudden, out of left field. The Reds have got something bigger, maybe better, than the bomb. That's what everybody is saying. What about that atom bomb that went off down in Texas? Blew three towns right off the map. You can't tell me that was any accident, mister. The Russians are jabbing at us now, trying to panic us and throw us off balance. And they'll be winding up for their Sunday punch any minute now."

David listened, fascinated. This air-line driver didn't know it, but he was putting his finger on the reason why he, David Hughes, was in New York right now with a locked and bulging brief case.

"And that ain't all, mister," said the man, leaning toward David confidentially. "I'll tell you something else, and it's straight from the horse's mouth. The Reds have found a way to stop our rockets and jets the minute they're airborne."

David stared at him. "That's just rumor."

"Yeah." The driver almost snarled at him. "Listen, mister. I'll let you in on a little secret. I drive this car for the air line. And naturally, once in a while, I drive pilots and some of the crews in to town. I've heard 'em talking in the back seat, and what they've said is enough to make a guy's hair stand on end."

"What do you mean?"

"I mean that the instruments on the stratocruisers have been going haywire, crazy. The radar, too. Some of the boys have had to navigate as blind as a bat. You think those crashes you've been reading about just *happened?* Nuts! The Reds *made* 'em happen. They've got some kind of magnetic gimmick in the air, and they've been turning it on and off. What do you think's going to happen to our jets and rockets if we let 'em go? They're all operated by instruments, aren't they? If we let a few go and the Russians use this gimmick, our stuff'll land in Siberia instead of in Moscow. Hell, maybe the Reds can make 'em turn right around and come back!"

David listened, stunned by what he heard. His face was impassive, but his mind was racing furiously. This air-line employee *knew.* He didn't realize how *much* he knew. David hadn't known it himself until early that evening. He had heard it from a source on a much higher level, and he would hear more about it tomorrow morning, at a meeting place he did not yet know.

He shuddered to think of the reaction, the panic, that would sweep the country if the information volunteered by the garrulous driver suddenly became widespread and public knowledge.

The man wheeled his limousine west, up Forty-second Street, and finally brought the car to a stop in front of the air-line terminal. And as he opened the door he growled:

"Those goddamn fools back there. Those diplomats. They should have kept trying. They should have sat down on their striped pants and *made* it work! The goddamn stupid fools!"

David left the car and went into the terminal to check his return reservations. One look was enough to discourage him. What he saw was a repeat performance of the terminal at Idlewild. The same milling crowd, the same weary clerks, the same babel of frightened voices:

*"But I've got to get out! I've got to! You've got to get me a reservation, clerk!"*

*"I've got Priority One. Right here. Doesn't that mean something?"*

*"Try the trains? What trains? Look through the window, clerk. They've closed the gates across the street at Grand Central and shut down the ticket windows!"*

*"Look, I've been down here two days, waiting for a cancellation. You can't tell me no cancellation has come through! One must have come through!"*

*"Listen, clerk, I've got a wife and daughter. I've got to get them out, I've got to! I'll take three seats on any plane, going anywhere, as long as it's out of town!"*

Yes, thought David, I've seen it before, heard it before.

The same voices, the same people with the same pale and frightened faces, surging forward toward the counters until they were checked and pushed back by grim, white-helmeted military police.

This was where the Fear was the most paralyzing, its hand the clammiest, its clutch the tightest.

This was the city.

David hung onto his bag and brief case, elbowed his way through the crowd, and rode down the escalator. He pushed the glass doors open and stepped out into the dark, wind-blown night.

For a moment he stood irresolute and stared west, up Forty-second Street. His skin prickled at what he saw. It was a sight that no man could ever forget, a memory that could never really fade.

The towering buildings rose on either side, their dark windows, like sightless eyes, looking down at the dimly lit canyon below. It was quiet here—strangely quiet—a place brooding, barely whispering with life, waiting to die. Not a vehicle was in sight, and the only sign of movement in the street itself was a few old newspapers which the wind had snatched from the gutter and propelled along the road. David could hear them rustle as they drifted along.

Finally one or two civilians and soldiers came along, huddled deep into their coats against the wind. The sharp click-clack of their heels on the sidewalk echoed and re-echoed dismally.

David turned up his own coat collar and walked west, toward Times Square.

He passed the darkened Fifth Avenue Library and suddenly became conscious that on his left there was a single dull red light hanging high in the sky, like a displaced moon. It was the glowing top of the Empire State Building. Finally, between Sixth and Broadway, he began to see signs of life. A taxicab and then two Army cars, their headlights slashing through the darkness. A few more people, a bar and grill open, a restaurant. They were dimly illuminated inside, and what patrons there were within seemed to be soldiers. Outside, the neon and electric signs, the great spectaculars, were dark—dead.

It's the biggest and the weirdest graveyard in the world, thought David.

David turned right at Times Square and walked up Broadway. He looked for a cab but saw none. Carol lived up on Cathedral Parkway, West 110th Street. And, as she had said, not even the subways were running.

There was nothing to do but walk.

This was the theater district. He could make out some of the darkened marquee signs—the hits that had been playing here not much longer than a month ago. *Stepping Along*—the big musical down the street on one side of the deserted Astor Hotel. *F.D.R.*— the biographical drama of a President whom many people still remembered and whose great dream had now gone up in smoke. There was a bit of grim irony, too, in a huge theater ad that said: *"The Narrow Alley* . . . A Great Tragedy . . . Coming Soon . . ."

"A Great Tragedy . . . Coming Soon . . ."

And then suddenly Times Square became suffused in an eerie glow—a bluish-white wash of light. Startled, David turned to look at the source.

It was a huge television screen, high up on the side of one of the buildings. One of the networks operated it as an advertisement, bringing the Broadway crowds athletic events, news, dramas, and political speeches. It had been an instant and tremendous success. David remembered reading, back in Palomar, that they had been forced to rope off the entire Times Square area while two hundred thousand people jammed the streets to watch the last world's heavyweight championship fight.

He blinked at the blinding light, and another memory stirred in him. The television screen was located on the exact spot where the big Camel cigarette sign once stood. As a boy he had been fascinated by the old sign. There had been a smiling man blowing smoke rings across Broadway. When the air was calm, the rings floated across like huge white doughnuts. But when it was windy, the man in the sign kept smiling, but all he could blow out were wispy puffs of smoke.

A small knot of pedestrians and soldiers stopped on a corner to stare at the screen, and David paused with them. For a moment he wondered why the television screen was working, since there were so few spectators. Then he realized that the same images would be seen on a network system, on millions of television sets from coast to coast, and that operating the sign would make little difference in the over-all cost. His mind slipped back to the observatory at Palomar for a moment. Francis, the steward, who had been with the Old Man for twenty years, would no doubt be taking in whatever this show was going to be on the set in the reception room on the main floor. Francis was a great video and radio fan.

The glare softened into a dull silver background, and then a title in red letters appeared:

## NEWS OF THE WORLD

The background dissolved into a scene showing a green-colored globe of the world spinning on its axis. Then came the voice of an invisible announcer:

*"News of the world! A five-minute documentary summary brought to you every night at this time by the GENERAL TEXTILE CORPORATION, makers of DOWNYSOFT blankets and DOWNYSOFT towels.*

*"And now, here is your telecaster—Arthur Morrow!"*

The spinning globe segued into a scene of a paneled study lined with bookshelves. A gray-haired man sat at a desk. He smiled at David and the others. Then the smile disappeared, and he looked professionally grim. He stared straight into the eyes of his watchers and then spoke.

*"Good evening. This is Arthur Morrow. Tonight the world waits and wonders. The tension grows, becomes almost unbearable. And on the end of everyone's tongue is the same terrible question: 'Will it come? Will it really come at last?' "*

The man on the screen leaned back in his leather chair, shook his head.

*"No one knows. We can only hope and pray that in this last desperate moment Man will come to his senses. Even now, at this very moment, Mr. William Allison, our Secretary of State and special envoy of the President, is on his way to the Kremlin to meet in extraordinary session with Mr. Bakhanov, the Foreign Minister of the Soviet Union. In a moment we hope to telecast this historic event for you direct from the new Kremlin at Kirensk, in Asiatic Russia. Permission for this strange raising of the censorship curtain comes from the Soviet government. It is their claim that they are doing this to illustrate to us, and to the world, that it, too, is willing to compromise. At any rate, they are making much of it in their propaganda line. . . ."*

Someone in the knot of spectators spoke up. It was a young soldier.

"So Allison's meeting Bakhanov. Geez, I hope they work out something!"

"I doubt it," said an older man. "Talk, talk, talk. Nothing but talk. That's all we've heard for years. The way it's going to end up, we'll talk ourselves into six feet under."

"Well, anyway," said the soldier, "nothing's gonna happen while they're sitting around a table."

"Oh no?" The older man laughed harshly. "Listen, sonny, ever hear of a man named Hull?"

"Hull?"

"Yeah. I guess you wouldn't remember, sonny. You were still pretty wet behind the ears. But Hull was our Secretary of State then. Back in '41, it was. He was sitting around a table with two Jap diplomats, and no one thought anything would happen. Not right then, anyway. Then all of a sudden—wham! Right in the middle of everything, the Japs let us have it at Pearl Harbor."

David listened and remembered. He'd been only eleven then. But he remembered his father, white-faced and shaking in anger, turning off the radio. He remembered the bewilderment, the surprise, the disbelief. The Stab in the Back, they had called it then.

David shivered a little as the gray-haired man on the screen went on:

*"It seems incredible that the peoples of the earth stand on the brink of holocaust tonight, that the lights have gone out in the great cities of the world. Tonight, like a great colossus, the Soviet Union stands astride Europe and Asia, while we have declared our defense responsibility through the whole of the Western Hemisphere, from Canada, through South America. Tonight the Soviet Union, as well as ourselves, has the bomb. And tonight the world waits for the zero hour—the hour that no one wants to come but everyone expects to come. . . ."*

A soldier on David's left muttered, "Yeah, it's the waiting. It's the waiting that's tough. It's the waiting that's driving everybody crazy."

"What I want to know is, Frank, what are *we* waiting for?" His companion was emphatic. "Why don't we throw it first, before they do? Somebody's going to throw it first, and it better be us. Or else . . . !"

"You can say that again." A sergeant was talking now. "Listen, you guys, I heard something, and it ain't from the latrine either. The Reds are supposed to have an atom cocktail planted in one of these here buildings, or down in the subway somewhere. I dunno, there may be ten of 'em, or a hundred, for all I know. They've got some kind of gadget where they can set 'em off from Moscow without getting off their fannies."

There was silence for a moment. The faces of the men looked white and set and unreal in the glare of the television screen. Then someone in the rear said:

"Maybe they're touching off a few rockets right now, headed F.O.B. New York. How the hell do *we* know? Why take a chance? Let's give it to 'em and get it over with!"

That was the popular opinion. Everyone said that when the pay-off came—not *if* it came, but *when* it came—New York would get it first.

It was the biggest city in the world, the prime target. It would make the loudest noise, illustrate the power of the enemy in the most potent manner, create the most dramatic devastation. Aside from Washington, which was now a ghost capital by orders of the Army, the big city had completed a state of evacuation much farther along than any other. It was possible that the Soviet *might* pick Detroit, or Chicago, or St. Louis, or Los Angeles, if they threw the first punch.

But everyone said, everyone whispered, New York. That was the one, the big one; that was where it would come first.

The telecaster up in the illuminated screen was saying:

*"In retrospect, the catastrophe that faces us now was not a matter of science, of atomic fission, of research or manufacturing techniques. It was a matter of the human mind, its ability to adjust itself to the fact that it had unleashed a terrible and*

*destructive power, and that men must either live with it, or be destroyed by it. But two decades were a pitifully short time to wipe away the accumulated mental debris, the accumulated prejudices and suspicions which had been bred in men for centuries. And we failed. For a while we thought we had succeeded. There was the United Nations, the various conferences of the Foreign Ministers at Washington, London, Paris, and Moscow. And after that the international control commissions and the nations' agreement to disarm. But then came the arguments over the veto power—the differences over the extent of inspection beyond national boundaries—the finger-pointing, the accusations of bad faith and subterfuge. And finally, the great blow—the dissolution of the United Nations—and separation.*

*"We might have succeeded, we could have succeeded with sincerity and mutual trust, and an awareness of how much we had to succeed.*

*"But we failed. And now, the world faces the consequences."*

A phone rang on the telecaster's desk. He picked up the receiver, listened a moment, nodded, and hung up.

Then he looked directly at David and the other men on the Broadway street corner and said simply:

*"We take you now to the new Kremlin in Kirensk, Russia."*

The television screen crackled, sputtered a little, faded, and finally blacked out. The darkness smothered David and the others huddled with him in an eerie, impenetrable blanket. They waited silently, shivering a little, listening to the sharp wind whining up the deserted side streets.

And then the glow came to the screen again and a voice with a Russian accent said:

*"This is Kirensk, capital of the Union of Socialist Soviet Republics."*

The screen showed a street in the Soviet capital in bright daylight. A crowd of people lined the curb, waiting impassively. They seemed quiet and well disciplined, not surging forward like American crowds. But perhaps the line of Red soldiers guarding the approach had something to do with their good behavior.

The invisible telecaster spoke briefly again:

> *"The crowd outside the new Kremlin awaits the coming of the American envoy, Mr. Allison, to confer with the Soviet Foreign Minister, Bakhanov."*

"Well, I'll be damned," commented the soldier named Frank. "Look at the people in that crowd. They look just like we do." He giggled nervously. "I swear to Christ, that big guy on the left with the fur hat looks just like my uncle Phil out in Detroit."

"Sure they look the same as we do," said the sergeant acidly. "What'd you expect 'em to have—horns?" He proffered a word of wisdom. "Hell, what's so tough about them? We can take 'em any time we want to, if you ask me. They put their legs in their pants legs one at a time just like we do, don't they?"

"Geez," a civilian said. "Look at their faces. What do you know? They're just as scared as *we* are!"

The voice of the Russian telecaster came again:

> *"Now the American envoy is arriving."*

An armored car came into view, bristling with Red Army men. It was followed by a huge black limousine, and another armored car followed the limousine. The camera moved with the procession. It stopped at a big gate in front of a building set back behind a wall. Soldiers pushed the onlookers away. A gray-faced man got out of the limousine, carrying a brief case. The gate opened, and he walked between two lines of grim Russian soldiers standing at attention. The gate closed behind him.

The Russian telecaster concluded:

> *"Thus the envoys of two great powers meet to confer in this great crisis. We of the Soviet Union want no war, and neither*

*does America, nor any of the other countries of the world. Let us hope that the envoy of your great country and mine come to an understanding on this historic occasion."*

That was the trouble, thought David. Everyone hoped the same thing, but nobody did anything about it. The grim game of waiting, the tension, could not go on forever. The fear of men for each other had been like a progressive madness, a subtle and cumulative poison seeping into the blood stream, and there was a limit to how much the patient could take, a limit to human endurance.

The scene shifted back to the United States, back into the paneled study again.

The gray-haired telecaster was at his desk, staring down at Times Square. He began to speak again, when a young man came from the left of the television screen and gave the man at the desk a note. He glanced at it briefly and then looked grimly at the men on the street corner:

*"I have a special bulletin here. Professor Albert Whaley, world-famous authority on atomic fission, and one of the scientists who aided in the preparation of the original Hiroshima bomb, committed suicide tonight. He was seventy years old."*

The telecaster paused for a moment. Then he nodded and smiled —a wooden, professional smile. You could see that his heart wasn't in it, that the smile was merely a signature, a way of signing off.

*"This is your telecaster, Arthur Morrow, speaking for the Downysoft Corporation and bidding you all—good night!"*

The paneled study swung around on a turntable and disappeared, and the commercial came onto the screen in colors. First there was a household scene. A motherly-looking woman opened the door of a linen closet and took a blue blanket from the top shelf. She examined the label and as she did, the camera panned down to the label—DOWNYSOFT! The woman nodded, smiled, and shut the door.

An announcer crowed:

"*Yes—it's DOWNYSOFT—DOWNYSOFT blankets!*"

The camera followed the woman into a nursery. Tenderly she placed the blanket on a tousle-haired child sleeping in a crib. Then she caressed the blanket and smiled again.

The announcer said in an unctuous voice:

"*For that soft and intimate touch—it's DOWNYSOFT. DOWNYSOFT blankets and DOWNYSOFT towels!*"

The first scene whirled out of sight on the turntable, and a new scene whirled in. This time it was the interior of an orchid-colored bathroom. A tall, lissome blonde who looked like the third from the left in a chorus line was standing in front of a glass-enclosed stall shower. She was dressed in a bright orange silk robe, and from the way it clung to her curvaceous body it was plain that she wore nothing else underneath. She turned to a small towel shelf and took out two towels. She hung them carefully on a rack, caressed them with her fingers, and smiled. The camera panned down to a close-up of the labels again.

Then the blonde began to take off her robe in a kind of televised strip tease. First there was a view of a smooth back, with the curved suggestion of the girl's breasts barely showing. Then, just as she dropped her robe, she opened the door of the stall shower and stepped behind it. She stood there for a moment in a side view, every feature of her body etched sharply in silhouette behind the translucent glass. Then she reached up and turned on the shower.

The announcer crowed again:

"*Yes! For that soft and intimate touch—it's always— DOWNYSOFT! DOWNYSOFT blankets and DOWNYSOFT towels!*"

The man on David's right spoke softly. "Soft and intimate touch is right. Oh, brother!"

"Geez!" said his companion. "Geez, Joe! That blonde! How would you like to have *that* little number?"

David felt a little sick in his stomach. He turned up his coat collar and started to walk up Broadway, his feet echoing dismally on the empty pavement, past the dull marquees, the empty boarded-up stores, the dead neon signs. The wind whistled down the darkened canyon, and its cold breath, too, smelled of the Fear.

**2.** At Columbus Circle, the traffic lights, blinking sentinels on the dark-shrouded, desolate streets, continued to operate stubbornly. As they went red, green, red, green, the click of their mechanism as they changed sounded abnormally loud in the brooding silence.

David Hughes watched the lights break into a long illuminated V, one arm of lights extending up Central Park West, another up Broadway. They changed in a kind of staggered beat and cadence, red and green, red and green, winking glassily in a ghostly and grotesque stone-and-steel fairyland.

It seemed fantastic to David that he was here now, in the city of New York, a lone pedestrian walking through a wind-swept graveyard, committed to the most dangerous and most important mission of his life.

Ten hours ago his day had started like any other day.

A rough hand shook David.

"Wake up, Dave."

Dave tried to push the hand away and draw the covers back over him. But the shaking persisted, and finally he opened his eyes to look sleepily at the grinning, freckled face of his roommate, Joe Morgan.

"Rise and shine, Reverend," said Morgan. "Time the priest was preparing for the pulpit."

Morgan, a long string bean of a man with a constant grin under his sandy hair, was the spectrograph expert at Palomar. He had worked with David at the Harvard Observatory, later served a term at Yerkes, then at Mount Wilson, and finally hooked onto the Big Eye under the Old Man. Like David, he was a bachelor, and the two of them lived in the dormitory, an ascetic, monklike place of soundproofed walls and doors and black curtains, for men who slept all day and worked all night. They called the place the "Monastery" and each other "priests."

As for Morgan's reference to the "pulpit," that was David's special province. It was the nickname for the telescope control board, where David flicked switches or pushed buttons to turn the dome, open it, and swing the Big Eye onto a star, at the whim and direction of the Old Man up in the capsule at the top of the tube.

"Just came back from the observatory," said Morgan as David began to shave. "And the Old Man's acting mighty strange. Dave, what the hell is going on, anyway?"

"I don't know."

"You're his assistant," said Morgan. "You ought to know."

David turned to Morgan. "I'm just as much in the dark as you are. He hasn't told me a thing, and his own wife doesn't even know what he's up to. He's found something, Joe, I'm sure he has. But you know the Old Man, you know how he's acted about these things before. Until he gets it on the line, photographs, calculations, and theory, with a solid conclusion to go with it, everyone on the observatory staff can just keep on whistling."

Morgan lit a cigarette and flung the match into the wastebasket. "Maybe. But I think this is something big, Dave, much bigger than anything that's happened before. I've never seen the Old Man act like this. Working all night and all day, skipping meals, taking an hour or two of sleep when he's almost dead of exhaustion. You can almost see his cheekbones popping out from under his skin." He paused and threw away his cigarette. "You know what happened to me a little while ago at the observatory?"

"What?"

"I'm supposed to be the spectrograph man here. But I tried to get into the spectrograph room in the telescope girder, and it was locked. Had some plates there I wanted to see. The Old Man was in there, and he told me to go away. Go away, mind you! He sounded a little wild, like a jealous kid guarding a toy. I don't know, I've never heard him talk like that before."

David was thoughtful. "It could be the times, Joe. The trouble with Russia, everything. Everybody's snapping at each other these days. You couldn't find a calmer, more even-tempered man than Dr. Dawson. But the generals have been hounding him, running him ragged, for months."

"Yes, I know." Morgan spoke soberly now. "They've been taking the Old Man off his mountain every now and then, and he doesn't like it. That trip to New Mexico on the rocket-projectile thing—that Maryland job. He's kicked like a steer each time, but he's had to go. And those security guards they've got posted around the place. You'd think the Russians were going to drop paratroopers right through the dome."

David adjusted his tie. "Hear anything new on the saber-rattling up at the observatory, Joe?" He spoke casually, almost too casually.

Morgan shook his head. "Same old stuff. The fuse is lying right out there in the open, inviting somebody to light it. Francis had the radio on, and to hear the commentators tell about it, this little two-bit planet is scheduled to blow up any minute now." He grinned a little sickly. "It's funny."

"*What's* funny?"

"I don't know. Up here, on this nice, remote, clinically clean mountain, it's hard to get excited about this cold war. But I was down in San Diego last night—and it's different. The place is like a morgue, most of the lights are out. And that suits me fine!"

David stared at him, and Morgan grinned. "Professionally, I mean. Or, to repeat the old saying, it's an ill wind that blows no good. And I'll show you why." He reached into a box he had brought from the observatory and took out a number of photographic plates. "Here. Take a look at these, Dave. Developed 'em a couple of days ago."

David picked up a plate, looked at it. It didn't look like much, a few faint smudges of silver granules on a film of gelatin. "You haven't got it labeled, Joe. What is it?"

"Messier 31. One of our more skittish island universes, way about beyond the suburbs of our own star system. You see how clear it is?"

David nodded, and Morgan picked up another plate, gave it to him. "Here's the same thing, taken months ago, before the lights went out in Dago."

This spectrograph plate was fogged. "Mostly the scattered blue light of mercury," explained Morgan. "From the advertising signs in San Diego. It's been ruining our plates. Remember the last mess with the 100-inch eye at Mount Wilson? Los Angeles was growing too fast for the observatory there. The lights began to creep way out in the suburbs, making a nebula of their own and cluttering up the sky. That white, acrid haze they called smog climbed right over Mount Wilson, dimming the sky nebulae." David returned the plate to Morgan, and he restored it to the box. "And now we've got the same thing, Dave. San Diego's grown almost as big as Los Angeles in the last ten years, and conditions have been getting worse every day because of those damned lights."

"I know," said David. "I went down into Dago with the Old Man when he delivered a speech before the San Diego-California Club, complaining about the new neon and electric signs they were putting up. Asked them for an ordinance to stop it."

"And what did they say?"

"Oh, they were very polite about it. But they said the Old Man was asking too much, he was trying to stop progress."

"And what did the Old Man say?" asked Morgan.

David grinned. "You should have been there, Joe. It was wonderful. The Old Man really laid into 'em. Told them that if they were more interested in advertising sausages and soap and the latest movie epic than in finding out the secrets of the universe, then they could have it. If *that* was progress, he told them, he was going back to his mountain, where the air was clean, and never step off it again. Then he walked out."

"Well," said Morgan thoughtfully, "the Old Man got his wish about the lights. They've gone out here, and everywhere else, and God knows if anyone'll ever get a chance to turn 'em on again. And if *that's* progress," he added a little bitterly, "we'd better start retreating backward, damned quick!"

The phone rang, and David answered. It was Francis, the steward, calling from the observatory.

"Dr. Dawson wants you in his office right away, Dr. Hughes."

David frowned. It was only eleven-thirty in the morning, an unusual hour to get a call from the Old Man.

"What's up, Francis?"

"I don't know, sir." The steward sounded excited. "General Hawthorne is due here at any moment. He's flown in from the East, and it's some kind of extraordinary conference. I've never seen Dr. Dawson so agitated."

"And you're sure he wants me there?"

"Yes, Dr. Hughes. At once!"

Francis hung up, and David, puzzled, told his roommate briefly what had happened.

Morgan was impressed. "Sounds like big stuff, Dave. Hawthorne's head of military intelligence and the key figure in this whole cold war setup right now. If he says the Russians are about to let us have it, then we'll try to beat them to the punch. One word from him, one opinion, and the dynamite goes off, all hell breaks loose. And he wouldn't be traveling to Palomar, right in the middle of this witch's brew, just to pass the time of day."

David agreed soberly. "But this is high-echelon stuff. Why does the Old Man want *me* there?"

Morgan shrugged. "You're his first assistant—number one boy. And the Old Man must have his reasons. All I'm sure of is that this meeting isn't going to be a love feast. You know how the Old Man feels about Hawthorne and the rest of the brass. And that goes, vice versa."

A half-hour later David was closeted with the general and Dr. Dawson in the Old Man's study.

The general was a big, hulking man with the face and look of a bulldog. His ice-blue eyes were set deep in his square face, and they snapped whenever he spoke. He had made his reputation as a young colonel in G-2 during the last World War, the one they called World War II, back in the forties. In 1955, under the growing tension of the cold war, Congress had broken up the Civilian Commission for the Control of Atomic Energy, originally headed by David Lilienthal, and turned it over to the military.

It was then that Matt Hawthorne had been given four stars, and with it control not only of the whole atomic program, but of every scientist connected with it. In the next five years, because of the obvious integration of this function with the intelligence branch of the military, he had been authorized to mobilize and use, at his own discretion, the scientific brains of the United States in every field of endeavor.

David sat there, fascinated, and watched the two men, General Hawthorne and Dr. Dawson. The Old Man was sitting back in his chair behind the desk, watching the general clamp a cigar in his teeth as he paced up and down the room. Dr. Dawson looked small and almost frail behind the big desk, a man of sixty-five with a finely chiseled face cast almost in an ascetic mold and topped by a shock of tousled white hair. Now, in the light of the hooded lamp on the desk, David saw how gaunt the Old Man's face had become, how deep the shadows under his eyes, and how sharply etched the lines around his mouth. He's tired, thought David; he's got the look of a man almost unbearably weary, a man stretched taut and close to the breaking point. Only his eyes seemed to be very much alive against the pallor of his face. They were unnaturally bright, almost feverish and crackling in their intensity, and as they followed the general they were wary and hostile.

They're a couple of heavyweights, thought David, champions in their line, the best in the business. And they had already squared off; the very air in that quiet room was electric with their hostility. They had clashed brusquely, from the moment the general strode into Dr. Dawson's study, over the question of David's presence there.

"I told you over the phone that this was to be a private meeting over an extremely confidential matter," the general had snapped, glancing at David. "I don't think we want any third party present."

"Dr. Hughes is my assistant," Dr. Dawson said quietly. "He is here at my request, he knows the details of my work for the military, and he has my entire confidence. I think you can count on his discretion, General."

The general started to say something in protest. Then, with an impatient wave of the hand, he forfeited the point. It was plain that he had some larger matter of argument on his mind.

"Dr. Dawson," he began, "we have just established a new defense headquarters at an underground location not far from New York City. At eleven o'clock tomorrow morning there will be an extraordinary meeting of the General Staff and a select group of scientists. This meeting will be of the highest importance, and I want you to be there."

The Old Man stiffened. "May I ask what this meeting will be about, General?"

The general stopped his pacing. He flicked the ashes from his cigar, very deliberately, into an ash tray. Then he turned to the Old Man and looked him squarely in the eyes.

"We shall make a rather important decision," he said. "By noon we shall decide whether we will strike at the Soviet Union immediately, with every weapon in our arsenal—*or* wait for a few more days."

The room was quiet. David sat there, stunned, watching the Old Man sitting immobile behind his desk, the general staring at him. Suddenly David heard the grandfather clock in the corner of the study. It seemed to grow louder as he listened. Now it was abnor-

mally loud; it seemed to tick faster and faster, with an ac-
celerated metronomic beat. David resisted a crazy impulse to rise,
to smash the glass face of the clock, to rip the hands off, to stop
that loud and obscene beat, the thing it was saying, war or peace,
war or peace, war or peace.

War or peace. They or we. Strike or wait. War or peace.

The Old Man stirred. Finally he spoke, quietly, almost inaudibly.

"General Hawthorne, why are *we* forcing this decision? Our
policy is, and has been, not to strike in an undeclared war without
moral justification. The President himself, the State Department,
has promised the people that——"

"Bunk!" The general swung around the desk, leaned down,
stared belligerently at the Old Man. "Moral justification! Ethics!
Do you think the Soviets care a damn about nonsense like that?"
He stopped, and then said slowly and deliberately, "Besides, we
have plenty of moral justification—self-defense. What would you
say if I told you the Russians have already attacked us?"

The general paused dramatically. But if he expected a reaction
from the Old Man, he was disappointed. As for David, he had
half risen from his chair, fascinated with horror, watching General
Hawthorne.

"I have heard no evidence of any attack," the Old Man said.

"No," snapped the general. "No, you wouldn't. Not up here on
this mountaintop, maybe. But down in the cities, my dear Doctor,
down where people live, it's different. They're going crazy with
rumors, and some of these rumors are true. We're holding them
together by discipline, in some areas by martial law, and faced by
the threat of a national panic if the people really find out the truth."

"*What* truth, General?"

"I'll give it to you straight, Dr. Dawson. The fact is that the
Soviets have a secret weapon, some kind of new super weapon. We
don't know what it is, we have no countermeasures against it, all
we know is that they're throwing it against us in controlled doses
and have been doing so for the past month. They're using it as a
technique of cold war, trying to smash our morale, to demoralize

us and break us down, so that we'll listen to a deal—*their* deal!"
The general spat out the word. "But they may be in for a little
surprise. After we finish this East Coast meeting tomorrow, the
whole thing may boomerang back into their damned Red faces.
We've learned a few tricks of our own!"

He's good, thought David, watching the general. He's hard, and
he's ruthless, and he doesn't scare easily, and he knows his way
around. The Soviet propaganda had built up the Red soldier to
scarehead proportions, a man of physical might with a fanatic contempt of death. But watching General Hawthorne, under the circumstances, was strangely comforting. If there had to be a final
holocaust, thought David, it was the Hawthornes who would save
the country, or die trying, and the United States was lucky to have
them.

Dr. Dawson stuck to his point. "How do you know there *is* a new
Soviet weapon, General?" he said, almost dryly, as though he were
posing a question to some student in a lecture class. "What facts do
you have, what evidence?"

The general started to pace the floor again. "Dr. Dawson, in the
past month we have undergone a series of phenomena—unex-
plained phenomena, without any scientific rhyme or reason—freak
disasters. The earthquakes in various sections of the United States
where no tremors have ever been experienced before. The tidal
wave that rose out of the sea without warning, swamping Havana.

"These erratic changes in the internal pressures of the earth's
surface suggested something possibly astronomical, or cosmic, in
nature. We know that the top men in the Soviet, scientists like
Kavenoff and Malvik, have been working on this type of grand-
scale weapon for some time. They've drawn on the best brains of
their satellites, in addition—Ferenz of Hungary, Dubois of France,
Migliore of Italy, Peterson of Sweden, and Dietz of Germany."
General Hawthorne paused, looked steadily at the Old Man, and
then said with gentle irony: "And as you know, Doctor, we have
been conducting the same line of cosmic research ourselves, with
your own enthusiastic participation."

David glanced quickly at Dr. Dawson and remembered. First, the New Mexico job, and later, Maryland. Over the Old Man's violent protests they had dragged him off Palomar Mountain and bludgeoned him into the top post with the Ballistics Research Laboratory where his knowledge of measuring the speeds of galaxies had been applied to measuring the speeds of projectiles. David had gone along on both trips. He had participated in all details, and he knew how much the Old Man hated the whole setup.

But Dr. Dawson ignored the general's thrust and asked:

"About these phenomena, General. Do you know whether similar ones have taken place in the Soviet Union?"

The general grunted. "If they have, I haven't heard anything about it. Neither have our agents. Anyway, a field mouse couldn't get through the Iron Curtain these days. But aside from that, my dear Doctor, the question is academic. Why should these disasters happen in Russia? If the Russians have this new weapon, they obviously wouldn't be using it on themselves."

"Obviously not, assuming that your arbitrary assumption is correct, assuming that they *do* have some kind of weapon."

General Hawthorne exploded. "There's no doubt about it! You can indulge in the luxury of scientific skepticism all you want, Doctor, but I'm a realist, and I know what I'm talking about. And the last two weeks have proved me right."

The general's jaw set in a hard block as he went on: "In the last two weeks, Doctor, the Reds have stepped up their damned offensive. They've begun to hit us in the belly, where it hurts, in ways that the public doesn't know about yet, thank God. Last Monday a flight of long-range jets set out for a routine flight over the North Pole. Their instruments suddenly went out, they lost communication with their base, and we never heard from them again."

The Old Man leaned forward now. He became tense, interested in what General Hawthorne had to say; he seemed to hang on every word.

"This weapon of theirs, we have discovered, can deflect and sabotage magnetic instruments," continued the general. "We've noted fluctuations in our own magnetic equipment from time to time. Our air navigators and pilots have been losing their directional beams, they've been going far off their course, their radar has ceased to function." The general paused. "You can see what effect that would have on our A-projectiles, my dear Doctor, on our rockets, on our air force. Apparently the Reds have found a way to deflect them at will."

The Old Man was silent, but his bright eyes betrayed his interest. Finally he said:

"And this meeting on the East Coast tomorrow morning, General?"

"We're going to pool our brains and try to figure out just what the Russians have. If you and the other scientists there can't figure it out, can't put it down to any naturalistic phenomena, then we have only one conclusion. The Reds have got something, and we've got to beat them to the punch." The general's face grew brick red, and he flung his cigar in the wastebasket. "If it was up to the General Staff and myself, we'd be throwing everything we have at the Soviet right now. But no! The President doesn't want to make any overt move. Neither does State. For the record," General Hawthorne snarled. "For the record. What the hell good is any record going to be in a couple of more days?"

David watched the Old Man as he rose from the desk. He seemed perplexed, as though trying to come to some inner decision. The general picked up his hat.

"That's all, Dr. Dawson. When you reach New York City tomorrow morning, phone military headquarters, R-Section. They'll pick you up and drive you to the meeting place."

The Old Man turned and then said slowly, "I'm sorry, General, but I'm not going."

"You're not *what?*"

"I'm not going," Dr. Dawson said levelly. "In the first place, I cannot morally be a party to any arrangement that may set off a world war. And in the second place, I am in the midst of a tremendously important piece of research here at Palomar——"

"Research be damned!" blazed the general. He slammed his hat down on the table. "Look here, Dawson, I've had enough of this nonsense from you and from those other fools you call your colleagues. You've sabotaged me every step of the way, like a pack of Reds."

The Old Man suddenly blazed back. "You know what I think of the Soviet system of government, General. You know how I despise it, what it's done to its men of science, how it's bent them to the will of the state. I hate anything that smacks of a totalitarian society. I am still technically a free citizen in a free democracy and not yet a member of the military. And I resent your inference that my colleagues and I——"

"Listen, Doctor, I'm not going to argue with you," Hawthorne interrupted. He pounded the table with his fist. "You're going to stop your stargazing for a few days, and you're going to get back down to earth and fly East and be at that meeting tomorrow morning. And those are orders!"

"I'm sorry, General," said the Old Man stubbornly. "I am willing to compromise and send my assistant, Dr. Hughes, here, in my place, provided he is willing to go. But I repeat, I cannot go myself —not now."

The general saw there was no moving the Old Man and changed his approach. His voice was suddenly very quiet.

"I warn you, Doctor this is treason."

"A matter of definition, General. It's *your* concept of treason."

"Suppose I told you that under the present military law it is conceivable that you could be shot for this."

"It would not change my mind, I assure you," the Old Man said calmly.

For a long time they stared at each other. Then finally General Hawthorne turned his cold blue eyes on David.

"We'll expect you at that meeting tomorrow morning, Hughes," he said curtly.

He put on his hat, turned, and walked from the room without looking back at the Old Man.

At Sixty-fifth Street a taxi swerved around the corner.

David hailed it, and it came to a stop with brakes squealing.

"One Hundred and Tenth Street, between Broadway and the Drive," he said, settling back. The driver made no attempt to operate his meter.

"That'll cost you ten bucks."

The man behind the wheel caught David's incredulous look through the reflector and turned.

"Ain't you heard, buddy? There's a war on. Now, is it a deal or ain't it?"

David nodded.

They drove through the darkened streets toward the place where Carol lived.

**3.**  He rang the bell, and Carol opened the door.

"David!"

Then she was in his arms. He could feel her body taut against his for a moment, then begin to tremble violently. Her nails bit into the back of his neck as he kissed her.

"David, David . . ."

Her body relaxed and blended into his now. He could feel the soft warmth of her; her lips inflamed him as she half cried, half laughed his name against his ear. After all, it had been three months since he'd last been East, since he'd last seen her.

He lifted her up, carried her into the room, and kissed her again.

Finally he set her down, and she said breathlessly: "Darling, darling, give me your coat and hat." She put them on a chair and turned back to him. "I'm not even going to bother hanging them up. Not now. Sit here, David, by the fireplace. Wait a minute, here's an ottoman for your legs; you have such long, long legs and you always like to lean them on something." She was excited now, nervous, all quick movement. "You've left the door open and your bag's still standing out in the hall. No, darling, don't move, I'll get it. Just sit here by the fire and don't go away. I've got scotch and soda ready in the kitchen—I know you never drink anything else."

He started to say something, but she put a finger on his lips and shook her head.

"No, David. Don't say anything. Not now. Not until I bring in the drinks and we can really sit down together. Not until I have a chance to really look at you again. Then we'll talk. . . ."

He watched her go into the tiny kitchenette, and he thought, She's coming back to Palomar with me. Tomorrow, right after that meeting, she's leaving this deathtrap and going back with me, if I have to beat her over the head and drag her with me.

He had written, wired, and telephoned her frantically to leave New York and come to the Coast. But Carol had refused, she had stayed on, she had business in New York. A talented and successful radio and television actress, she was making half-hour film television transcriptions for shipment to isolated military outposts. But more important, with her fluent knowledge of French and German, she was broadcasting short-wave to Occupied Europe.

The Department of Information was responsible for Carol's being in New York. The department, a super-streamlined agency, and a long cry from the old Office of War Information of World War II, had finally managed to tear itself away from the State Department. Now it stood on its own feet, its Secretary occupied a seat in the Cabinet, its power over all media was far-flung and virtually authoritative. It did not order an editorial line—not yet. It merely "suggested." But there was hard steel in the suggestions. And every day, in the temporary capital somewhere in the Middle West, the Secretary of Information lunched with the Secretary of National Defense.

"Information" had "suggested" that Carol and others like her volunteer for the hazardous New York post. It would be only temporary, the Secretary had pointed out. In another week the networks would complete the transfer of their entire New York radio and television operation to a new and emergency Radio City in Kansas.

David leaned back on the couch and listened to the clink of ice in glasses in the kitchenette. It was a relief to be here, in this warm and comfortable room, away from the graveyard outside. He looked about the room, noted that the furniture had been changed since he had last been in town three months ago. It was the new plastic and non-inflammable furniture—the kind they called "Modern Translucent." It was, he decided, a little too modern for his taste.

But then, he thought, he might have become a little stuffy, fallen behind the times, in his roost at Palomar. He could never quite understand how a lovely and talented girl like Carol could have fallen for a rather prosaic person like himself. True, he had a certain amount of prestige in his own field; he was first assistant to the Old Man himself.

But you couldn't eat prestige. And the fact that Carol made four or five times as much money as he did sometimes nagged him.

"David!" She spoke suddenly from the kitchenette. "I know you said you wouldn't tell me, but I just can't stand it. Why are you in New York *now?*"

"Military secret," he said lightly.

"Something in that brief case you brought in with you?"

"Yes."

"And you can't even tell your own wife?"

"You're not my wife yet." He grinned. "But that reminds me—there's something I *can* tell you." Then he paused dramatically. "I've found a place for us to live."

"David!" she cried out in delight. "No!"

"Yes! Right in the observatory colony. A cottage—fieldstone and white shingles, *and* two bathrooms. Wait'll you see it!"

"But, David, how on earth——?"

"Just one of those lucky breaks. That is, lucky for us—unlucky for someone else. The place belonged to one of our research associates—the man who ran the Schmidt camera. Anyway, he and his wife broke up, and they moved. He went to Lick Observatory, and she took the children and went back to her mother's. Anyway, there it is, all furnished and everything, waiting for our new name plate. We'll send out a hundred invitations for our housewarming."

She sounded surprised at that. "A hundred? Are there *that* many people at Palomar?"

"Sure. On the staff alone we've got four research associates, twenty-one research workers, and twelve computers. Not to mention their wives and children. And then there's all the other personnel—the cook, and steward, and chauffeurs, and engineers, and telescope mechanics." He listened to cupboards slamming and the pop of a soda bottle from the kitchenette. "But never mind that. What's taking you so long?"

"I'll be right in." A pause, and then: "David, did you *really* miss me?"

"Hurry up and come back in here," he said. "And I'll show you how much!"

She laughed. "Why, darling, you sound positively dangerous."

Maybe I do, he thought. He was one of the few bachelors at the observatory colony, and for him it was rather a lonely life. Palomar was a graduated society, in the manner of a small and isolated Army post, and its social life was restrained and somewhat clannish. Couples naturally entertained couples, and he was always the extra man.

As such, he was an irritant to the staff wives in the colony, and they had tried their hardest to marry him off, at least in the beginning. They had invited "friends" up from Los Angeles or elsewhere for week ends and thrown them into David's company.

Even Emily Dawson, the Old Man's wife, had made a special effort to marry David off. The Dawsons were childless, and when she learned that both David's parents were dead she had taken him under a motherly wing. She had a niece in San Francisco, and she'd brought the girl to Palomar just to meet him.

But the experiment had failed, and finally she had told David almost reproachfully:

"I had hopes for you and Ann, David. It would have done my old heart good to have you in the family. Why, I was even dreaming of a big wedding right here in my own house." Then she had shaken her patrician head and sighed. "I'm afraid you'll just have to bring this young lady, Carol, back to Palomar here, before we all burst a collective blood vessel!"

Now that he thought of it, he had spent most of his time with Dr. and Mrs. Dawson. It had been monastic, almost like living in a lighthouse without a woman. But there was blood running in his veins, good red blood, and sometimes, just before dawn, when the domed roof finally closed over the Big Eye like a great halved eyelid, his need of Carol had become a gnawing hunger.

Carol came in carrying a tray on which there was a bottle of scotch, soda, and glasses filled with cylindrical tubes of ice. David looked at the frozen cylinders curiously, then remembered seeing them advertised in magazines. They were a feature of the latest refrigerators—individual frozen ice tubes instead of the old and clumsy cubes. You merely pressed an ejector button in the refrigerator, and the ice tubes popped out, one by one. They fitted into a glass very neatly, one to a drink.

They think of something new every minute, thought David a little cynically.

Carol sat down beside him, gave him his drink. "How's His Eminence?"

"Who?"

"Dr. Dawson."

"Oh," grinned David. "Working his head off—on something big."

"What is it?"

He shrugged. "I don't know. The Old Man's keeping *this* one close to his chest."

"Poof!" She laughed at him. "I thought Dr. Dawson told you *everything!*"

He grinned back at her. "He usually does. But this time he hasn't seen fit to consult me and get the benefit of my vast experience. He never does till the job's all over." He put down his glass suddenly and looked at her. "But never mind the Old Man. It's been a long time, Carol. Come here."

They were in each other's arms again, and as David held her he thought, The hell with it all, the cold war, and the dark city outside, everything. It was bound to come; they could conceivably be blown up tomorrow, or now, tonight, at this moment, when he held Carol close. The world outside was complicated; you could worry yourself crazy just thinking about it, living in it.

This was the stuff, this was the idea, the way to live while living was good. A warm and comfortable room, the feel of a woman against your chest, and in your arms, and on your mouth, the touch of warm, throbbing, living flesh under the thin dress, the scent of her hair against your face, the sound of her tiny moans in your ear, the leaping, exciting hope that tonight, maybe tonight . . .

The phone rang.

It jangled with a kind of obscene insistence. It was an intruder there, unwelcome, coarse, inconsiderate. They did not stir, but it would not go away.

It rang again, and again, and again.

"David," whispered Carol. "David, let me go."

He released her finally, and she arose a little unsteadily. She smoothed her dress and walked toward the phone, and as she did, David thought shakily, She's lovely, she's wonderful. Everything about her—the way she walked, the way she talked with that low, husky voice of hers, the pale skin, the oval face, the way her jet-black hair was brushed up and back over her head, and her mouth, luscious and full.

Carol lifted the receiver, said: "Hello." She listened for a moment, and then:

"Dr. Hughes? Yes, he's here." She held the phone toward David. "It's long distance. Palomar calling."

"Palomar?"

He rose from the couch, suddenly worried. What had happened at the observatory? Why did they want him now? As he came to the phone Carol asked:

"How did they know you'd be here?"

"I told the steward he could locate me at your apartment, and if I wasn't here you'd know where to find me." He took the phone and said:

"This is David Hughes."

The operator told him to wait a moment. He heard a crisscross of vague filtered voices. Someone was trying to locate someone else in New York; someone wanted a St. Louis number. The voices were remote and mysterious; they began and were cut off abruptly, like disembodied wraiths.

David waited a full minute, then jiggled the receiver.

"Operator! Operator!"

The operator's voice came on again, told him to wait again, and he hung on impatiently. He glanced at his watch. One o'clock. That would be ten on the Coast. If it was clear, if the sky and seeing were good, the Old Man should be taking settings now, with Bill Forrester at the pulpit. . . .

The operator came on suddenly:

"Here's your party."

It was Francis, the steward. His voice sounded shaky, agitated; it was trembling.

"Dr. Hughes, Dr. Hughes!"

"Yes, Francis? This is Hughes. What——"

"Come back to Palomar at once. On the next plane. Dr. Dawson——"

Francis's voice was suddenly snapped off abruptly. There was a buzz, and the phone went dead. David swore, jiggled the receiver. The instrument buzzed again and then cleared; the phone was alive again for just an instant.

An operator spoke somewhere, very faint and very far away.

"Rio is ready for you, Palomar. Rio is waiting. We'll hold the Amsterdam circuit until——"

The operator's voice cut off. The phone went dead again.

What in hell was going on? thought David. Why were they calling Rio, Amsterdam, and God knows where, all of a sudden?

And why did Francis tell him to come back? Before his voice had been snatched off the circuit he had said something to David about the Old Man. But the Old Man had sent him on this mission; the Old Man knew he had to be at that meeting tomorrow morning, or else!

He got the New York operator, asked her to try Palomar. He told Carol briefly what Francis had said, and then he began to worry.

"I don't like it, Carol," he said. "Francis sounded like a scared rabbit. Maybe something's happened to the Old Man. His heart isn't any too good—angina—carries around nitroglycerin pills. Mrs. Dawson packs a vial of pills in every suit he's got, in his desk, and there's even a vial of the stuff up in the observer's cage at the top of the Eye. But the Old Man's pretty absent-minded; he's left 'em home more than once. And when he needs one of those pills under his tongue, he needs it fast!" He shook his head. "I don't know, Carol. He's been working his head off lately, and the generals have been running him ragged, and maybe his heart—maybe he's had a collapse. Otherwise, why would Francis sound the way he did?"

"David, you mustn't fret like that." Carol came over and twined her arm into his. "Perhaps it isn't Dr. Dawson at all. Those calls to Rio and Amsterdam you just told me about—maybe they mean something."

David jiggled the receiver, called for the operator. "This god-damned phone," he raged. "First they cut me off, and then I can't even get an operator!"

"The trouble's probably at the New York end, darling," said Carol. "They've only got a skeleton crew working. Most of the switchboard girls have left, and you can't blame them."

Finally an operator came on. She was maddeningly calm. She told David the circuits to California and to Palomar were busy. He begged her to get him through. She was properly sympathetic but very professional.

"I'll call you when we make the connection," she told David.

He paced up and down the floor, jittery, confused. He had to get through to Palomar, to get more details.

Francis had told him to come back, to take the first plane back. But there was that all-important meeting in the morning at military headquarters, wherever that was. He had some very important data in his brief case, and his presence would immediately be missed.

He was, in short, under orders to be there. From General Hawthorne. Maybe the Old Man was big enough to defy the top brass.

But *he* was only David Hughes.

And he could be slapped down, and hard, for not showing up at that conclave. It could mean a drumhead trial, a prison, a firing squad, maybe. In times like these they weren't too particular. The area between the civil and the military had faded into a nebulous no man's land.

No matter how much the Old Man protested that David had returned to the Coast under his, Dawson's, orders, an Army court would be sure to take the simple and disastrous view that General Matt Hawthorne, four stars, had ordered him to be there.

There was also another, and far more important, consequence.

Suppose the data in his brief case was valuable, *really* valuable?

Suppose the figures, diagrams, and conclusions, all neatly itemized on paper in his brief case, proved the key on which the men at the meeting made their decision?

Suppose, on the basis of what he was bringing to that all-important meeting in the morning, they decided to throw any further caution out of the window and strike at Russia immediately?

It was possible. It was horribly, damnably, and obviously possible that he, David Hughes, might be carrying the match for the fuse there in that shiny leather bag on Carol's table. By his not going to that meeting, by his failing to present that data and interpret it for the group, they might make a mistake and start the inferno.

Or, failing David's presence with vital information, they might make a different mistake and hold their attack, when the sound decision would be to strike. They might hold it a little too long, and the Soviet might beat them to it.

At this moment, David realized miserably, at this hellish moment, he was an unwilling giant on a world stage, carrying a hot torch he didn't want and couldn't handle.

It was too much, he thought. It was too much to ask of any one man. Even if the Old Man himself had asked him to come back.

*But had he?*

David didn't know, he wasn't sure. He didn't know whether the order for his return had actually come from the Old Man, or whether something had happened to Dr. Dawson, and Francis had called David on his own authority.

He turned suddenly to Carol. "Can I send a telegram out of New York?"

She shook her head. "The telegraph offices closed two weeks ago, David."

Then the only way to reach the Coast was by phone. The instrument lay on its cradle now, a black and shiny demon, grinning at him. The operator hadn't called him back. He yanked the phone up in a sweaty hand and tried again.

"I'm sorry, sir," the operator said. "All circuits to California are busy. I'll call you when we have one clear."

There was a faint note of irony in the operator's voice. She gave the impression that he'd be lucky if they phoned him back by morning. David frantically tried to explain that it was vital, an emergency.

She was sympathetic, she was sorry, but there was nothing she could do. What with the evacuation, with every relative trying to call every other relative, with most of the circuits already given over to the Army, there was nothing she could do.

She could only keep trying.

David slammed down the receiver.

"Sit down, darling," Carol said soothingly. "Sit down. Try not to worry for a while, David. Whatever it is, I'm sure everything will be all right."

She didn't know about the meeting, she didn't know on what kind of hook he was impaled. And he couldn't tell her. But she sat there, looking up at him and holding a fresh drink toward him.

He took the drink, had another. And another. Then he went to
the phone and tried to get Palomar again.

The operator was very sorry. The circuits were still busy, and
there was no way of telling when they would be free. There was no
point in David's calling every ten minutes; she would call him when
the lines were open again.

And finally David thought, The hell with it, the hell with everything. There's nothing I can do except wait.

And if worst comes to worst, if I hear nothing from Palomar, I'll
go to that meeting anyway, no matter what Francis said. I've *got*
to go!

But as he talked to Carol, as they sat close together, as the liquor
began to take hold, he recalled Francis's voice before it had been
cut off on the long lines, how it had shook and trembled, as though
he were terrified, and the fear that something had happened to the
Old Man nagged David like the throbbing of an exposed nerve.

He tried to forget it for a while. He asked Carol about the city,
about New York, what it had been like living there in the last few
months. Her face sobered, and she was suddenly afraid. He could
see it in the quick brightness of her eyes, in the drawn, taut look of
her face, in the sudden trembling of her fingers as she deliberately
crushed her cigarette in the ash tray.

Finally she took a deep breath and then she started to talk, as
though she'd been dying to talk to someone about it for a long time,
to get it off her chest. The words came tumbling out in quick,
rambling sentences, and as she went on they came faster and faster,
as though she were determined not to leave any space between
them, not to give the incipient hysteria a loophole in which to creep
in and take possession.

"Of course it's like a bad dream, David. You wouldn't believe it
—living here in the city now, I mean. It's simply fantastic. Even so,
you can get used to it after a while, in a way. When Mother was
alive—well, I remember what she used to say, 'You can get used to
hanging, if you hang long enough.' I don't know. Anyway, it's not

so bad during the day, really it isn't. It's the nights. Without the lights, the streets simply pitch-black—well, it's pretty nerve-racking. There've been all kinds of holdups and muggings. It's not that the authorities are trying to black the city out—that wouldn't do any good against those guided missiles or whatever they call them. It's just because they haven't enough men to run the power plants. That's why the subways and the els aren't running either, even if they had the men to run them. And food—David, you just can't imagine. You have to walk blocks before you can find a place that has anything to sell, and when you buy it, you pay fantastic prices. It's all black market, of course. People want to make money fast and get out before it's too late—and you pay ten times what food is really worth. Five dollars for a pound of butter, David. You can't get it for less anywhere, if you're lucky enough to find it. But if it's an apartment you want, that's different. They're just giving them away. A penthouse on Park Avenue—you can have it for the asking. It's ridiculous, David. There are just thousands of empty apartments going begging. People just left with what they could carry in a suitcase—left their furniture and everything behind. There aren't more than a few thousand people left in town, so you can imagine.

"Of course nothing makes sense any more. But I forget, there's the heating problem. Lucky for me this building is fairly new, and we have individual heating units for each apartment. The people left in the old buildings with a central heating system didn't get any heat, and so they simply moved to one of the new buildings—just like that. As for getting around the town—well, you know something about that, David, you already know how hard it is. The only way is a taxi—if you can find one. The drivers have thrown away their meters, and they charge you what they think you can afford, and of course they think you're all millionaires.

"And oh, the network studios—not to mention the Telecast Building—they're all madhouses now. You have to show your pass and wear a badge and go through the third degree at least five times, and show them your handbag to prove you haven't got an infernal machine in it, before you can get in to broadcast. It's insane, of course, but everyone's on edge; it's what they call Security. I know you think I'm mad to stay here, David, but we were asked to volunteer, at least until they set up new short-wave transmission studios in the Middle West. It won't be for much longer, darling, just another week, they say, and——"

She had averted her face from him ever since she started to talk. Now she stopped as he gently took her chin and turned her face up toward his.

Her eyes were blurred with tears, and they were scared, and suddenly she was in his arms.

*"David! Oh, David, David!"*

She was a terrified child, clinging to him, shaking violently in his arms, crying his name hysterically over and over. He held her tight, comforting her, soothing her, murmuring to her, pressing his lips against her cheek so that they became sticky with her tears.

It's all been building up in her, thought David; it's been building up for days and weeks.

Finally Carol drew away and wiped her eyes. "I'm sorry, darling. I'm sorry."

"Sorry for what?"

"For blowing up like that." She sat down and said faintly, a little ashamed, "I made up my mind I wouldn't cry, I wouldn't break down, I wouldn't get hysterical, like so many of the others. *Now—* look what happened!"

"You had it coming," said David. "Anybody would in a setup like this." He lit a cigarette and gave it to her. "But that's all over with now. You're going back to the Coast with me tomorrow."

She shook her head. "But, David, I can't."

"You're going back with me, and that's that!" he insisted. "I've got a plane reservation back tomorrow afternoon and a super-high priority in my pocket. I'll get another seat for you on that priority if I have to tear down the airport."

She tried to reason with him. "David, David, you don't understand. We promised to stay on the job; it's supposed to be important. The Department of Information says our broadcasts are getting through—to Europe. The people over there are hearing them, David, in spite of the Russians, in spite of everything——"

"To hell with all that," he said roughly. "It's too late for that boring-from-within propaganda stuff. They're all whistling in the wind. The blowoff'll come any hour now, and it won't be a question of propaganda, but of a lot of other weapons a million times more lethal. You've done enough, Carol; you've been here long enough, longer than anyone has a right to ask. After all, you haven't been drafted, you're just a volunteer——"

"That part of it doesn't matter, David." She was looking at him steadily, and it irritated him. He took the expression in her eyes as accusation and blazed at her.

"All right, all right, maybe I'm not a great patriot. Maybe I've no right to talk, sitting up on my nice, safe, remote mountaintop back at Palomar. But maybe I've got some information you don't know about, Carol. And I'm just not patriotic enough to let them murder my own fiancée." He walked about in a rage. "The damned fools! The crazy idiots running this government, and the Soviet government, and the others. If somebody could persuade these morons in striped pants to look upstairs for a minute and take a good long look at the stars, they'd find out that this infected speck of dust they call the earth isn't big enough to fight about, isn't worth the trouble——"

"David," she said gently. "You don't have to make a speech."

He looked at her, and suddenly he felt awkward and foolish, like an adolescent kid on a high school platform. I'm a little drunk, he thought, that's it, I'm a little drunk, and shooting off my mouth like a street-corner reformer.

Get off the soapbox, Hughes, get back to earth.

"Carol," he said, "all I know is that you're inviting suicide every minute you stay here. You've got to come back with me tomorrow."

She shook her head, and he knew it was final. "David, David, believe me, I'm not trying to be noble or anything like that. But I've *got* to do what I'm doing! I've *got* to go through with it!" She pulled him down to the couch with her and pressed her cheek against his. "Darling, darling, please, let's not quarrel. Not now."

She clung to him, and to David the room became a kind of blur, like a background out of focus, a hazy cubicle hemming them in. He was drunk now, drunk with the whisky, drunk with the feel and the scent of her, drunk with the warmth of her body against his, the perfume of her hair, the caress of her lips on his ear.

"David, will we really be married soon?"

"As soon as you get out to Palomar." He almost added "if."

She kissed the lobe of his ear again, his cheek, his throat, his mouth. He was afire with the feel of her, and he thought, I can't, Carol, I can't take any more of this. Carol, Carol, I can't take any more!

"What are we waiting for?" he whispered. "What are we waiting for?"

"No, David, no, darling, no."

She drew away from him, held him at arm's length, looked at him. It was perverse of her, he thought wildly, one of those baffling things women do without rhyme or reason. There was compassion in her eyes, but he resented it, he didn't want compassion now.

He could have fought it, tried to overwhelm her.

He could have shouted: "Now, now, or maybe it'll be never. Maybe there'll never be any tomorrow, or the day after tomorrow. Carol, for the love of God!"

But he didn't.

Instead he rose abruptly and glanced at his watch.

"Two-thirty," he said, almost too casually. "I'd better go."

Carol nodded.

He picked up his brief case, and the feel of the leather and the bulging papers within brought him back to his dilemma. He went to the phone again, dialed the operator.

"I'm sorry, sir," said the operator. "But the Army took over all long-line circuits ten minutes ago. They may be released by morning. I'll call you."

He hung up, and he thought, That's that. It's out of my hands, there's nothing I can do. Nothing, except—wait for tomorrow.

He turned to Carol. "What was the name of that hotel again?"

"The Rutherford," she answered mechanically. "It's east of Fifth, on Fifty-sixth."

"The Rutherford," he repeated.

He waited for her to rise, to say something, to see him to the door. But she did not stir from the couch. Instead she lay there motionless, watching him, appraising him, measuring him. Something had come into her eyes. They were hard to read at the moment; they said nothing, really, except that they expected *him* to do something, to make the next move.

The wail of a siren screamed up suddenly from the dark canyon outside. It tore the silence of the room with its shrieking din. Then it threaded away somewhere in the night, fading as fast as it had come.

They were apart now, out of each other's arms, and the Outside had come between them again. The realization was in her face, and he knew it was in his. The little island they had inhabited briefly and together had slipped into the dark sea, and they were both afraid and swimming for their lives again. The Fear, by some subtle osmosis, had penetrated through the walls; it was in the room again, a cold and oppressive shroud enveloping them both.

"Hope I can get a cab," he said.

His voice sounded strangely false. Still she said nothing, made no move to get up. He turned his back on her, acutely conscious that she was watching him intently as he walked toward the foyer. He picked up his coat and hat deliberately from the chair where she had left them, and turned to her.

"David," she whispered suddenly. "David—don't go!"

He stood there transfixed, staring at her. Mechanically, unaware of what he was doing, he put his hat and coat down again. The blood rushed hotly to his face, his heart pounded, and he began to tremble violently.

"Carol . . ."

"Don't go out there, darling." Her voice was husky. "Don't go out there—and leave me alone."

The morning light was streaming in the window when Carol said:

"David, I've got to get down to Radio City. We've got an early broadcast, and one of the announcers still has his car in town. He's picking me up on the corner, and if I don't meet him I'll never be able to get down to the studio."

He made a last try. "You won't change your mind about flying back with me this afternoon?"

"No, David," she said quietly. "I can't."

Then Carol thought of something, made a sad face. "I didn't realize it was so late. And, darling, I *did* want to make your breakfast. There isn't much food in the refrigerator, the times being what they are, but——"

"Forget it," he said cheerfully. "I'll throw something together."

He turned on the small portable television set in the bedroom. A Negro girl at a piano came on with some wake-up-and-sing stuff. She was dressed as a maid and was obviously at her mistress's piano, her broom and mop leaning against the instrument.

The mistress came into the picture, and the Negro maid grimaced in alarm, as though caught poaching on her employer's time. But the woman of the house was very pleasant about it. She motioned the girl to stay at the piano; it was apparent that she would rather have music than have her house cleaned.

A moment later, the woman of the house, caught by the music, joined the girl in a duet. They laughed and swayed and made eyes to the rhythm of the song. There was a clock on the piano to give a visual picture of the time, and there was a face painted on its dial. The face grinned and grimaced, too, and had a wonderful time. Now and then it waved its hands jerkily, like an agitated and happy puppet.

It was pleasant stuff, early-morning stuff for the housewives, and David and Carol couldn't help smiling at it.

But then the scene was wiped out abruptly into a blank screen.

A surge of documentary news-of-the-day music came up, and a spinning globe of the world appeared. A streamer brightened and swept around it, and the legend announced:

## NATIONAL NEWS

David's smile froze. He and Carol stood there, motionless, hypnotized, listening.

The announcer underplayed his news and made it effective. His words were measured and somber, and his voice was a steady monotone.

> *"Early reports from the Soviet Union indicate that the last-minute conference between Mr. Allison of the State Department and Foreign Minister Bakhanov has failed. There is a rumor that Allison has already left Russia by plane, and the tension is mounting hourly.*
>
> *"Meanwhile, the Army has announced that Washington has been completely evacuated, the last government bureau moving out two days ago.*
>
> *"The President, it is reported, is waiting a personal report from Allison at his secret headquarters somewhere underground. It is reported that he is resisting strong pressure from some of his advisers to take the initiative before it is too late. The health of the Chief Executive has given some concern. Since Congress stripped itself of power to declare war and gave the President authority as Commander in Chief to make whatever instantaneous decision necessary, the strain and responsibility have been overwhelming.*
>
> *"Flashes of unexplained light were detected early this morning over Labrador. Observers at Hopedale and Northwest River are unable to account for the phenomena, except to say that they resembled the tails of illuminated rockets. . . .*
>
> *"There are rumors that New York, Chicago, Detroit, Philadelphia, Los Angeles, and, in fact, every city of over five hundred thousand will be totally evacuated by Army order*

*this week end. Emergency facilities have been set up in the
hinterland for those without relatives or friends residing
in——"*

"David, shut it off!" Carol's voice rose hysterically. "Shut it off!"
He turned the switch and the picture dissolved to a tiny rectangle
of bright light, which finally drowned in the dull, gray screen.
"Why don't they stop?" Carol cried. "Why don't they stop?"
"They don't know how to stop," David answered quietly. "Not
any more."

After Carol had left, David tried the long-distance operator
again.
The lines were still tied up, and he swore softly as he hung up.
He prepared a hasty breakfast, but he had no appetite. His
ignorance of what had happened back at Palomar kept gnawing
at him; the trembling in Francis's voice over the phone haunted
him.
He checked his watch.
It was nine o'clock. And General Hawthorne had named the time
of the meeting at eleven, somewhere outside the city itself. He had
to make a decision, and make it quick. He might be too late by now,
as it was.
He went to the phone and asked the local operator for military
headqarters, New York area, R-Section.
A couple of voices finally routed him to a Colonel Hatch.
"Hughes?" The colonel was curt. "Where have you been? We've
been waiting for you."
"Sorry, Colonel, I——"
The colonel interrupted, asked for the address. "You damned
near missed that meeting, Dr. Hughes. As it is, we'll have to work
fast to get you out where you have to go. We'll send a car up for
you right away!"
The colonel hung up, and David fidgeted about Carol's apartment, waiting. He washed the dishes, put·them away, turned on the

television set, turned it off again, sat down, got up again, paced the room.

*What had happened at Palomar?*

He looked at his watch again, did some rapid calculating. The meeting was at eleven. It might take hours, probably would. He would be lucky if he got out of it by late afternoon. The decision they expected to make wasn't a quick, cut-and-dried affair. There would be a lot of argument back and forth.

In any case, he couldn't get to a phone and find out what was going on back at the observatory. Once in that meeting, they'd lock the doors and seal them with MPs.

Maybe they'd be through at five, he thought. Maybe. He might be able to call the Coast then, the lines might be clear. Might, might, might. He'd try Carol once more over the phone; he'd know something then, know it for sure. If they decided to let go, to start it rolling, to throw the first punch, he'd have to come back and get Carol.

It might be very tough getting out of town. He had a reservation, a high priority. But only for one seat, not two. He'd have to find a way, some way to——

The phone rang.

David sprang to the instrument.

"This is the long-distance operator calling Dr. Hughes, Dr. David Hughes."

"I'm Dr. Hughes," he almost shouted.

"The lines have just been cleared, sir, and Palomar, California, is calling." There was a pause, and David waited rigidly. Then the operator said: "Here's your party."

A voice came thinly, distantly, over the wire.

"Dr. Hughes. Dr. Hughes, is that you?"

"Francis!" David yelled into the mouthpiece. "Francis, what's happened out there?"

The steward's voice came over clearly now. "Dr. Hughes, I've been trying to get you all night. I wasn't sure you got my message before we were cut off."

*"What happened, Francis? What's it all about?"*

"We had hoped you'd be on your way by now, sir. Dr. Dawson wanted you here. Oh, one moment." There was a pause. "Here's Dr. Dawson now, Dr. Hughes."

Thank God, thought David. Thank God the Old Man was all right.

Dr. Dawson came on. His voice was strange, feverish; it shook a little.

"David, I want you back here as fast as you can make it. Take the first plane out. Don't delay a moment, do you understand?"

"But, sir, what's it all about?"

"I can't tell you over the phone."

"But the meeting, Dr. Dawson. They expect me there——"

The Old Man's voice suddenly became harsh. "Forget the meeting, David. There is no necessity for you to attend. I'll guarantee you immunity for any consequences resulting from your absence. You have my word for it. The important thing is to get back here to Palomar—*at once!*"

The Old Man hung up.

David Hughes put the receiver back on the hook numbly.

There was no rebelling against an order like this—not the way the Old Man had put it.

The hell of it was, he *still* didn't know what was happening at Palomar.

Dazed, his mind whirling in a pinwheel of confusion, David put on his hat and coat and tucked his brief case under his arm.

Then he walked out of the door and heard the lock snap shut behind him.

**4.** Thursday morning, on the seventeenth of November, in the year 1960, was crisp and sunny.

The air was invigorating; it had a winy snap to it and was cleaned and sweetened by a northwest wind.

The sun was bright; it razzle-dazzled the rivers and glinted on the windows of New York and warmed the brick and stone walls of the canyons.

As David walked rapidly up Cathedral Parkway and then turned right down Broadway, he reflected on the incongruity of the weather.

It was not the kind of morning to expect sudden death, not the traditional backdrop for cataclysm. In the operatic and literary tradition, such events were augured by black skies, flashes of lightning, roars of thunder.

But the weather was not being literary or operatic this morning. It refused to be moody and provide a stage. Whatever schemes man was contriving, it was having none of it. It simply insisted, contrarily, on being itself.

Thus Nature, in what might have been its own version of an unfunny jest, had provided the kind of morning lyrics were written about, topcoat weather with a tang, the kind of morning to walk through the park, or to take that long ride through the country and forget the office.

To David Hughes, visually at least, Broadway presented rather a cheerful appearance. True, there were only a few vehicles on the street, but there seemed to be more pedestrians abroad. The night before had been desolate, the street a black graveyard, but perhaps the sun had drawn the inhabitants from their concrete warrens, lured them out with warm promise, infused them with its own optimism.

But the faces of the people belied the mood of the morning.

They were still stamped with the Fear; its imprint was indelible. They were gaunt and strained, and they did not smile. They knew that the Fear was still there, that it walked in the sun as well as in the darkness.

And David Hughes, as he hurried down Broadway, knew it too.

He kept watching the side streets, on the alert for a cab. Two or three taxis went by, but they were loaded with passengers. David kept on the west side of the street, going downtown. The traffic, or what there was of it, seemed to be moving in that direction.

At 180th Street, David heard the sound of a siren shrieking up Broadway.

It was an Army car, and moving fast. Instinctively he shrank back into a doorway. Then when the car sped by he stepped out on the walk and watched it.

He saw it swerve, with brakes screaming, and turn left into Cathedral Parkway, two blocks away.

It was the vehicle the Army had sent for him.

The men in it would find him gone; they would find Carol's apartment empty. The big strategy meeting, wherever it was being held, would go on without him now. And whatever decision the generals, the Secretary of Defense, and the consulting scientists made, it would be made without Dr. Dawson's data in the brief case David carried under his arm, and without David's interpretation of it, as the Old Man's representative.

They would miss him, and General Hawthorne would find him and ask some pointed questions. He, David Hughes, was in effect and at this moment a hunted man, a fugitive from military law, and subject to its consequences.

He quickened his step, and now and then, furtively, he turned his head to look back up Broadway.

The olive-drab car from intelligence would emerge in a few moments, when they found him gone. Its occupants would be watching the streets, looking for him. By their very lack of numbers, all pedestrians were conspicuous, and suddenly David felt almost naked on the wide Broadway sidewalk. It was possible that he might be picked up before he had hardly started.

Between 106th and 105th streets he found a candy-and-tobacco store open, one of the few still doing business. It occurred to him that it would be a good place to hide, to get off the street until the Army car went back.

David opened the door and went in.

There were several men in the place, all apparently regulars. At least they all seemed to know the man behind the cigar counter, a short, bald man with thick glasses. David had entered in the middle of a discussion. One of the men lounging on a stool at the now inactive soda fountain was saying to the proprietor:

"So you sent your family to the Catskills, Sam?"

The proprietor nodded. "Ellenville. I figured they'd be pretty safe there till I sell out and close up." He glanced around at his depleted stock. The store was almost empty of goods. "And that won't be long, Bernie. Tomorrow or the day after, maybe."

He turned to David, and David bought a pack of cigarettes. The price was a dollar, the transaction matter-of-fact. The man behind the counter continued:

"The way I figure, Bernie, if the Reds hit us with a bomb, the blast won't get up into the mountains."

"Yeah," said Bernie. "*If* they hit us with a blast. But they won't."

"What do you mean?"

"The Russians are too smart for that. They got something else up their sleeve. Radiation."

The proprietor was fascinated. "Radiation?"

Bernie nodded knowingly. "Radiation. That's it. That's the pay-off. I was reading a piece in the *Daily News* before all the papers folded up in town," he said. "It was something one of these big-shot scientists said, Sam. He said there's no place that's safe any more. Not even the mountains. Nowhere. And all on account of radiation."

"How do you mean?" Sam was suddenly worried.

"Here." The man named Bernie took a torn sheet of newspaper from his pocket. "I got the clipping right here." He spread it on the fountain top. "Listen to what it says at the end."

Bernie paused for a moment, then read the final paragraph slowly. " 'In any case, there is no defense against these lethal particles, no place of escape. There is no cave too deep to hide away, no mountaintop too high or remote. As long as men must breathe air and Nature provides winds, the human being, no matter how fast he runs or to what destination, is helplessly and pathetically vulnerable.' "

The man at the counter folded the clipping, his fingers trembling, and thrust it into his pocket. The bald head of the proprietor, Sam, was shiny with perspiration, and there was agony in the eyes behind the thick lenses. It was easy to see what he was thinking. People breathe air in the Catskills; the winds blow there too. . . .

"Christ," someone said, breaking the silence. "Christ, what a world!"

Amen, thought David, watching through the window.

The conversation turned to rumors. Everybody had heard a rumor. A fat man with a mottled face said:

"I heard that they stopped the salt-water fishing fleets from going out and won't let anyone sell any more deep-sea fish."

"Yeah?" Bernie wanted to know. "Why?"

"They think maybe the Reds dropped a lot of pills in the Atlantic and the Pacific, near the coasts. Made the fish radioactive. Lights 'em up inside like Christmas candles. Eat 'em—and good-by!"

"That's a new one on me," said a man thumbing through a magazine on the wall rack. "Remind me to eat hamburgers from now on."

"God," said the proprietor, finally joining the discussion again. "I had fish last night—mackerel."

The fat man laughed harshly. "I hope your wife doesn't divorce you, Sam."

"What do you mean, Paul? Why should she?"

"Once you get these radioactive particles in you, they tell me, you're no good in bed. A lot of guys working around this here plutonium stuff found that out. So did their girl friends." He grinned at the others and turned back to Sam. "But I wouldn't worry about it, Sam. You're no kid. You've had your fun."

No one grinned back. The would-be humorist said good-by and eased his huge bulk through the door.

The proprietor was still worried. "How do we know what's going on right now? Maybe we're all standing here and breathing in this stuff now, without knowing it. How about it, Bernie? How do we know we ain't radioactive right here and now?"

"One thing's sure," said the man with the magazine. "None of us have any Geiger counters. We couldn't tell if we wanted to."

"Maybe you guys can't" said Bernie. "But I can."

They looked at him curiously, and he drew a small camera from his pocket. It was the ordinary and popular type which developed film within the camera itself, after a few moments of waiting.

He held up the camera to the others. "I got my own Geiger counter right here," he said triumphantly. "If you did a lot of reading up on this radiation stuff like I have, you'd know film can give you the tip-off."

They watched him hypnotically. The man called Bernie, now a savant, savored his moment.

"Like to see whether there's any radiation around right now?"

They pushed in close to him without replying, their faces tense. David moved in with the others, as interested as anyone else, already knowing what the man was up to, knowing that the camera was capable of indicating, at that moment, life or possible death.

Bernie did not touch the shutter. Instead, with the air of a demonstrator before a spellbound audience, he pressed the developer button and pulled out a paper tab. He ticked off the seconds on his wrist watch as the developing reagent worked on the unexposed film within.

Finally, with a flourish, he opened the back of the camera and took out the print.

The print was clear.

"Well, gents," said Bernie impressively, "we're still okay. There's no radiation around. Y'see, if there was, it'd go right through the camera like X rays and fog up the film. If this picture came out all fogged up, brother, *we'd* be in trouble."

There was a moment of silence.

Then someone said: "You've got something there, mister. But won't you find out a little late? What I mean is, if the picture's fogged, you'd already be radioactive, wouldn't you?"

"Yeah," agreed Bernie. "No getting around that. The question is: how *much* would you be lit up inside? They tell me you can take a certain amount without dying. But the minute you see any fogging at all—that's the time to scram."

"Scram where?" asked Sam.

Bernie shrugged. There was no answer to that one. Still, the men in the candy store seemed impressed. It was something to *know* whether you were dying or not, even if it might be too late. Automatically their eyes strayed to a case in back of the cigar counter, where there was a stock of film. The proprietor took out a fistful of the rectangular yellow boxes and stuffed them into his pockets. The others quickly bought the rest of his stock.

David turned toward the window again, watching for the Army car. Bernie's demonstration had been a simple but familiar one. Back at Palomar he had seen the effect of radiation on sensitive film many times. There were other ways to detect it, of course: by the comet's tail of ionized particles in what was called a Wilson cloud chamber; by the action of an electroscope in discharging; and of course by the clicking of a Geiger counter.

But now, in David's mind, there was a serious doubt. *Was the attack, when and if it came, going to be atomic at all?*

Back at Palomar General Hawthorne had been sure that it was something else, something bigger, something perhaps on a cosmic scale. He had come to Palomar to talk to the Old Man personally, so strong was his belief, so determined was he to recruit Dr. Dawson, the greatest of them all in the affairs of the heavens. He had been convinced that the Russians had a secret weapon and that they were applying it when it suited them, as a series of steps to resolve the cold war and break the American morale without entering a full-scale atomic battle.

If the Russians *had* something new, thought David, their use of it in this respect made sense, from their point of view. The United States was a rich land, and if the Reds could bring it down and exploit it without too much damage, that would be to their benefit. The trouble with a victorious radioactive attack was that it left nothing to the victor. It was fatal, not only to humans, but to live-stock and animals. It polluted the waters and the crops, the build-ings, and bridges, the very land itself, contaminated it all with a coat of death. And in the end it left nothing but a vast, desolate, and diseased waste, of no good to the Russians or anyone else.

Suddenly, through the window of the candy store, David saw what he had been watching for.

The olive-drab Army car came in view. Its siren was silent now, providing no warning. It cruised down Broadway slowly, and David saw the soldiers in it scanning both sides of the street.

He shrank back from the window guiltily, and the vehicle went by.

The skin prickled along his back. He was hunted now, and Hawthorne would be the hunter. He was a fugitive, and there would be harsher names the general would call him, deserter, saboteur, traitor. The brief case he held burned hot in his hands.

The thought occurred to him that if General Hawthorne were informed of his disappearance early enough, he, David, might be stopped at the airport before he had a chance to take off.

He began to regret the decision he had made, almost wished he had disregarded the Old Man's order to return to California without attending the meeting.

At any rate, it was too late to do anything about it now. He had to get out to Idlewild, and get there fast.

David opened the door and was just about to step out on the sidewalk when a cab drew up to the curb. The driver got out and walked into the store, leaving his motor running. David saw that there were two other men in the cab, and for a moment he found it impossible to believe his luck.

The driver was buying cigarettes from the proprietor when David asked:

"Got room for one more?"

"I might," said the man. "Where you going, buddy?"

"Idlewild Airport." David tried hard to keep the eagerness out of his voice.

"That's a long way out of town, Buddy," said the driver, his blue eyes studying David greedily. "Clean out to the end of Queens, and these days there ain't any fares coming back. It'll cost you some dough."

"How much?"

"A hundred bucks," said the man casually.

David nodded. He had no disposition to haggle. He had the cash, and it was worth everything for him to get to the airport in a hurry.

The driver stuck out his hand. "In advance, buddy."

David paid him, and as the man stuck the money in his pocket he said:

"I've got a couple of other guys to drop off first. Then we'll get going."

David squeezed into the back seat beside the other two men, and they started to move down Broadway. The others showed no inclination to talk, and David was grateful. He had a lot to think about.

First of all, he wondered how the Old Man was going to protect him when he got back to Palomar. The Old Man was one of the world's great scientists, a Nobel prize winner, a power in himself. But even Dr. Dawson couldn't countermand an Army order and get away with it. Not these days.

It would take some kind of special magic, thought David grimly, to keep him out of trouble now.

And then there was Carol. . . .

The cab stopped at Columbus Circle, and one of the men got out. Then the driver swung east on Central Park South, toward Fifth Avenue.

As they were rounding Fifty-ninth Street into Fifth, at the Plaza, it happened.

It began with a noise, a low, deep, rolling ominous rumble.

The rumble blended into a subterranean roar, a throaty booming sound.

"Christ!" yelled the driver. "What the hell is that?" He stopped the cab in the middle of the street.

The booming continued, grew louder, echoed and re-echoed like an artillery salvo. David, in that terrible moment of panic, had a single objective moment, a flash of light on the lens of his eye. He saw a few pedestrians on the avenue, standing still, frozen, listening, their faces blanched with terror.

And then it came.

The street seemed suddenly to undulate in a slow wave.

The taxi began to shiver, then shake, then do a crazy, awful, lurching dance. It tossed from side to side, like a mechanical toy, as David and the others clung to their seats for dear life.

"It's the Reds," shouted the driver. "The goddamn Reds! They've hit New York!"

The roaring became louder and was mixed with sharp snapping sounds, as though great blocks of stone were being torn and ripped apart deep underground.

The buildings started to sway, and dance, and shiver.

David watched, fascinated, in sweaty terror, unable to move, unable to breathe. He saw whole panes of glass fall from the windows of the Plaza Hotel, the Savoy-Plaza, Tiffany's, Plummer's. They fell in sheets, in a great glassy, deadly rain, crashed to the street. He heard people screaming, saw them running for building entrances. One man fell, his head a mass of blood, almost decapitated by flying glass.

It thudded and smashed on the roof of the taxi, crashed against the cab windows. The shatterproof glass of the vehicle bent back and cracked but did not break.

The man sitting next to David suddenly screamed: "Let me out! Let me out of here!"

David grabbed him, tried to keep him inside. The man's eyes were bulging with fear, they were mad; his lips were flecked with saliva, his teeth bared in an awful grin.

"God damn you, let me out!"

He slammed David in the face, ripped open the car door, ran out toward the lobby of the Plaza. He had just passed the statue in the center of the Plaza when a large sliver of glass whistled down and slanted into him. He fell on his face, the blood gurgling from his body.

*Carol!*

David yelled her name above the awful roar. It vibrated on his lips as he was shaken and tossed in the rear of the cab. She'd be inside the RCA Building now, broadcasting in the studios at Radio City, nine blocks away.

And God knew what was happening within the buildings!

The marquee of the Savoy-Plaza broke off and hung at a crazy, limp angle over the sidewalk.

The water mains on the avenue broke, sending geysers of water shooting skyward. From somewhere far downtown there was a tremendous explosion, and a great cone of smoke puffed straight up and mushroomed in a swirling ball.

Glass was still falling out of the yawning windowpanes, slamming to the road and disintegrating in a shower of slivers, till the road was covered with it.

There was a single sharp tremor, and then suddenly the vibrating stopped. The roar faded to a rumble, which rolled off in an uptown direction.

It was still. It was over.

The driver and David stared at each other stupidly, white-faced, numb with the shock.

Outside a single pane of glass fell from somewhere far up, splintered in the road with a shattering report.

"They've started it," said the driver hoarsely. "It's the war— they've started it. Those Soviet bastards have started it."

He babbled on in the same vein, incoherently, still in shock, half-hysterical.

A man ahead, lying in a pool of his own blood, screamed. People started to pour from the entrances of the buildings, crazy with shock, shouting at the top of their lungs uncontrollably, retching at the sight of those who had been caught by flying glass, slipping and slithering over the glass-covered sidewalks.

They were all running across the street toward the open, toward Central Park.

The driver started his motor. He stepped on the gas; the car skidded on the slippery pavement. He spun it around in the middle of the Plaza.

"Driver!" yelled David. "Driver, get me down to Radio City!"

"You're crazy," babbled the man. "You're crazy, mister. I'm heading for the park, for the open. They may give it to us again any minute. It ain't over yet. We'll get it again. I'm going for the park with everyone else!"

"But I've got to get to Radio City."

"Then walk, God damn it, walk!" the driver yelled savagely. "Get outa my cab and walk!"

David opened the door. The driver, in his hurry to get to the park, hardly slowed down the vehicle. David jumped, fell, cut his hand on a piece of glass. He lay there for a moment, stunned, inert.

Then he looked at his hand. The blood was streaming from it, but luckily it was a superficial cut. He bound it with his handker-chief, unsteadily got to his feet.

Then he dazedly realized that he was without his briefcase. He had left it in the taxi, and the cab was gone.

To hell with it, thought David. It doesn't matter now. It's too late for that and everything else.

*I've got to find Carol.*

He began to run down Fifth Avenue.

It was hard going, slippery going. The glass-covered pavement was treacherous; he almost fell headlong twice. He dodged a number of white-faced pedestrians running in the opposite direction toward the park, heard others on the sidewalk and on the road, crying out, hurt.

But he did not stop.

He ran blindly through the spray of a spurting water main at Fifty-seventh Street, came out drenched to the skin, moved past the once proud giants of the most glamorous street in the world, Bonwit Teller's, Tailored Woman, Cartier's, DePinna, all long closed, their plate windows shattered out.

At Best and Company he saw what appeared to be a group of victims, all naked, flung crazily over the sidewalk. As he came nearer he saw that they were display mannikins which had been stripped and left in the window when the store had closed.

Saint Patrick's was windowless, but its doors were wide open, and people were running inside for shelter, anywhere to get off the street.

David fought for air; his lungs ached as he ran doggedly on, turning the corner into Fiftieth and Rockefeller Plaza.

A siren sounded, then another.

An Army truck came roaring up Fifth, its solid rubber wheels crunching the thick carpet of broken glass. It was filled with goggled men in monstrous costume: galoshes, gloves, coveralls, and masks. They were hunched over small black boxes and listening to earphones.

This was the Radiological Squad, and these absurd gnomes were the Geiger men.

The clang of ambulances added to the din; the special flying squads of first-aid men began to roll up in trucks. These were the catastrophe units of the Army, specifically designed for disaster action.

The wounded city began to swarm with mobile units carrying uniformed men; it was obvious that the Army had taken over.

David came into the center of Rockefeller Plaza.

It was a weird sight.

The pavements were hidden by piles of jagged, broken glass. The towering buildings surrounding the square—the RCA Building, Time and Life, Eastern Airlines, Associated Press—all glowered down blindly, their glass eyes gouged out.

The sunken rectangular plaza, which once had served as a skating rink in winter and a café garden in summer, was like a box of broken glass.

The great statue of Prometheus, standing watch over the sunken plaza, tilted crazily. David caught a glimpse of the legend:

*Prometheus, teacher in every art, brought the fire that has proved to mortals a means to mighty ends.*

David ran into the RCA Building, where the broadcasting studios were located.

It was jammed with people milling around, herdlike, afraid to go out, expecting another blow. They were white-faced, shouting, talking hysterically. They had been lucky. They had been safe within the building, and there was no apparent damage to the interior of the great corridor.

The babel rose and fell:

*"Earthquake—felt like an earthquake."*

*"Earthquake, hell! There's never been an earthquake in New York, not even a tremor. There can't be. This town's built on solid rock!"*

*"It was the Reds! This is just the beginning!"*

*"Everybody said New York would get it first. Well, we have!"*

*"Must have been a bomb planted deep in the subway. Or maybe in the river."*

*"Tried to phone home. The phones are all dead."*

*"They may hit us again—any minute now."*

*"God, what if this whole place is radioactive right now? Maybe it is. Maybe we don't know it. If it is, we're done!"*

*"I could have got out. I could have got out a week ago. But like a damned fool, I stayed."*

*"Charlie, we're done for. We're standing here and dying. It's the radiation. It gets into the marrow of your bones, eats up the blood, gives you tumors like cancer. God, we're standing here and taking it and dying!"*

The place was alive with white helmeted military police trying to keep the crowd in order.

David tried to get to the studio elevators. Only one was in operation, and that was guarded by an MP. He flung David back.

"Better check with the sergeant at the information booth, buddy."

David told the sergeant that he was looking for a Carol Kenny, an actress who, as far as he knew, had been broadcasting in some studio on the upper floors.

The sergeant wasn't inclined to be of much help; he let David know that he didn't have any time at the moment hunting up girl friends for a lot of guys.

"Remember?" said the sergeant. "We just had a little trouble around here."

David suddenly recalled his priority. It had been countersigned by General Hawthorne. He showed it to the sergeant, who immediately became co-operative. He opened a tally book, ran a thick finger down the last page.

"Carol Kenny. Yeah. She had a short rehearsal and then went out."

"She went out?"

"That's right. Just before this thing went off. With an announcer named Ray Graves, it says here. Probably went out for coffee or something. They were due back for broadcast ten minutes ago, but I guess that's out. They won't be broadcasting around here for a little while."

So Carol had gone out. Carol had gone out into the street. And that deadly rain of glass . . .

David felt a little ill. He thought, Maybe nothing happened, maybe she found shelter, maybe she's all right. Maybe . . .

He decided to wait.

An hour passed, and Carol did not show up.

He looked at his watch. It was almost noon. There was no way of finding out what had happened to her, not the way things were now. And he had to get back to Palomar. Something big was going on out there. The Old Man was waiting for him.

He could only hope that Carol was all right, that she hadn't been caught in the street, that she was alive.

David waited another fifteen minutes, then contacted the sergeant at the information desk, told him that he had to get out to Idlewild Airport and that it was an urgent matter of military importance.

The sergeant was very helpful now; the name of Matt Hawthorne was magic. He escorted David through the Forty-ninth Street entrance, hailed an Army car, gave the corporal driving it an order.

"Take this man to the Fifty-ninth Street Bridge, Corporal." He turned to David. "There's a staging point there for Army vehicles moving to the island, sir. If you'll show your priority to the officer in charge at the bridge, I'm sure you'll be able to get a hitch."

An hour later David walked into the terminal at Idlewild. He had just reached the reservations counter when he heard:

*"David!"*

He whirled and saw Carol running toward him. Stunned, unable to believe that it was she, he stood there, gaping foolishly. And then she was in his arms.

"Carol, what happened? How did you get here?"

"Darling, darling, I thought I'd go out of my mind. I didn't know what happened to you." She was crying on his shoulder. "All I knew was that you were coming out here to the airport. But they didn't have any record of your leaving—and I waited and waited, and finally I thought, back in town, maybe you'd been hurt, maybe you were dead. Oh, David!"

It was a little while before she was coherent enough to tell him the rest.

"I'd just gone out for breakfast, David. With our announcer, Ray Graves. We usually do that between rehearsal and broadcast on a morning show. Anyway, we went over to Sixth Avenue, and we'd just gone into the restaurant when it happened. Everything. After that I knew there wouldn't be any broadcast or anything else. And I kept thinking of you. You'd be out here at the airport, or on the way out. I had to meet you then, to go out with you to California, and Ray—Ray was wonderful. First we went to his place to see if his wife was all right, and she was. Then he drove me out here, went way up to the Triborough Bridge and up the parkway, that way, because the Army wouldn't let any civilian cars cross the Fifty-ninth. Oh, David, I was so afraid something had happened to you. I've been here, waiting and waiting for—well, it seems *years!*"

There was still the problem of getting a seat on a plane for Carol.

David had his reservation and priority, but the reservations clerk swore that he couldn't assign another seat on the next plane going to the Coast.

At the last moment, however, there was a cancellation. One of the passengers hadn't been able to make it, had been delayed in town for a reason unknown. But it could be guessed at, and the guess was pretty grim.

At Chicago they had been delayed for three hours. Now it was just getting dark as the stratocruiser glided across the Arizona border and began to eat up the last lap to San Diego.

The radio was on in the lounge cabin, and an announcer was broadcasting from a Chicago origin. Suddenly he was cut off, and an announcer from New York came in, told his listeners that the transmitters were working again from that city. The passengers in the cabin sat up and listened as he gave them the first news fragments from the metropolis:

". . . *the over-all damage to New York, it can now be reported, was surprisingly small. The modern structures in the city stood firm, although a few antiquated wooden buildings collapsed. Casualties, according to early estimates, amounted to some five thousand persons, killed and injured, for the most part, from flying glass.*

*"The main damage has been to morale. The vibrations, although doing little damage in a material sense, caused panic among those still left in the city. The Army has declared the city under martial law and has ordered the population evacuated.*

*"The rumor spread through the shaken city that the Russians had struck with an atom bomb buried deep underground, that they would strike again. Army authorities deny this, pointing out that an atomic underground explosion would cause far more serious effects. They report, too, that their Radiological Squads have found no sign of deadly radiation. I repeat— there is no indication of any lethal particles in the air.*

*"Seismologists are at a loss to explain the strange vibrations. They point out that New York has always been considered tremor-proof and earthquake-proof, that it stands on solid bedrock, and that it would take a tremendous internal force to cause a fault in the rock.*

*"Meanwhile, the entire nation is being swept by the rumor that the Soviet Union has a secret weapon quite different from but more potent than the atom bomb. The rumor states that the Reds have used the weapon before, and used it to create a tremor in New York this morning as one of the final stages in the war of nerves. The Department of Defense has not confirmed or denied this.*

*"A sensational story is now going the rounds that America's top-ranking military men, at a special meeting this morning, have confirmed the existence of this secret weapon. This story, entirely without confirmation from any official source, states that the decision has been made to attack the Soviet Union in self-defense, that tremendous pressure is being brought on the President as Commander in Chief to give the signal. The story goes on to say that he is, at the moment, resisting all pressures and awaiting a fuller and more complete seismological report, on the off-chance that the tremor may have been a natural phenomenon.*

*"There is even a wilder story, put forth by a former Washington correspondent now at the temporary capital, that the President was about to yield to the advice of his military advisers, when he received a mysterious long-distance phone call from California. According to Frank Landon, the newspaperman responsible, the President was on the phone a half-hour. When he emerged from his office he was deathly pale and changed his point of view abruptly, refusing to order the attack.*

*"I repeat, these are only rumors; there is no official confirmation from any responsible quarter."*

The stewardess came in and turned off the radio.

"Please go back to your seats and fasten your safety belts," she said. "We'll be coming into San Diego in a few minutes."

**5.** At Lindbergh Field, David immediately went to a phone booth and called Palomar.

It was Francis who answered. "Dr. Hughes! Where are you, sir?"

"In San Diego. I've got Miss Kenny with me, Francis."

"Oh. Dr. Dawson was worried about you, sir. We all were. After hearing what had happened in New York—well, you understand, Dr. Hughes. Was it very bad?"

"Bad enough. Tell you more about it later, Francis——"

"They say the Russians——"

"Yes, I know," interrupted David impatiently. He wanted to know, he wanted to find out fast. Everything. The phone calls. The urgent order from the Old Man to return. "Francis, what's going on at the observatory?"

"I don't know, Dr. Hughes." Francis sounded dead tired. "All I know is that I've been on the phone, calling astronomers from all over the world, ever since yesterday evening, asking them to come to Palomar at once."

David remembered the operator's remote voice the night before, as he had tried to get Francis, calling Rio, Amsterdam. . . .

"They've been coming in ever since last night and early this morning," continued the steward. "There must be twenty of them in all. Dr. Dawson's been locked in his study with them for hours. They're in there now."

"Francis, who are they? What are their names?"

"Well, Dr. Hughes, there's a Professor Ellender of Harvard, Professor Manning of Mount Wilson, Van Vreeden of Leyden, in

Holland, Dr. Perez of Rio de Janeiro, Bornson of Stockholm, Professor Varanov of the Pulkovo Observatory in Leningrad, Dr. Graves of Cambridge Observatory in England, Dr. Smythe of the Royal Astronomical Society, and oh—several others."

David hung on the phone, spellbound.

*Ellender, Manning, Graves, Van Vreeden, Varanov.*

These were names, the Greats and the near Greats, the select of the Who's Who of astronomy. Ellender in stellar interiors, Manning in stellar evolution, Van Vreeden in astrophysics, Perez in novae and nebulae, Varanov in comets and meteors, Bornson and Smythe, quantum mechanics.

These were the giants, almost as big as the Old Man. And now, for some fantastic reason, they had flown to Palomar from all over the world.

*But why? Why?*

The question drummed and throbbed in David's head as Francis continued to talk:

"It started only about an hour after you left for New York, Dr. Hughes. Dr. Dawson came out of his study and he looked—well, I've never seen him look that way. He looked pale—almost *wild*. For a moment I thought he'd had an attack. He gave me the list of names and told me to switch the astronomers to the private phone in his study after I made the connections. Then he asked for you." The steward's voice shook a little through its weariness. "He was so excited that he'd even forgotten you'd gone to New York. After that I tried to phone you and the wires went dead, and finally this morning we managed to get in touch with you."

"And you've no idea what the doctor said to these other men, Francis?"

"No, sir."

"Francis, listen," said David, watching Carol through the glass door of the phone booth. "If you can get to Dr. Dawson, tell him we're going to have a bite to eat here at the air terminal and then start out for Palomar. I've got my car parked in a garage in Dago. And by the way, have you any room for Miss Kenny?"

"Yes, sir. It's quite crowded in the colony now, Dr. Hughes, but I think I can arrange it."

"Thanks, Francis. See you in a couple of hours."

David hung up and walked out of the booth. Carol saw the stunned expression on his face.

"David, what is it?"

He told Carol briefly what was happening at the observatory. But she was unimpressed.

"With the earth ready to blow up, David, does it really matter what happens up there in the sky?" She smiled at him wanly. "And, darling, can we get something to eat now? I'm famished."

He relaxed a little over sandwiches and coffee, and they talked of other things, mostly themselves. And Carol asked finally:

"David, when will we be married?"

"Tomorrow, if you like. We can come back down to Dago here in the morning and stay at a hotel."

Her eyes suddenly filled with tears. "Here comes the bride, darling." She smiled. Then she leaned over the table and kissed him. "And speaking of brides, I'm going to be practically naked. All I've got is the dress I'm wearing, not even a toothbrush. David, I know you're in a hurry, an awful hurry, but when we get your car in San Diego, will you give me a little while, just a few minutes, so that I can buy a few clothes, anything, as long as it fits? Be a darling, say yes."

He grinned and said yes, and kicked himself mentally for not meaning it.

He needed the time; he begrudged it to her.

He wanted to get to Palomar—fast.

They were well out of San Diego now, speeding through the starlit night along the broad road to Palomar.

David kept his foot down hard on the accelerator. They turned off Route 101 at Solana Beach, raced past Rancho Sante Fe, Lake Hodges, through Escondido, the southern gateway to Palomar. And then they began the long, tortuous climb up through the

San Jacinto range, pointing for the solid hogback of granite that was Palomar itself.

"So *this* is what the newspapers call 'The Highway to the Stars,' " said Carol.

"Yes."

She sniffed. "It looks like any other road."

"Naturally. Why shouldn't it?"

"I don't know," she said. "I expected it to look more—well, *glamorous*."

He smiled. "It will after we get off the plain here and start to climb."

The country grew progressively rugged, a vast and silent wilderness of broken hills and canyons, the star-bright sky painting the patches of snow in old silver and playing weird tricks with the shadows deep in the gorges.

David felt Carol shiver close to him.

"Cold?" he asked.

"No." She laughed apologetically. "I guess I'm just a little scared."

"Why?"

"Well, in the first place, you're driving awfully fast. And in the second place, it's so wild and lonely up here in the mountains. And the way this road curves around and around the mountain with those deep canyons dropping off on both sides——"

"Don't worry," he reassured her. "I've driven this road so many times, I think I could do it with my eyes shut and one hand tied behind my back."

They kept climbing for a few minutes before either of them spoke again. Then Carol said thoughtfully:

"Funny what a difference a little distance makes, David. Back in New York—and yes, even in San Diego—there was always that terrible pressure, that awful *waiting*. But this mountain seems so remote, so far away from everybody and everything. It's another world—a whole new peaceful world."

He nodded. He, too, felt the release. What had happened back in New York seemed now an ugly and nightmarish dream. Whatever happened to the cities, he had thought, even if they were blasted clean off the earth, these mountains would still be around.

But then he remembered the group in the candy store back on Broadway. The talk of neutron radiation, the proprietor, Sam, worrying about his family in the Catskills.

And he thought, The mountains would still be around, but not for man or any other living thing.

Carol leaned her head on his shoulder and dozed a little. He drove on, now and then looking up through the Plexiglas roof of his car, up into the cold night sky. The heavens were blazing, as though some mighty hunter had raised his gun in glee and spattered the black backdrop with a million silver buckshot. His practiced, professional eye picked out the buckshot one by one—cold, dull red Betelgeuse, yellow Capella, familiar Polaris, white-hot and blue-hot Vega and Rigel, and the brightest of them all, Sirius.

He had seen them often enough, studied them through the months and years, and yet he could never get over the wonder of them. There they were, up there now, swimming around among the deep-sky objects—the galaxies, open and globular clusters, diffuse and planetary nebulae, and the bright riot of the Milky Way. They had been moving in their courses billions of years ago, and they would go on, thought David. They would go on in their preordained courses, through astronomical and infinite time, long after the earth had ceased to be.

The Old Man and he had enjoyed many a long talk over early-morning coffee, after the night's work was done and the droning motors closed the dome against the paling sky. On cloudy nights, when the dome stayed up, they played chess in Dr. Dawson's study, and after that, over their brandy, they had often talked all night. And more often than not, the Old Man talked of the sky in non-astronomical terms. David recalled something now that the Old Man had said in one of these sessions.

"Consider the sky, David," Dr. Dawson had said. "The nonprofessional, perhaps, has never realized that what he sees overhead on a clear night is the most amazing drama ever offered. The curtain rises for him, on any clear night, to reveal a superb play written by a divine hand, and the layman barely gives it a glance. But to you and me it has always been a wonderful antidote for sanity when we compare it to the agitated and unpredictable little madhouse on which we live and quarrel and come to blows and die.

"Yes, David," the Old Man had continued. "You and I are astronomers and, therefore, fortunate. We can always retreat from the turbulence around us to our sanctum sanctorum, the sky. It gives us an exact ruler to measure by, a precise order of ideas. And in the presence of the orderly march of illuminated worlds up there in the void, this cold war, this new threat which currently plagues our fourth-rate planet, seems to be only a local affair of some badly run asylum."

Carol stirred and lifted her head from his shoulder. "How far is it to Palomar?"

"Only a little way. We'll be there in a few minutes now."

Carol pressed her nose against the car window and stared out into the night for a minute. Then she asked: "David, why did they pick *this* isolated mountain for an observatory, anyway?"

"For two reason," he answered. "In the first place, the 'seeing' is good."

"The seeing?"

He laughed at her blank look. "Astronomical argot. It refers to the degree of unsteadiness of the image in the observing instrument, as it's affected by the atmospheric refraction of light rays. And the atmosphere itself here is clear the year round—makes for ideal observation. It's comparatively windless. Oh, there are storms during the winter, of course, but they're pretty short—blow over fast."

"You said there was another reason why they built it here."

"Yes. Palomar's almost earthquake-proof."

"Why?"

He grinned down at her. "Are you really interested?"

"Of course I am. If I'm going to marry an astronomer and live up in the observatory colony, I've got to know *something* about my husband's business! Now then, Doctor, you were saying about earthquakes . . .?"

"Well, it's a little technical, but you asked for it. You see, darling, a few million years ago the flat top of Palomar was on a level with the plain round it."

"Well, I must say it's changed since then," she murmured. "It's certainly grown up to be a big boy."

"And still growing. Geological forces from within have pushed it up until now it's six thousand feet above sea level. This mountain happens to be a solid rock of granite, bounded by two fractures, and it can't be shaken very much by any faulting or quake tremor from within. Any shock spreads through it in a fast-moving wave which has a very small force—too small to damage seriously the instruments and 'scopes in the dome."

"Thank you, Doctor," she said gravely.

He grinned and bowed his head elaborately. And at that moment they plunged out from among the trees and into the open, on the summit of the hill. Carol gave one quick gasp.

"Palomar," said David.

The great central dome leaped out of the ground and thrust itself upward with almost breath-taking suddenness. With the great burnished hemisphere reflecting the sky in a silvery sheen, it looked like a half section of some fantastic, inverted dirigible. Behind the central dome, like some infant it had spawned, stood the tiny dome that housed the eighteen-inch Schmidt camera, and distantly, on an outer ridge, glinted the dome of the forty-eight-inch. The power-house topped another rise, flanked by a brood of shining water tanks. A cluster of small buildings and houses hugged the slope of the mountain, close to the dome. It was an austere sight, and yet a kind of silvery fantasia, a geometric fairyland.

"Well, Carol, how do you like it?" There was a note of pride in David's voice.

She groped for words. "I—why, it's almost fabulous, David—it takes your breath away! It looks just like one of those pictures you see in nursery books about the Wizard of Oz or Puss in Boots. You know, where the king's castle is balanced on top of a mountain, surrounded by little cottages perched crazily around on the sides, and a winding road going up."

David grinned. "Come to think of it, it *does* look like that."

As he spoke he saw that the dome of the big building was up, and for a moment it didn't register. This was a clear night, the sky nearly perfect. Then suddenly he remembered. The Old Man wasn't running any takes of the sky tonight. He was closeted in his study with the big shots of the world's observatories and discussing . . .

*What?*

With mounting excitement he drove through the gate of the high wire fence and parked the car in the yard. They stepped out into the sharp, sub-zero cold, and once out of the car, the heavens seemed to come down and blaze and crackle about them, so that the stars seemed almost tinselly artificial in their brightness, and Carol almost fancied that she could actually hear them pop around her shoulders.

They walked halfway around the great, squat, round building before they came to a small door, not much bigger than a house door and almost lost in the massive circular wall. Through this, after identifying themselves to a sergeant at the door, they entered a foyer tastefully and simply furnished in early American and softly lighted by hidden lamps. The reception room beyond the foyer was in the celestial motif, topped by a miniature dome supported on oval arches.

A stout man with iron-gray hair, ruddy-cheeked and neatly dressed in a suit of shiny alpaca, rose from a desk and came forward to meet them. It was obvious that he was dead tired. His face was lined with fatigue, and there were shadows under his eyes.

"Hello, Francis," said David. "Dr. Dawson still in the study with the others?"

"Yes, Dr. Hughes. I didn't dare disturb him—even to tell him you were here. They've been in there for hours."

"Maybe I'd better not barge right in then. I'll wait till they've finished." David suddenly remembered that Carol was at his side. "Oh, darling, this is Francis, our steward, receptionist, and general major-domo of Palomar. He arranges for all the earthy wants of this stargazing colony, and if you ever need anything, call on him. Francis—this is Carol Kenny."

The stout man smiled. "In a way I've already met her face to face, sir. Welcome to Palomar, Miss Kenny."

Carol looked puzzled for a moment until David grinned and said: "Francis is a great radio and television fan. One of your admiring public. He's seen your lovely face on the video screen many a time. In fact, he never fails to keep me posted when you're scheduled to go on."

"Oh." Carol looked gratefully at Francis. "Thank you for reminding him. And of course he's written a lot about you in his letters. He spent half of one whole letter raving about the veal paprika you serve."

Francis blushed. He was obviously pleased as he took their coats and hung them in a closet. When he turned back David looked at him solicitously and said:

"You look all in, Francis."

"It *has* been hectic, sir. Getting all those phone calls through for Dr. Dawson—ordering extra food and setting up extra cots in the auditorium—and then of course arranging for Tom and Guido to drive the station wagons down to San Diego to meet the planes and pick up the astronomers as they came in." Francis shrugged. "Well, sir, you can imagine, none of us have had much sleep in the last twenty-four hours."

"How's Dr. Dawson taking it?" David was concerned. "You know he can't stand too much, Francis—not with his heart."

"Yes, sir. I know. Mrs. Dawson phoned the observatory here from the house three times in the last hour. She's tried to get through to the doctor, and I know she wants to get him home for some rest, but he won't talk to *anyone*. He's just locked himself in the study with the others, and he hasn't had a bite to eat since early this morning."

David thought of the galaxy of names closeted with the Old Man. Then he asked:

"Did you say, Francis, that Varanov of the Pulkovo Observatory was here?"

"Yes, Dr. Hughes."

"Funny they let him leave Russia at a time like this."

"He wasn't in Russia, sir. We located him in Mexico City. He was working on something with Professor Martinez down there. Dr. Dawson had some trouble with the officer in charge of the military guard here. At first he wouldn't admit Varanov into the observatory, but finally Dr. Dawson won out." Then the steward abruptly changed the subject. "Was it really terrible in New York, sir? The radio and television have been broadcasting all kinds of stories."

"It was bad, Francis," admitted David. "But not as bad as a lot of people think. The buildings weren't damaged, outside of the windows, and those people who got hurt were caught in the streets."

Francis shook his head. "I don't know, Dr. Hughes, up here we're so far from everything. They say the Soviets are responsible, that they've got some kind of new and terrible weapon. But I don't know. I just don't understand how it ever got to this. Another war, after the last one . . ."

Suddenly the steward remembered his duties and turned to Carol.

"Oh. You must be tired after your trip, Miss Kenny." And then to David: "I've saved her one of the small guest cottages, sir."

"Thank you, Francis," said David. "I appreciate it."

"And so do I," added Carol. "But somehow I'm not the least bit tired right now——"

She broke off abruptly as a tall, regal-looking woman with snow-white hair came through the foyer door.

"Well, David!" Her bright eyes showed relief as Francis hurried to her and helped her off with her coat. "We were half afraid you weren't coming back!" Then she looked at Carol. "And this is Carol."

"Carol," said David, "this is Mrs. Dawson."

"You're right, David," Emily Dawson looked at Carol appraisingly. "She is lovely. And I'm glad you came, Carol; this young man was eating his heart out." She took Carol's hands in her own and smiled warmly. "Welcome to Palomar."

"Thank you, Mrs. Dawson."

Emily Dawson had met the Old Man when he was a student at Harvard. David could never look at her without thinking that she must have been a beauty in those days, in the days of her youth. Her features were chiseled so straight that they were almost severe, but her warm smile and the gracious welcome in her lively blue eyes belied any reserve. Her hair was startling, almost showy in its whiteness, and her skin was smooth, delicate in texture, and gave the illusion of being almost transparent.

It struck David, as he watched Emily Dawson and Carol standing together, that the Old Man's wife was still a beauty, in a great and gracious way, in a different, antique frame.

Those who knew the Old Man said she provided the only earthbound competition to the stars in his affection. She fussed over him, worried about his food, bought his clothes, saw that he carried his heart tablets in every suit. And, as Mrs. Dawson once said to David:

"I'm not a wife to the doctor, David. I'm just his caretaker."

But she was his wife. The Old Man was utterly helpless without her. And now Emily Dawson was holding Carol at arm's length and smiling into her eyes.

"Well, my dear! You're going to be an astronomer's wife. How do you think you'll like it?"

"I think I'll like it very much."

"Wait, child, wait!" The Old Man's wife shook her head dismally. "You'll be the most miserable woman in the world in a little while. No sensible girl in her right mind should marry an astronomer."

"But why not?"

"Astronomers work nights, my dear. You'll never have any social life. If you want to go to the theater, you have to consult the weatherman and make sure you buy your tickets on a cloudy night. If you want your husband to take you to a concert, you pray for rain. Sometimes, when the weather is clear and you've been home alone night after night, you could scream for a few friendly clouds to come along and cover the sky, so that your husband can come home from the observatory and keep you company."

She shook her head again, dolefully. "Take the advice of an old woman, Carol. Learn to knit or take up solitaire—anything to occupy those long evening hours. Otherwise you'll be horribly bored and start thinking of how nice it would be to be married to someone in the plumbing-supply business."

David grinned at the Old Man's wife. "Before Carol has a chance to answer, Mrs. Dawson, and before you have any more chance to break up my happy home before it begins, *I'd* like to put *my* two cents in."

"Yes?"

"I've known you for a few years, and I can't remember ever seeing *you* knitting, or playing solitaire either. And I'd be willing to bet you aren't bored."

The phone buzzed. Francis answered it and then stiffened tensely at his desk.

"Yes, Doctor," Francis was saying. "Yes, sir, Dr. Hughes is here. He just came in with Miss Kenny. Yes, I'll tell him. What was that, sir? Bring the small radio into the study? Yes, Doctor, at once."

Emily Dawson went to Francis quickly. "Tell the doctor I want to speak to him."

She took the phone. "Charles, you've got to stop. You've got to come home and get some rest. . . . I know, I know. It's important, it's always important. But this time, Charles, you're overdoing it. I don't know what you're up to—you've never told me—but nothing is that important." She listened for a moment and then hung up.

Her eyes were dull now, her lighthearted mood gone; she looked tired, worried.

"I can't do anything with him. I can't do a thing with him, David. It's the first time. And whatever this thing is, he'll kill himself."

So the Old Man wanted the radio in his study, thought David. Ordinarily Dr. Dawson hated the radio and television both. They intruded with affairs that didn't interest him, that disturbed him, that violated the tranquillity of his own kingdom.

But now he was asking for it. Funny, thought David. The Old Man was closeted in his study with a group of top men, the greatest astronomers of them all, whose only horizon was infinity.

But a radio was an earthly affair, confined to earthly matters. It had nothing to do with nebulae or island universes millions and billions of light years away.

They must be talking about something very close to home, guessed David.

But if so, *what?*

He thought of the wild rumors sweeping the country, the phenomenon at New York, the Russian secret weapon General Hawthorne had talked about. Hawthorne had said that it was something on a cosmic scale.

Maybe, thought David, maybe the general was right. Maybe Hawthorne had something, after all.

Maybe that's what they were discussing in the Old Man's study right now—looking down at their feet instead of over their heads.

"Dr. Dawson wants to see you in a few minutes, Dr. Hughes," Francis was saying. "He told me to tell you to stand by."

David nodded. Then, as the steward was helping Emily Dawson on with her coat, David took Carol's arm.

"Carol, you don't have to wait——"

"I'd like to, David," she said. "I'm not tired at all, and I'd like to see the observatory. I'm terribly curious."

"If you wish, Dr. Hughes," said the steward. "I could——"

"Thanks just the same, Francis," interrupted David. "But you've got plenty to do as it is. Anyway, I'd like to show her around myself while I wait for that meeting to finish."

Mrs. Dawson offered Carol the hospitality of her home for the night, but David thanked her on Carol's behalf and told her that Francis had already made arrangements. Then the Old Man's wife turned to Francis and said:

"Francis, I'll be waiting up. The moment the doctor finishes, call me. I'll come for him myself." Her face sagged a little now, it was haggard, but she smiled as she turned to Carol.

"Please come and see me tomorrow, my dear."

After Emily Dawson had left, and as Francis was disconnecting the small radio from his desk, David said with an attempt at lightness:

"Come on, Carol. I'll take you on the dollar tour."

He led her through a door and onto the ground floor. This was a circular corridor, severely simple and paved in rubber parquet. From it, on each side, ran the astronomers' offices. Then he conducted Carol past the small auditorium and lecture hall, the library, the cafeteria, and the kitchen, gleaming in white tile and monel metal. They walked by a series of darkrooms, and finally he led her into his own office.

"Like it?" he asked.

She studied the leather furniture, the bookshelves recessed in the paneled walls, the deep gray rug, and the illustrations: David's graduating class picture at Columbia, an etching of the original Harvard Observatory, a drawing of Galileo peering through his telescope lens, an air view of Palomar itself, and finally a picture of herself on the leather-topped desk.

"It's very nice, David," she said. "But it's so plain—it needs a little color——"

"Oh no, you don't." He grinned. "No frilly feminine touches for me—not here, anyway. This is my retreat, and if it's monastic— well, I like it that way. I don't care what you do to the cottage we're going to live in—that's your department—but in my office, no colored pottery, no chintz curtains on the windows——"

"*What* windows!" She laughed. "There isn't a window in this whole darned mausoleum!"

He took her back in the rotunda and up the stairs to the mezzanine. He pointed out the lounge, rest rooms, drinking fountains, exhibits of meteoric rock under glass, a model of the observatory itself, literature in racks, illustrations of the planets, and finally a large reception room displaying the history of the 200-inch reflector, in photographs, drawings, and text.

"Now *this* looks a little more comfortable," Carol remarked.

"Yes. The mezzanine here is our concession to the public. People come up here in droves every Sunday, not only from San Diego, but even from Los Angeles."

David had forgotten his somber mood of a few minutes ago. This personal little tour was something he had planned for a long time, and now that Carol was here, he was enjoying her reactions.

"But, David, why should they come here? Isn't the Mount Wilson observatory much nearer to Los Angeles?"

"Sure." He smiled. "And ten years ago, back in 1950, before Palomar was really open to the public on a tourist basis, Wilson used to get all the business. But now *we've* got the biggest eye in the world, while Mount Wilson has to struggle along with a puny 100-inch. And you know people—they like to see the biggest and the best."

"What on earth do you do with them when they get here?"

"Oh, show 'em around—lecture 'em on the theory of operation— open and close the dome for them—let 'em look at the telescope."

"That must keep Dr. Dawson pretty busy on Sundays."

"The Old Man? *He* doesn't wet-nurse the tourists." David made a wry face. "*I* do!"

She laughed up at him. "Well, the public is lucky to have a handsome barker like you. But, David, what do you do, line them up one by one when they want to look through the telescope?"

"Look through *what* telescope?"

"Why, the big one that's here." She was taken aback by his sudden and mock-stern expression. "David, what's the matter? What did I say?"

"Oh, nothing. Nothing but blasphemy, heresy, and sacrilege—at least for an astronomer's wife. I'm glad no one overheard you."

"But all I said was——"

"I know. You see, my darling, you don't *look* through a reflector or mirror telescope. Not a big one like this, anyway. You just take photographs."

"But in all the pictures I've ever seen," she protested, "the astronomer always has his eye screwed up against a little eyepiece at the bottom of the telescope when he's looking at stars and heavenly bodies and things."

He looked even more pained at that. "Sure. But they were looking through a refractor, or lens telescope. They're more romantic— much more photogenic for movies or magazines. As I said, we don't *look* through a reflector like the Big Eye here at Palomar—we get *into* it."

"You what?"

"We ride up to the top of the telescope and climb down inside of it. Or at least the Old Man does. He takes all the observations and makes all the complicated calculations. I just stay below near the switchboard and give him the position settings."

She looked incredulous. "You mean you really get *inside* the telescope?"

"Come on." He grinned. "I'll show you."

He led her out past rows of switchboards protected by roller sheets of metal, and they climbed another flight of parquet stairs into a kind of transparent cubicle completely enclosed by glass, walls and ceiling alike. A tiny glass sign said: "No Visitors Allowed Beyond This Point."

"Well," said David quietly, "there it is—the Big Eye."

"Oh, David!" Her whisper was almost inaudible.

It was a thrilling, awe-inspiring sight. The huge telescope, like a great monstrous robot, loomed up almost vertically, sheer into the shadowy arch of the dome, where its soaring spiderwork disappeared entirely. It was big—big beyond description—almost frightening in its vastness. Its north and south piers, squat and solid and massive, came out of the floor and held up the great apparatus like two hunched shoulders. The two cylinders in its yoke were bigger than railroad cars as they reached out for support into the horseshoe of the frame. The telescope tube itself rested silently, delicately, on its trunnions.

It was still, motionless, now. Yet Carol, as she stared at it, almost had the feeling that it was alive, that it had a beating heart and nerves and muscles, that it was sleeping now but soon would bestir itself, yawn, and then reach up and up toward the stars, its five hundred tons creaking and groaning in the joints as it stretched itself.

"It gets you, doesn't it?" said David softly.

"Oh yes, yes," she whispered. "David, what—what does a Thing like that *do?*"

"More than any man ever dreamed would be possible." He spoke almost reverently. "The Big Eye right out there has reached up into billions of light years of cold space, Carol. It's pulled down stars and nebulae and supernovae we never knew existed before, and dropped them right into our laps. It's discovered new and remote worlds—millions and millions of them—some of them vast enough to make our own look like a microscopic speck of dust floating around in a stadium." He was staring up into the dome, talking half to himself now. "It's brought enough light down through what we call the tube and onto that big mirror to make real studies of the galactic systems, the binary stars and their separation, and the secret of the expanding universe itself——"

"I'm not sure of what you're saying," she interrupted. "But just hearing it makes my head swim."

He nodded. "Unless you're an astronomer, Carol, I suppose this *is* so much Greek. But putting it in layman's language, that big 'scope out there is already giving us the story of how stars are born, how big they are, how hot they get, and how long they have to live. And that isn't all. From that kind of data we're already getting a hint of how long *we* have to live right here on earth."

She stared at him. "How?"

"Well, it's this way, Carol. The sun itself is a star—and pretty small potatoes, a poor relative, as far as stars go. In terms of stellar distance, the earth is practically glued to it. When we find out how old the sun actually is, we'll be able to predict how much longer it's going to shine, giving us light and heat." He smiled. "See? We're kicking around in this particular universe on borrowed time. We've hitched our earthy wagon to a star, but someday that star's going to lie down and slowly die on us!"

She shuddered. "What a horrible thought!"

"Don't worry." He laughed. "We're still good for a few billion years yet." Suddenly he sobered. "Or—we were. Now—I don't know. It looks as though man, with his little atom bomb, is going to beat the sun to the punch and get rid of himself first." He took her arm. "Come on, Carol. I'll take you up to the top."

"You mean—way up there?" She looked apprehensively up into the shadowy dome.

"Sure. Up to the observer's cage, inside the top of the 'scope." He led her back down the stairs and into the corridor. "We never take the public into the observation room itself. You see, Carol, crowds generate heat from their bodies, and just a couple of degrees' rise in the observation-room temperature would be enough to throw several of the delicate instruments right out of whack. And of course we rarely give anybody a ride to the top. You ought to feel very flattered."

"Thank you," she said weakly. "But right now I'm beginning to feel scared."

He went to a locker, pulled out two heavy fleece-lined suits, fur hats with ear muffs attached, heavy mittens, and scarves. "We'd better put these on," he said. "If we're going for a ride to heaven, we'd better be dressed for it. Gets pretty cold up there in the dome. From the way it felt when we got out of the car in the yard, it's well below zero."

They wriggled into the heavy clothing, and then David led her to a small automatic elevator. In a few moments they stopped at the main floor, and as the elevator door opened, a cold blast of air hit them. David stepped out, went to a control board, and pushed a button. A motor droned somewhere, and the hemispheric roof opened into two halves. Only an almost imperceptible hum and a faint lightening of the shadows indicated that the roof was opening at all. Carol, craning her neck and looking straight upward, finally made out a faint segment of blue-black sky and two or three faint stars almost hanging onto the end of the 'scope as it thrust up vaguely into the slice of night between the parted dome.

David came away from the control room, smiling. "Of course this is just a demonstration. We're not going to take any observations or anything like that. I just wanted you to know what it was like when the dome was down."

He led her back into the elevator, and they stopped on a narrow balcony. From here they climbed a short, circular iron stairway to what David called the "jump-off" bridge. They were already at a dizzy height, and he could feel Carol holding his hand with almost frantic pressure. A blast of icy-cold air blew down upon them through the open dome.

"All right, darling?" he asked.

"I think so," she said in a small voice. "But as far as I'm concerned this is the end of the world."

He held her close. "In a way it is. From here on we take a scenic railway to the stars."

He pressed a push button on the bridge. Carol gasped as a flying conveyor car raced down a curved track from an invisible perch far up under the dome and stopped at the bridge. David grinned at her discomfiture and motioned her to step onto the narrow car.

She looked at him and shook her head, a little pale. "Don't be afraid," he said gently. "Just hang onto me." He held her by the arm, and gingerly she stepped across the abyss beneath and onto the car.

David closed the small swinging gate on the conveyor car and locked it. "Hang onto the rail with both hands," he said.

Then he pushed a button, and somewhere below motors began to sing a muted song. The cage glided away, then soared outward and upward in a dizzy, fantastic ascent toward the top of the telescope. Now they were two fur-covered pygmies whirling up into the vault of the dome, riding a steel carpet toward the stars. Finally the car slowed and came to a stop next to a catwalk. The observation floor yawned far below, and they were almost fifteen stories from the ground level itself.

For a moment Carol clung to David, trembling as he held her. He was immediately penitent. "Maybe I shouldn't have brought you up here."

"No, no," she said faintly. "I—just for a moment I felt—well, a little sick. I'll be all right."

"Sure?" He was really concerned now.

She nodded. He held onto her and pointed down into the top of the telescope. She saw a cisternlike cubbyhole, a cylindrical steel well, with a curved bottom and an instrument desk coming up through the floor. There was a strange-looking little chair at the desk which rolled around on rails within the well, and an instrument panel opposite the desk, set with dials.

"This is the observer's cage," said David. "The Old Man sits in that chair and through the voice-power phone signals to me down at the control board for star settings. When I start the Big Eye moving, he rides along down there inside of it, watching those luminous dials until they indicate the exact observation position. Then he pushes his photographic plateholder into position, pulls out the slide—and that's the 'take.' "

He said nothing more for the moment. They stood there, clinging to the catwalk. Carol felt David's arm slip around her waist, and she leaned against him. A strange, almost wild feeling of exaltation filled her, and she looked up through the dome into the indigo sky. The stars seemed to be floating by across it, moving through it like tiny lighted ships at sea.

They had escaped from their own planet now, and they were standing in space. They had stepped off the earth and ridden up into the mysterious bosom of the heavens and thrust their heads among the stars, into the vault of the universe itself. Up there the illuminated stars moved along their ordained paths through infinity, through everlasting tranquillity. The earth was not a few feet below, but a million light years below, a remote and troubled and diseased speck of dirt swimming around in the void, crawling with microscopic and cannibalistic organisms.

"It's wonderful," Carol whispered, "wonderful. I've never felt so exhilarated, so *free*." She stole a look at David's face, saw his reverent, faraway look.

It's like being close to God up here, she thought, so close that you could almost see His face.

The phone suddenly buzzed down in the cisternlike cage. Like a noisy burglar, it broke the silence and the spell. Up here at the top of the telescope, they had for a moment soared into the heavens, but now they knew that it, too, was earthbound.

David turned to Carol. "Somebody below wants us," he said. "Do you think you can hang onto the catwalk here for a moment?"

She nodded. He walked to the top of the telescope and clambered down a series of pipe rails into the cage. The phone buzzed again, and he hunched over it like a furry dwarf, fumbling with the receiver in his heavy mittens.

He spoke briefly, put the receiver back on the hook, and then looked up at Carol from the cistern below.

"That was Francis. We'd better go right back down. The Old Man wants to see me now."

**6.** As they descended to the ground-floor corridor they heard the news coming over Francis's radio, muffled in the Old Man's study.

They were back on earth again.

Outside of Dr. Dawson's study they saw small knots of men gathered, talking in low voices. David was struck by the fact that their faces were taut and grim, that they seemed strangely quiet, without animation.

He picked them out one by one—Ellender of the Harvard Observatory, the shaggy man with the ill-fitting suit; Manning of Mount Wilson, a giant of a man, bald as a billiard ball; Van Vreeden of Holland; Perez of Brazil, rotund and swarthy; Varanov, the Russian from Leningrad, a white-bearded man with ice-blue eyes; Dr. Smythe of the Royal Astronomical Society, a wizened hunchback.

There were others, too, whom Francis hadn't mentioned. Duval, who watched the heavens from the Swiss Alps, Wallace of Aberdeen, Alvarez of Chile. Many of them were refugees from Soviet-dominated Europe and Asia.

What was the matter with them? thought David, bewildered. Where was all the excitement of the new discovery, *if* there had been something new. Why were they speaking in hushed tones? Why were their faces so grave, so pale and rigid, like puppet masks?

David walked up to Dr. Ellender and extended his hand. Ellender had been his mentor at Harvard and had been largely instrumental in getting the Old Man to invite David to Palomar. But Ellender seemed hardly to recognize him; his gray eyes seemed to look through and beyond David.

"Hello, David," he said absently. That was all. Ellender turned and followed the other men down the corridor. His hand, in the brief moment it had touched David's, was damp and limp and cold. And his forehead, too, was wet with perspiration.

As they drifted off, Francis came out of the reception room and met David and Carol near Dr. Dawson's door. Then he added almost apologetically:

"Dr. Dawson just rang for me, Dr. Hughes. He asked me to bring in both of you."

David looked puzzled for a moment and then knocked on the door. A gentle voice spoke from within, almost inaudibly.

"Come in."

A man was seated at a desk piled with a jumble of books, slide rules, photographs, pencils, and yellow scratch pads covered with computations. Carol looked at him curiously as he rose to greet them. So this is Dr. Dawson, she thought. This is the Old Man of the Mountain, the Wizard of Palomar, one of the great men of all time, whose back yard was the universe itself.

Carol lived in a world of celebrities, of Big Names, and she was used to them. She was one herself, in a modest way. Yet in the presence of this man she suddenly felt an almost embarrassing humility. There was nothing blatant about his appearance, nothing particularly bizarre or striking. Yet in a roomful of men you would pick him out among all the others for some baffling reason. You would know instinctively that here was a great man, a man who attracted others by a personal magnetism of sheer intelligence glowing from within and radiating outward.

"Dr. Dawson," said David. "This is my fiancée, Carol Kenny."

The Old Man offered her a thin, blue-veined hand. "Welcome to Palomar, Miss Kenny."

He spoke mechanically, almost without interest, as though he were hardly aware she was there. He seemed preoccupied, a million miles away. He was courteous enough, but there was no warmth in his voice, no welcoming smile.

The Old Man's just going through the motions, that's all, thought David.

It was unbelievable, he thought, unbelievable. He'd never seen the Old Man act like this before. Ordinarily Dr. Dawson was an unfailing gentleman in his relations with others. He put them at their ease, and they took to him immediately. No matter whom he met, in whatever station of life, he gave others the impression of humility, made them feel that it was *his* privilege to meet them, listened intently to what they had to say, as though every word they spoke were a word of wisdom. David knew that this appreciation of others was genuine. The Old Man was no poseur. Yet now he was almost rude.

It was plain that something had shaken him deeply, that he was laboring under some kind of tremendous tension. There was no other answer. After all, he wasn't meeting a perfect stranger in Carol. He had always been keenly interested in her, had asked David a hundred questions about her, had looked forward to meeting her. Now . . .

"You must be tired after your trip, Miss Kenny. Francis here will take you to your quarters if you wish."

His voice was gentle, but it was an obvious dismissal. David, shocked, glanced at Carol to see how she was taking it. He wondered: What is she thinking of the Old Man now—especially after the way I built him up?

But Carol was sensitive and a good actress. She could see that the Old Man wanted to be alone with David. She only smiled gratefully and said: "I *am* a little tired, Dr. Dawson. Thank you for being so thoughtful." David saw her to the door with Francis and squeezed her hand. "See you in the morning, darling," he said. Then he closed the door and turned to face the Old Man.

"Sit down, my boy," said Dr. Dawson gently.

David sank into one of the deep leather chairs. His curiosity was like a mouse in his belly, gnawing away at his innards. What was the Old Man waiting to tell him?

Slowly, almost deliberately, Dr. Dawson reached into his desk, took out one of the small cigars he favored. He lit it, and as he did David saw that his hand trembled.

"My boy, I don't have to tell you that something tremendous has happened. You know that I would not have countermanded General Hawthorne's order and exposed you to grave charges without a very good reason."

David nodded. The Old Man puffed on his cigar for a moment and looked steadily at his protégé. Then he said suddenly:

"David—do you believe in God?"

David's mouth dropped half open at the question. It stunned him by its very suddenness, by its irrelevance to anything he had even remotely expected. But the Old Man was dead serious, his eyes demanded an answer, and David managed to falter:

"Of course, sir, of course—I believe in God."

The Old Man paused. He seemed to look deep into David, weighing the sincerity of his answer. Then he said quietly:

"I know what you must be thinking, my boy, and I don't blame you. But I have not gone suddenly mad, and I am not yet senile. We have known each other for some time, David, and for some reason we have never touched upon this subject, this subject of faith, or religion, if you like. Now, in view of what has happened, I had to ask you, I had to know."

*In view of what has happened*, the Old Man had just said. Well, thought David, what *has* happened? And what did God have to do with it?

Dr. Dawson seemed to anticipate what David was thinking. He went on:

"Here at Palomar, David, you and I, as astronomers, have seen the great procession of stars and planets move in their immutable courses. We have named and classified them, measured them in precise terms—positions, orbits, velocities, temperatures, luminosities, compositions, and absolute magnitudes. If, in doing this kind of work, we have thought of our relationship to God at all, we have marveled at the orderly manner in which He has arranged the expanding universe."

Dr. Dawson put his cigar on a tray and leaned back in his chair, his eyes half closed. Then he continued:

"There are men of science who, since they cannot measure God, weigh him, or produce Him in chemical synthesis, are not concerned with his existence. Yet even *they* must have reflected that once, at the beginning of time, there was an original nebula that filled the void of the universe with equal density everywhere. They must have asked themselves, 'Where did it come from? How did it get there? Who put it there?' If a Creator did not create it, *who* did? If the agnostics and atheists among us do not admit the role of a Creator here, they must at least admit that it is an undefinable mystery.

"At any rate, David, whatever the innermost conviction of each man, it is only the fool who does not at least admit the mystery of creation—who thinks that everything just 'happened' somehow."

Dr. Dawson paused, looked steadily at David. "Forgive me, my boy, for all this preamble. But it is very pertinent to what I have to say." He measured his words. "In the past few months, David, I have seen a miracle. I have witnessed the *hand of God* suddenly appear in the universe."

"*The hand of God?*" echoed David stupidly.

The Old Man nodded. He reached forward on his desk, picked up a batch of enlarged photographs.

"Look at these."

David stared at the top photograph. So *this* was the project Dr. Dawson had been working on so feverishly through the Big Eye. This was why, at the Old Man's urgent request, Ellender, Perez, Varanov, and the others had come running to Palomar from all over the world. They *were* concerned with the sky, after all, and not with earth-bound matters.

He studied the photograph eagerly. It was that of a familiar constellation, and his practiced eye picked out at first glance what seemed to be a normal astronomical pattern. His mind clicked over like a comptometer, identifying the various members in the group.

Then suddenly something jarred his vision.

It was a tiny patch of light where no light should have been.

Dr. Dawson hadn't even labeled it.

David tried to place the intruder, tried to identify it. But it was foreign to him; he had never seen it before. He shuffled through the other photographs. There it was, again and again, the annoying and insistent extra patch of light, hanging on like a bright little leech. It changed its position as the dates of the observations changed, but it was there every time, sharp and clear.

It was all the more mysterious because Dr. Dawson had neglected to give it a name.

David stared at the photograph again, and his mind leaped to the possibility of asteroids or a new comet, but as quickly abandoned the idea as he shuffled through the other photographs.

David looked up at the Old Man, bewildered.

"I don't understand it, sir. It's something I don't recognize— something that doesn't belong——" He caught his breath as he saw the expression on the Old Man's face. "You mean it's something brand new—something we've never seen before?"

The Old Man nodded. "You and I are among the first to see it, David, with the help of the 200-inch telescope. But in the not-too-distant future it will be visible not only to other astronomers with smaller telescopes, but finally to the naked eye of the whole world. It was only by sheer accident, by the most remote chance, that I stumbled on it first, late in September, while doing some routine observations."

"But what is it, sir," asked David, "that extra point of light?"

"A new planet," answered the Old Man quietly.

*"A new planet?"*

"Yes, David. A strange new intruder into our solar system. Not an ordinary planet in the conventional sense, for it doesn't revolve around our sun at all. But a planet in size and mass and every other detail."

Dr. Dawson paused a moment as David kept his eyes glued to the tiny patch of silver. Then he continued:

"As you know, the last planet discovered was Pluto, back in 1930, at the Lowell Observatory. At the time of its discovery, before it was officially named Pluto, it was designated as Planet 'X.'

"Therefore, I shall name this newcomer—Planet 'Y.' "

*Planet "Y"!*

David was staggered. He stared at the Old Man stupidly. For a moment he could not believe what he had heard. No wonder the greatest astronomers alive had dropped whatever they were working on and answered the Old Man's summons!

This was one of those dream discoveries, the greatest triumph of the Big Eye, an astronomical miracle. He thought dazedly of what would happen in the observatories of the world when the news came out officially. That is, if the world was still around.

They'd go crazy, he thought, crazy!

So *this* was the answer! *This* was what the Old Man was talking about—the *hand of God*. This was it, this extra patch of light. There it was, planted on those photographs, sharp and clear.

For as long as men could remember there had been only nine planets revolving around the sun.

*And now—now there were ten.*

Now, as the Old Man had put it, there was a strange new intruder in the sky, a kind of heavenly stepchild, a celestial Johnny-come-lately.

Planet "Y."

"It's a massive body, as planets go," the Old Man was saying. "Much bigger than the earth. And it's traveling through space with fantastic velocity, far greater than that of the earth. It made the orbit difficult to calculate. In fact, two years ago it would have been impossible, before Morrissey built us his analogue computer."

Dr. Dawson's voice leveled off into a monotone, as though he were delivering a lecture before a science forum. "Although we can now see it and trace its orbit, we don't know where this wildcat planet came from, and we never will. The origin of Planet 'Y,' David, does not fit into any of the present cosmogonies. If we accept the Weizsäcker hypothesis as correct for the formation of our own solar system, we must reluctantly conclude that there are exceptions to it as a rule. For Planet 'Y' must have been born in the fiery explosion of a supernova."

David nodded. "I would agree, sir. It seems to me only the expanding wave front of a bursting sun could have given it the initial velocity necessary to bring it toward our system at its present speed."

As he spoke he reflected on what a triumph this would be for the Old Man. To discover a new planet was tremendous enough, but to add to it a major contribution to the theory of planetogenesis was enough to shatter the calm in every observatory in the world.

"At any rate, David," the Old Man went on, "Planet 'Y' was born. It was hurled off into space, traveling like a fantastic juggernaut, drifting through space for thousands or millions of years.

Then at last it came into the gravitational field of a star, was caught
and held. It is plunging toward that star now."

"And that star," said David, "is the sun."

"Yes."

"It's a great discovery, sir." David's voice shook a little. "No
wonder you called those men to Palomar. It'll create a sensation."

Yet as David spoke he wondered, even so, even in the face of this
tremendous new phenomenon, why had the Old Man ordered him
back in such a hurry?

"As you say, David," continued Dr. Dawson, "this new intruder
into our solar system will create a sensation. But it is more than
just a new planet. The consequences of its appearance are staggering beyond the limits of human imagination and there is no doubt
it will profoundly change the pattern of human life. If this new
planet is anything it is the hand of God."

There he goes again, thought David. The hand of God.

The Old Man seemed obsessed with the idea. Dr. Dawson was a
scientist, through and through, and yet what he was saying now
was curiously unscientific. Of course, David said to himself, it was
a miracle, but you could figure it on a cause-and-effect basis. A
fragment from a distant star coming within the sun's gravitational
field and swinging in an orbit around it.

It was the longest long shot possible, but theoretically it could
happen.

In fact, it *had* happened.

But that wasn't all, apparently. There was more that the Old Man
was getting ready to say. David could see it in his face, read it in
his over-bright eyes.

There was something else coming. Something big.

But *what?*

What could top a discovery like this? The Old Man had said
something about the planet's changing the way men lived. It struck
like a jagged fragment in David's mind. Where did *that* belong
in all this?

"David," said the Old Man, "everything I have discussed up to now has been a kind of preamble, by way of preparation for what I have to tell you now. A minute ago I asked you if you believed in God, and I said I had a reason for the question. If your belief is sincere, if your faith is deep-rooted, then it will give you strength to meet the revelation I am about to make to you, and even help you gain some comfort from it." Dr. Dawson hesitated a moment. "Now, David, I must ask you to prepare for a shock—a very great shock."

David sat rigid in his chair, fascinated, watching the Old Man. His collar suddenly seemed to be unnaturally tight, and he felt the goose flesh rise on his body. For a moment neither of them spoke.

Finally the Old Man picked up a chart from his desk.

"This chart illustrates the future orbit of the new planet, David. I've been plotting it for days, but I got my first result about an hour after you left for New York on Wednesday."

David looked down at the chart.

Then suddenly it swam before his eyes as the full implication of what he saw smashed into his brain. The sweat broke out in a cold ooze on his forehead, his mouth went dry, a cruel hand seemed to be curling itself around his throat, stifling his breath.

It was right there before his eyes. The awful and incredible denouement to the Old Man's discovery.

Planet "Y" was headed for an elliptical orbit around the sun. But its orbit intersected that of the earth, and the chart showed both bodies reaching the intersection point simultaneously.

Long before the geometric point of intersection, Planet "Y" would come close enough to exert a tremendous gravitational pull upon the earth, send it flying out of its orbit and toward Planet "Y" itself. And that would mean—*planetary collision.*

*The end of the world!*

It was right there, right there in neat circles on that crisp piece of graph paper. Dr. Dawson had indicated the point where the clash would come. He had marked it with a tiny "x." X marks the spot, thought David foolishly; x marks the spot where the accident would occur.

Like a man in a dream, he put his finger on the point.

The Old Man nodded. "The point of final gravitational attraction, David. The cosmic collision point."

It was impossible, of course. In the infinite sweep of space, the earth was merely a speck of dust. So was this new planet, this Planet "Y." Every law of chance was against it. A billion billion billion to one.

But there it was, right there in the diagram. There were the orbits of Planet "Y" and the earth.

And there was the point of collision. And nothing, nobody could stop it.

The end of the world.

The end of the world! The end of tne world! It beat through David Hughes's head like an awful refrain.

It was fantastic. It was something you toyed with in your imagination, or read about in those weird fiction stories. Soothsayers from the beginning of time had been predicting it, religious fanatics had seen it in their visions, and every year some crackpot predicted the exact day and hour of the catastrophe.

But people just laughed or shrugged and went about their business. The newspapers sent a photographer to take pictures of the cranks and their followers, usually kneeling and praying on some mountaintop as the appointed hour drew near.

But the hour came and went, and the earth kept right on rotating on its axis, and the photographers got their pictures. And the crackpot and his followers finally gave up and sheepishly went home.

And the next year there was always a new prophet and a new flock, a new day and a new hour. And a new picture in the press for the people to smile at the next day.

But this new prophet was not a crank. He was the man sitting at the desk, the man watching him with compassion in his eyes. He was Dr. Charles Dawson, a man of science, who placed no reliance in visions or dreams.

"At first I couldn't believe what I saw," the Old Man was saying. "I went over my calculations again and again. And invariably I always came to the same result—the same staggering result.

"It was then that I called the men from the other observatories —the only men in the world who knew the necessary mathematics for this problem—the best research astronomers in the world. I wanted them to check my calculations. I didn't dare trust myself.

"Furthermore, David, I could not announce this terrible phenomenon to the world alone. The responsibility would be too great, and there would be skepticism. After all, the world would have only my word, only one man's word, that the catastrophe would occur. But if the announcement came simultaneously from a group of the greatest astronomers in the world, then there would be no room for doubt, it would then be accepted as the truth it is."

Yes, thought David, this white-haired man sitting here in this quiet room was the true prophet, whose gospel and predictions were made on cold, hard facts. And these facts had been attested to by other true prophets like himself.

"Then that tremor we had in New York—those other phenomena General Hawthorne spoke about . . ." began David.

"Are all the result of natural stress and strain from the intrusion of this new astronomical body in the solar system," said the Old Man. "The fact is, they should have been even more violent and widespread, and in our discussion here we were puzzled as to why they were not. The only explanation we can offer is that, curiously enough, the other celestial bodies in our system seem to have moved into a new position of balance, compensating the strain. And so we can count on a little more time than we had expected."

It was clear to David now—*too* clear.

"Then there's no Russian secret weapon, after all."

"No, David. And as far as I know, there never was. What happened in the city of New York was a cracking of the bedrock, a minor earthquake fault in the rock. The other phenomena can no doubt be similarly explained."

David could have sworn that he saw the flicker of a smile on Dr. Dawson's face as the Old Man continued:

"Professor Varanov of Leningrad is here at Palomar, David, as you probably know. And I have it from him that the same kinds of baffling phenomena have taken place recently, not only in the Soviet Union, but in Soviet-dominated Europe and Asia. There has been an earthquake in Warsaw and tidal waves at both Naples and Vladivostok, to name a few. The Russians are sure *we* have a new and terrible weapon of some kind."

David suddenly recalled the news broadcast aboard the strato-cruiser as they were coming into San Diego a few hours ago.

"Then it was you who called the President, Doctor?"

The Old Man nodded. "I told him about the planet, told him it was on its way, and begged him to hold off any positive move for a few hours, until we were absolutely sure there would be a collision. Now—we are." Dr. Dawson paused for a moment. "We had to stop the fools from destroying each other before the planet ended their natural time."

*Before the planet ended their natural time.*

*When? When would it strike?*

That was the question, the question he avoided, the question that stuck in his throat, that he did not dare ask.

But now it was insistent, it wouldn't stay down, it demanded an answer.

"Do you know when the collision will come, Dr. Dawson?"

The Old Man nodded, but he did not answer immediately. It was still in the study, very still, except for the regular ticking of the clock in the corner. Then finally he spoke.

"A decade ago, as you well know, David, even a rough conclusion would have been impossible. But we have come a long way since then, with the new instruments we have developed and the new mathematical techniques we have evolved, and indeed with the 200-inch reflector itself. But now, although it is too early yet to calculate the exact hour, we have been able to calculate the day."

"When will it be?" asked David. He was impatient; he wanted the Old Man to get to it, and get to it quick. "What day will it be?"

"The end will come in two years and one month," answered the Old Man quietly. "On Christmas Day, 1962."

*Christmas Day, 1962!*

"A date not without its irony," Dr. Dawson was saying. "And yet an appropriate day, when one considers that almost two thousand years ago a miracle had been ushered in by a new heavenly body shining in the sky. It had heralded the birth of a new idea and then disappeared off into the void." The Old Man's voice was hushed now, almost inaudible. "It would almost seem, David, that it had made a complete circuit of the heavens and returned, this time in a different and final role."

Yes, David thought wildly, one thing was certain. Planet "Y" didn't just happen, it *couldn't* have just happened; the odds were stacked against it, millions and millions to one.

Whatever it was, it was a sign, a sermon in the sky, a divine wrath, a terrible judgment upon the creatures who called themselves men.

There could be no other answer. The Old Man was right. It *was* the hand of God!

David stared at Dr. Dawson. "What do you think will happen to people when they find out, sir?"

The Old Man leaned back and closed his eyes. "No man can tell, David. All we know is that there'll be profound changes, not only in our social and economic patterns, but in our mental processes. In a way, I got a preview of that this morning. When we started to go over my calculations, two of the astronomers present were confirmed atheists, and others were agnostics. They had believed in a kind of divinity of order, because the system of the heavens had functioned according to a kind of heavenly Hoyle ever since time began.

"But when they learned about this outlaw, this huge gob of matter, plummeting into our lives from nowhere, it smashed their faith or lack of it. The runaway planet up there was the great dissenter, the disrupter of order, the harbinger of chaos. It was the first and final exception to the rule they had worshiped, and they could not escape its timeliness and significance. And when they walked out of here a few minutes ago, David, they were men of religion."

"Two years and one month," murmured David. "It isn't very long."

"No. It's precious little time, David, for man to put his house in order after cluttering it with the refuse and the mistakes and the prejudices of centuries. But I suspect that Planet 'Y' will turn out to be a large and efficient broom."

They sat there silently for a minute, each lost in his own thoughts, listening to the methodical ticking of the clock. Finally David roused himself and asked:

"When will you break the news, sir?"

"Tomorrow morning. Better phone the news syndicates and the radio-television people immediately, David. Oh—and have Hartschorn make slides of those photoplates so that they can be used in the auditorium projector. I'll want you to run the slides off for the press while I lecture."

"Yes, sir," said David mechanically. "I'll call them for tomorrow at ten."

The Old Man nodded. "I'll inform the staff of what's happened at a preliminary meeting and then meet with the other astronomers before we go in."

David hesitated. "You're sure you want to break this—this whole thing, Dr. Dawson?"

"Yes. We decided at the meeting that there was no point in withholding the news. In the first place, we wanted the world to know before it had a chance to blow itself up. In the second place, people would know sooner or later anyway, if they survived themselves. The planet's traveling at tremendous speed, David. And of course it will become visible long before the end comes."

The Old Man rose, put his hand on David's shoulder. His voice was marvelously gentle.

"David, I'm an old man. This coming catastrophe may rob me of some of the years of my life—but not many. It's people like you —you and Miss Kenny—who'll be cheated. I—I don't know what to say to you now. I don't know what any father would say to his son at a time like this." The Old Man hesitated a moment. "I can only say this, try to console you with this—there's still faith. You must have faith."

"Faith?" echoed David. He thought of Carol and the future they had looked forward to. His calm suddenly disappeared, and a wave of bitterness took its place, and he began to tremble a little. Faith. The word stuck in his throat. He looked at the Old Man.

"Faith? Now? Faith in what, sir?"

"In a miracle," said the Old Man quietly. "Another miracle. A miracle of redemption, David."

Not much chance of *that,* David told himself cynically. That planet was on its way, on its regular course up there around the sun, and the earth would be drawn into it, and slam against it on schedule, sometime on Christmas Day, 1962. That was the scientific fact, that was what the Old Man's calculations and charts had said, and they were never wrong, they were as final as doom.

But now the Old Man seemed helpless, seemed to be groping for another sign in the sky. Now he had no calculations, no charts, no telescope photos, no slide rules to conjure up any future miracle. He was without benefit of these comforting things now; he could only fall back on an intangible they called faith and pass it on to him, David Hughes.

And another miracle in another two years was a little too much to hope for.

At the door to the study the Old Man suddenly took David's shoulders and turned him around so that their eyes met.

"Don't let it get you down, my boy. Face it. Try to live normally. Get married. Have a child."

Funny, thought David as the door closed; he had been shaken for a moment, but now he felt better. The Old Man's eyes had been compassionate, they had been serene with a strength of their own, and somehow they had poured that strength into David.

*Try to live normally. Get married. Have a child.*

That was what Dr. Dawson had said. But the Old Man was tired, he wasn't thinking.

If Carol had a child, if she became pregnant almost immediately, it would live hardly more than a year.

**7.** It was well past midnight when David made the last phone call from his office.

"Corey talking." The tired voice over the receiver belonged to the managing editor of the World Press in Los Angeles.

"Mr. Corey, this is David Hughes, Dr. Dawson's assistant here at Palomar Observatory."

"Yes?"

"Dr. Dawson has an important announcement to make. Will you have a representative here at ten o'clock tomorrow morning?"

There was a moment of hesitation at the other end. Then: "What's it all about, Mr. Hughes?"

"I'm sorry. I can't tell you over the phone."

Corey's voice became a little querulous. "You don't seem to realize, Mr. Hughes, that L.A. right now is a ghost town and I've only got a skeleton staff on hand. Under ordinary circumstances anything that Dr. Dawson had to say would be big news, and naturally we'd be more than glad to cover it. But with all hell due to break loose at any moment, you understand I couldn't let a man go all the way up to Palomar unless it was a really big story."

It was all David could do to stop himself from yelling what he knew into the phone. That fool down there in L.A. prattling about how big a story he wanted, thinking in terms of columns and half columns and paragraphs!

Instead David said quietly, "It's a bigger story than you think, Mr. Corey. So big that some of the world's greatest astronomers have flown in to Palomar here to consult with Dr. Dawson. They'll be at the press conference tomorrow."

Corey seemed to be somewhat impressed at this. Then he said:

"Look, Mr. Hughes, if you could just give me an idea of what it's all about over the phone, I could have a rewrite man take it down and give you my solemn promise that we wouldn't break it until you gave us a release with the others."

"No," said David. "I'm sorry. Your man will have to be here. Dr. Dawson will make his announcement personally."

"I see." Corey seemed a little bored now, weary. "And who'd you say would be there besides Dr. Dawson?"

"Well, to name a few, Ellender of Harvard, Bornson of Sweden, Smythe of the Royal Astronomical Society, Van Vreeden of Holland, Varanov of the Pulkovo Observatory in Leningrad——"

"Varanov? The Russian?" Corey's voice leaped suddenly like an electric spark. *"He's* at Palomar?"

"Yes."

David could almost hear Corey's mind clicking over, savoring the news value of this. "How'd he get out of the U.S.S.R. at a time like this? They won't let a sparrow across the Soviet border now."

"We located him in Mexico City."

"I see." Corey was eager now. "Do you think he'll talk?"

"Talk?"

"Yes. About the threat of war, I mean. About the Soviet point of view. As a Russian scientist, he——"

"I can't say," interrupted David sharply. "But he'll be here at ten o'clock in the morning."

"All right," said Corey crisply. "We'll have a man up there then. Thank you very much, Mr. Hughes."

David hung up. He felt a little ill. Corey had been no different from the others. They had all been a little difficult, the press and radio people alike. Not so long ago, as Corey had implied, the mere announcement that the Old Man would have something to say was enough to send a horde of reporters scurrying up to Palomar.

Now, what happened in the heavens was small potatoes, compared to what *might* happen on earth.

It was almost amusing, thought David, in a macabre sort of way. He had actually been forced to "sell" the greatest story of all time.

He felt tired, very tired now. He snapped out his hooded desk light and shuffled out into the darkness of the observatory. It was quiet in the great circular hall, a kind of brooding and unearthly quiet, almost sinister in its overtones. He started for the light switch and then changed his mind. Somehow he didn't feel like facing the glare of lights now.

He walked noiselessly along the corridor, his feet making no sound on the rubber-inlaid floor. He passed the cafeteria, the library, the auditorium and lecture hall. Then he paused for a moment as he saw a crack of light coming from under a door.

The Old Man was still up.

David hesitated, debated whether to knock on the Old Man's door and tell him the press meeting was all set for the next morning. Then he decided against it and went through the door and down the stairs to the ground floor. The night light was on in the reception room, dull blue under its shade, but Francis was gone.

David took his hat and coat from the foyer closet and stepped out into the night.

The cold wind hit him broadside, making him gasp. He turned up his coat collar and walked out of the yard and onto the road, heading for his room at the Monastery a short distance down the road. It was a moonless night, but the heavens, nevertheless, suffused the entire area with light. He had never seen the constellations blaze so brightly. They tipped the domes of the observatories with silver and similarly etched the various buildings of the mountain colony —the water-supply works, the electric plant, the cottages down the road.

David's eye swept the heavens as he walked, glancing momentarily at each illuminated island universe—and then moving on. Yes, they were really putting on a show tonight—Hercules, the Kneeler; Pegasus, the Winged Horse; Sagittarius, the Archer; Cassiopeia, the Lady in the Chair; Canes Venatici, the Hunting Dogs.

And finally his roving eye caught and held the patch of sky where, plummeting onward, cold and lifeless and remorseless,

Planet "Y" was moving on its inexorable and fatal arc, bent on cosmic destruction.

Two years and one month . . .

How long was that? Figure it out. Two times fifty-two. One hundred and four weeks. Plus four, more or less.

One hundred and eight weeks—seven hundred and fifty-six days.

You could go on like that. You could break it down into hours, minutes, and even seconds. But it all added up to the same thing.

Two years and one month. And then—*Merry Christmas.*

How much life could you pack into two years and one month, even by living desperately, with the ticking of the clock loud in your ears? In two years and one month, he, David Hughes, would be thirty-two. A man in his prime. Young enough to enjoy life vigorously, old enough to know how precious it could be.

And even now, as he walked along Observatory Road, he was walking on borrowed time. It was beginning to slip away from him already. These minutes and seconds here on top of Palomar Mountain were now part of a precious stack of chips.

And they were beginning to slip away, he was already beginning to lose. And there was no way of winning them back.

He looked up again, fascinated, at the constellation in which the Old Man had first sighted the killer planet. One night in the not-too-distant future that empty patch would be punctured by a tiny silver pin point. The pin point would get bigger until it became a disk, and then a bigger disk, and then bigger and bigger as it came nearer and nearer, night after night.

And it would have your name on it, and the precise time and date.

And that was the agonizing thing about it—to know exactly when you were going to die. Like the convict in the death house awaiting execution, you would live with your eyes on the clock, cherishing every miserly minute.

But unlike the condemned man who awaited the chair or the hangman's noose, you could not hope. You could not hope for a pardon, or clemency, or a stay of execution, or even an escape.

For you there was no hope, no clemency, no escape.

David Hughes was suddenly afraid—afraid to be out there in the open, in the sharp night, alone. He had been all right back in the Old Man's office, but now—now it was beginning to get him. He began to hurry, to walk faster and faster, like a boy hurrying past a graveyard, his feet crunching on the graveled road.

A kind of panic swept through him as he hurried along, his head up, staring at the sky. Somewhere back in the recesses of his memory he recalled a Mother Goose story, something he had learned as a child in first or second grade:

> *One day Henny-Penny was walking in the woods. An acorn fell from a tree and hit her on the head. "My, my," said Henny-Penny, "the sky is falling, and the world is coming to an end. I must go and tell the King."*
>
> *Then Henny-Penny met Ducky-Lucky. "Where are you going in such a hurry?" said Ducky-Lucky. "The sky is falling," said Henny-Penny, "I must go and tell the King." "Wait for me," said Ducky-Lucky. "I will go with you and tell the King."*
>
> *Then Henny-Penny and Ducky-Lucky met Turkey-Lurkey. "Where are you going in such a hurry?" asked Turkey-Lurkey. "The sky is falling and the world is coming to an end," said Henny-Penny and Ducky-Lucky. "We are going to tell the King. . . ."*

The panic possessed him. It shook him, drove him on, so that now he was half walking, half running past the rows of darkened cottages on each side of the road. He envied the people who slept in them, the telescope mechanics, the steward and the cook, the janitors, the chauffeur, the handy men, the power-plant and Diesel personnel, the others on the Old Man's staff. They and their families slept peacefully now, with nothing on their minds, not even tomorrow.

But tomorrow would be another day. Then they would know what he knew now. And after that they would never again sleep soundly. . . .

He came to the small guest cottage where Carol was staying, and abruptly he stopped.

The cottage was dark, like all the others. Carol was in there, and by now she would be asleep.

Carol . . .

He remembered that night back in her apartment, back in New York. He had been afraid then, although it was nothing like the awful Fear that clutched him now. He had held Carol in his arms, close, very close, and the Fear had gone away, it had ceased to possess him. He had lived for the moment then, and the hell with tomorrow.

He needed Carol again, now. He needed her more than he had then. He needed her more than anything on God's earth. His need of her was like a crying hunger.

He turned and went up the walk and onto the porch. He knocked on the door, softly at first, and then louder and louder, in an almost frantic tattoo.

The lights went on inside the cottage. A curtain parted in a window. Then there was a sound of a key turning, and the door opened.

*"David!"*

She was standing there in the doorway, shivering in a thin robe, staring at him.

He shut the door behind him and without a word swept her into his arms.


It was two minutes before ten o'clock in the morning.

The reporters, the radio and television men had already been shown into the small auditorium by Francis, and the buzz of their conversation filled the room. But the Old Man and the other astronomers hadn't come in yet. They were holding a last-minute meeting in the study.

David stood in the glass-walled projection room of the auditorium, fumbling with his slides, nervously tinkering with the projector. Throwing sky images up there on the screen above the platform was nothing new to him. He had gone through the routine a hundred times, not only for Dr. Dawson and his colleagues, but for the tourists who visited Palomar.

But now he was jittery, and his hands were all thumbs. He wondered how the Old Man would break the news to this press and radio crowd.

He wondered how they would take Planet "Y."

How big did printers' type come, how black and bold? How loud could headlines scream? And would there be any of those silly melodramatic affairs you saw in the movies, those rapid-fire conversations between the city editor and the foreman of the pressroom?

> *"Stop the presses, Joe. We'll need a first-page replate!"*
> *"Make it the next edition, Mac. We're already rolling."*
> *"I said stop the presses!"*
> *"Okay. Okay. I suppose you got something big, Brisbane!"*
> *"Big? Listen, Joe, this is terrific—the greatest story of all time. The world is coming to an end!"*

At a time like this, thought David, you could think of the damnedest things. You felt a little lightheaded; your mind played tricks on you, with fanciful images. . . .

He looked at the clock. Five minutes after ten. He wished the Old Man would come in and get it over with. He was getting more of the jitters all the time. And he had a busy day ahead.

Late in the afternoon Carol and he were driving down to Dago to get married.

It was wonderful the way she had taken it, the way she had taken the news early that morning. He had made love to her first, savagely, as though it were his last chance on earth, and she had responded wordlessly, without questions, without asking an explanation.

She had sensed how much he had needed her, and that was enough.

Later, when he was spent and the Fear had gone and he was calm again, he had told her. He had given her the whole story, simple and straight, and he had expected hysterics afterward. But there were no hysterics. She was funny, he told himself, she hadn't even cried. She was funny, and wonderful. She had rested there in his arms, saying nothing for a long time. And then finally:

"We'll still have two years together, David. We can make it a lifetime together."

"Then you're not afraid, Carol?"

"No, David. I'm not afraid. Not like this. Not with you."

She was funny, and she was wonderful. She hadn't even cried.

He listened to the conversation of the newsmen as they waited for the Old Man. They were frightened, you could see that. It was plain in their taut faces, in the way they spoke.

They were, in a sense, beaten men, thought David as he watched them through the glass-enclosed projection room. They had no hope in themselves, saw no hope of anyone else averting the tragedy. They had already accepted the war as a *fait accompli*, and now they looked backward at what had gone before.

David listened to their chatter eddying up to the projection room:

*"Look, Ed, we had a temporary monopoly of the bomb back in the forties. Remember? And what did we do with it? We muffed it. We sat on it and watched the Reds gobble up Europe and Asia, watched them like a hypnotized bird watching a snake, gave them a chance to dream up a firecracker of their own."*

*"The Baruch proposal, the Marshall Plan, the Atlantic Pact, the Eastern bloc, and the rest. And the Reds playing it cagey all the way . . ."*

*"Christ, Frank, when you think of it, the whole thing's like a bad movie. And now here it is, right around the corner— A-Day!"*

*"In a way, I suppose it's partly our fault. Maybe we could have made it one world. We had a world weapon, and we made a nationalistic gimmick out of it. You know, we've got a gun and you ain't. Be good guys now. Do it our way—or else!"*

*"I could have sworn it was going to be all right, Fred. Roosevelt and Truman, back a few years ago—they were trying. And all those conferences later . . ."*

*"Talk, talk, talk, talk. Everybody talking about the international control of atomic energy and nobody doing anything about it . . ."*

*"Funny how it all happened, Ed, when you look back at it now. For a while, there, it looked swell. The Russians finally dropping the veto power in the Security Council and even agreeing to international inspection . . ."*

*"Are you kidding, Frank? It was what they call 'agreeing in principle.' But they weren't putting that one over, not on me! I was with Globe Press at the time, and I drew the assignment with the Control and Inspection Commission in the Soviet. Sure, they showed us Moscow and Kiev and Leningrad. But when we started to head east, into Siberia and Manchuria, we began to be 'delayed.' And it was the 'Mystery Cities' we wanted to see—Dudinka, Norylsk, Petrovsk, Yakutsk, Seimchan, Magadan, and the others. Well, we never did. And, brother, that's where the Reds were really radioactive. Anyway, we hung around awhile and finally came home. What was the use?"*

Joe Morgan, David's roommate at the Monastery, joined David briefly in the projection room. The Old Man had just broken the news to the rest of the staff, and the spectrograph man was pale under his sandy hair.

"Listen to them," said David. "They're like mourners talking at a wake."

"They don't know what we know," responded Morgan dully. "They don't know that there won't be any wake because there won't be any mourners. Listen to 'em, David. What they're saying now sounds like prattle—childish prattle."

They were two men playing God for a moment, it occurred to David, he and Joe Morgan. Knowing what they knew, they could see these men as crawling microorganisms in a laboratory test tube, crazily running around and around the inside of the glass in awful and pitiful futility.

"*What the hell is the President holding out for, I ask you, Fred? Look at what happened in New York. It's obvious that the Reds have got a new gimmick! What's he trying to do, get us to commit national suicide?*"

"*I hear they got him backed against the wall. He's getting it from the generals, from senators, from the Cabinet, everybody but his wife. They're all in favor of lighting the fuse quick.*"

"*Yeah. But what's he holding out so long for?*"

"*Wants to be morally sure we're right, I guess.*"

"*Hell, that's what I call old-fashioned. Someone ought to give him the facts of life. You can't even spell 'morally' in Russian.*"

"*It's ten-fifteen already. I've got to get back to the office. What's holding Dawson up, anyway?*"

"*I don't know. I kicked like a steer, Al, when the boss assigned me to this. I said, 'Look, Manny, the excitement's down here, right here in the office, and to hell with spending half a day way up at Palomar.' Well, said Manny, it might be a new comet or meteor Dr. Dawson's discovered, you know, one of those things he pulls out of the sky now and then. And I said: 'So what, Manny, and who cares? What's an item like that worth now? Page 10? Page 20?*"

"*I wish the Old Boy would walk in and get it over with, Frank. I've gotta get out of here and be back in L.A. by one.*"

"*Maybe this clambake will turn out okay, Ed. After all, Varanov's here. A big-shot Soviet in the U.S. now. It's a good angle.*"

"*Yeah. I'm going to try to get to him, like the rest of you guys, right after this lecture, or whatever it is. But if I know these Reds, we'll all be lucky if we get a 'nyet' out of him.*"

"*Wait a minute. Here comes Dawson.*"

The door at the rear of the auditorium suddenly opened. The chattering of the newsmen suddenly stopped as Dr. Dawson came in, followed by the others. One by one they filed in—Smythe, the gnomelike hunchback of the Royal Astronomical Society, his face like a wrinkled gray mask; Perez, the muscles of his round face working with emotion; Manning, the giant of Mount Wilson, his thin mouth a hard line, his bald head shining with perspiration; Varanov, the massive white-bearded Russian, his eyes hard and cold like two blue agates; Perez, Van Vreeden, Wallace, Ellender, Duval, and the rest.

The newsmen stared at them with sudden respect and a kind of awe. These were, after all, scientific men of international reputation, and the simple fact that they were here, gathered in one room, was an event out of the ordinary. But these days, when it came to news, everything was out of the ordinary.

The news- and radiomen were there to get a story. They would listen politely, even expectantly, to what Dr. Dawson had to say, and spot it on an inside page or after the middle commercial on the news broadcast. But they had their minds on other things.

Grimly and quietly the astronomers took their seats together on the left-hand aisle. All except the Old Man. He walked up to the platform and turned to face his audience.

For a long moment he stood there, his eyes straying over each of the newsmen. He's a born showman, thought David Hughes. He's a showman in the way he's standing there now and looking at them. He commanded their deference and held them.

The auditorium was quiet as the Old Man began to speak.

"Gentlemen, as representatives of the press and radio, you are preoccupied at the moment with current events of a highly unusual nature. But now, for a few moments, I ask you to take your eyes from the affairs of our own planet, the earth, and look at the sky.

"I summoned you here this morning because something completely extraordinary has taken place up there in the domain of the heavens—something not only extraordinary, but completely unprecedented. I stumbled upon this phenomenon a short time ago, and upon learning of its overwhelming implications I immediately summoned these gentlemen, my colleagues, from their posts all over the world. They have checked my observations and my calculations, and they will attest to all I am going to tell you now."

The Old Man paused for a moment. Then he said with gentle irony: "Gentlemen, I ask for your undivided attention for five minutes, and I promise you a story for page 1."

The Old Man looked over the heads of his audience and nodded to Francis, who was standing at the light switch in the rear of the auditorium.

The auditorium was plunged into darkness.

"All right, David," said the Old Man. "Give me the first slide."

The Old Man was through.

David shut off the projector. Its whirring sound slowed and died in the dead silence of the darkened auditorium.

Then the lights went on.

The men in the auditorium sat there in the bright glare, stunned, paralyzed, as though under a powerful narcotic. They sat stiffly, like waxen images in a museum gallery, like rigid figures in a still picture. They stared fixedly at Dr. Dawson, their jaws slack and sagging, their faces ashen with shock and horror.

"My God!" someone moaned softly in the back row. "My God, my God!"

That was all. The one voice—and that was all. Then silence again, dead silence. And finally another voice, rising and cracking, shrill in hysteria:

"It's not true! *It can't be true!*"

It was Langley, a radioman. He had half risen from his seat, his eyes bulging, his face dead white.

"I'm sorry, Mr. Langley," said the Old Man quietly. "It *is* true, and there is no chance of error. My colleagues are ready to substantiate what I have said."

The others began to stir and sigh and rustle in their seats, like men coming out of a dream. The first smashing impact was beginning to wear off. Then, with almost a single accord, their voices rose, loud, protesting, incredulous, hysterical. They rose from their seats almost all at once, talking in a wild babel.

"Please, gentlemen." The Old Man raised his hand. "Please. If there are any questions, please ask them one at a time."

The babel stopped as suddenly as it had started. Some of the men fell back in their seats, others remained standing. Finally a newspaperman named Graham spoke, his voice breaking into a cracked falsetto.

"Dr. Dawson."

"Yes?"

"Is there any chance of this catastrophe being averted? Is there any chance at all—of this Planet 'Y' taking some other course?"

The Old Man shook his head. "Nothing I know of can stop it." He paused, then said softly, "Nothing but a miracle."

"But the end of the world! It *can't* happen! It's crazy—fantastic!" The man from World Press, the man Corey had sent up, was sobbing out the words. "I've got two kids. They're young. Why, they won't even have a chance to grow up. Two years and one month!" Then he blurted foolishly, "Dr. Dawson, for God's sake, there *must* be something we can do!"

The Old Man looked at him for a moment. Then he spoke, gently and compassionately.

"It's out of our hands. I know it's clear to you, as well as to myself, that this is a divine punishment. Any man, whether scientist or dreamer, minister or atheist, can draw no other conclusion. In a sense, even in the face of the coming catastrophe, we are fortunate——"

"Fortunate?" someone cried hoarsely. "How?"

"We have been preparing to exterminate ourselves by our own hands in the very near future. Tomorrow, or the day after that, or the next week, perhaps, or next month. Now, at least, the immediate tragedy will be averted. We have been given the opportunity to live a little longer. Perhaps we will make good use of the time remaining to us, make our peace with God."

A thick, foreign voice came from the left. "Dr. Dawson is right, gentlemen."

The news- and radiomen turned their heads and stared at the speaker.

It was Varanov, the Russian.

"When I walked into Dr. Dawson's study yesterday, I did not believe in God. I do now. So, too, will all my people in the Soviet Union. There can be no other answer to what has happened.

"Neither can there be any further conflict. Now it is over, this threat of war is over. Communism—capitalism—these systems are nonsense now. Our Red soldiers will lay down their arms, as yours will. For there is no use destroying each other, when all will finally be destroyed. Men who are facing the same execution for the same reason do not hate each other. And two years is not a very long time to live."

Varanov sat down. The men in the auditorium stared at him, fascinated. For a moment there was dead silence. Then Perez, the Brazilian astronomer, rose.

"Senhor Varanov is right. One must concede that there is divine purpose in this terrible miracle. I am no philosopher, senhores, and I am no politician. But even I understand one thing. We have been given these years of grace, this little time that remains, for a purpose. It did not just happen that way. Consider this and call it a curious kind of logic, if you wish. But if God wished to destroy us by the cosmic explosion of a star, if this was the method He chose, He did not have to reach far out into the universe and explode the distant star from whence this Planet 'Y' came. The sun is a star, senhores, very near and quite convenient for this purpose. Had He been instant and quick in his wrath, had He chosen the sun instead of this other and far-distant star for His cosmic explosion, this little planet of ours, the earth, would have vanished instantly in a blast of heat and a puff of smoke."

There was a moment of silence. Then a reporter named Brewer cried out hysterically: "The hell with all this double talk. Nobody wants any sermons or platitudes now!"

He jumped to his feet and, his face livid, pointed his finger at Dr. Dawson.

"We're going to die!" he cried shrilly. "You and me and every damned one of us! Why didn't you keep it quiet? Why did you and all these other scientists tell us about it?"

"We had a moral duty to do so," answered the Old Man. "We discussed it, my colleagues and I, in my study. We felt that if men had been given these two years of grace, they should be so informed before they took matters into their own hands and destroyed each other. Furthermore, had mankind, by some miracle, compromised their differences and let each other live a little while longer, they would have seen this planet come into the sky and come closer and closer with each succeeding day. They would have asked questions then, and these questions would have had to be answered."

"You should have kept quiet about it," insisted the newspaperman sullenly. "What kind of a life do you think we're going to live, knowing the date of our own execution, watching that damned thing in the sky come closer day after day?"

"I think we'll all live a better life," answered the Old Man quietly.

"I'm not interested in your theories of reforming, Dr. Dawson," flared Brewer hysterically. "All I know is that on Christmas of 1962 I'm going to die. So is my wife, and so is my little girl and my little boy. As far as I'm concerned, that's the only important thing."

"Is it?" The Old Man spoke patiently. "I wonder. No doubt death is a great tragedy to all of us. But in a larger sense, an astronomical sense, what does it amount to? Man is, after all, merely a microscopic organism living on a grain of sand revolving around a fourth-rate star." He paused. "As a matter of fact, we really have no right being alive in the first place."

"No right? What do you mean by that?" Only Brewer and the Old Man were doing the talking now. The others hung on the discussion, quiet and absorbed.

"Did you ever hear of an English astronomer named Eddington, Mr. Brewer?"

"No."

"Well, Eddington pointed out that actually we are interlopers in creation, intruders. We really have no right to be here. We are here because one chemical element out of the whole ninety-two—carbon—happened to be able to combine with others in thousands of different ways. We are, in short, here on this earth as a freak of nature, unique in all the universe.

"Think of this, Mr. Brewer, consider this extraordinary state of affairs. We are alive only because we cling to a tiny bit of dust just the right distance from the right sun. Around us the vast bulk of cosmic material is either blazing at temperatures of millions of degrees, or else scattered remotely in the cold absolute void. A small deviation in either direction, a slight jarring of our lucky position—and we would be wiped out in an instant." The Old Man stopped and then said very quietly, "That deviation has now come."

There was a full minute of silence. The Old Man waited on the platform for someone to speak further. No one did.

"Are there any further questions, gentlemen?" the Old Man asked.

No one broke the silence.

"Very well. I know you gentlemen will want to contact your offices immediately. You'll find a telephone in the reception room and others in the various offices off the corridor. You're welcome to them." The Old Man nodded. "Good morning, gentlemen—and thank you."

David Hughes, standing by the projector, watched the newsmen curiously as they rose and slowly moved toward the door.

They had the greatest story on earth, but they did not rush for the phones in a frantic race to get the story in. On the contrary, they seemed almost reluctant to leave.

They shuffled out of the auditorium as though they were walking in their sleep. The look of the condemned was already upon their pallid faces. Already their heads were shaved and their trousers slit for the electrodes and they were hearing the last rites.

**8.** An hour later the whole world knew about Planet "Y."

The shock radiated outward from Palomar and shuddered through the earth like a great earthquake.

The phones at the observatory rang incessantly, and already the Highway to the Stars was choked with cars racing upward into the San Jacinto range, toward the new magnetic center of the earth. The military guard at the observatory was alerted for trouble.

The people of Palomar were nearest, and they came to the observatory first. Almost with a single accord the staff astronomers, the physicists, the mathematicians and calculators, the telescope mechanics and maintenance men, the janitors and Diesel workers had dropped whatever they were doing. They had gone to their homes, gathered their wives and children, and, like the Israelites drawn to the temple in time of crisis, had headed for the main observatory, as though somehow they would find salvation there.

Now they gathered in little voiceless knots, their faces white and dazed. Some of them, without knowing why, had dressed in their Sunday best, they and their wives and children, as though it were a holiday. They searched each other's faces dumbly, looking for hope, but they saw no hope. All they saw in each other's faces were mirror reflections of their own. They wandered about aimlessly, like pale automatons, eddying and flowing through the corridors and foyers and reception rooms.

They gathered before the closed door to Dr. Dawson's study, waiting for a word.

But there was no word.

And finally, inevitably, they climbed the parquet stairs toward the transparent partition blocking off the telescope from the rest of the observatory.

The Big Eye seemed to hypnotize them. They pressed their noses against the glass wall and stared at it mutely, as though somehow it could rectify what it had done, as though, by merely stirring itself, it could make amends for its crime.

*"What have you done to us?"* the staring eyes on the other side of the glass said. *"What have you done to us?"*

But the monstrous apparatus, soaring up into the semi-darkness of the dome, was silent. It stood there, unmoved, vast and massive and triumphant. It seemed to leer back at the white faces malevolently, as though it were well aware of what it had done, as though it knew the havoc it had wrought.

Yes, the great telescope was conscious of its power and proudly flaunted it. It had a right to revel in its own strength. After all, it had created all the havoc merely by producing only a tiny glint of light deep in its Pyrex cornea.

To those who watched it through the transparent wall, it was a Thing, it was alive. Its massive piers, its yoke, its girders and cylinders were muscles which it flexed in glee on ball-and-socket joints. Its burnished eye was invisible, but they were aware that it was mocking them. They almost expected a bellow of triumph to roar up and out from the yawning mouth of the giant and echo through the dome.

It was the telescope who was alive, not those who watched it. They were inanimate, dead. They could only stand and stare, like images of fleshy wax.

Had the heavily armed soldiers not been there, as stunned as anyone else, but still watchful for the first sign of violence, the hatred might have bubbled out of the onlookers and exploded into hysteria. They might have come to life, a wild and avenging mob. They might have found axes and sledges somewhere, surged forward, smashed through the glass partition, and rushed toward their leering tormentor, chopping and hammering at it, blinding its eye and hacking at its muscles until it came crashing to the floor.

Elsewhere the great observatories of the world were attacked by mobs. Unlike Palomar, they had been unprotected, caught off guard. The attacks came simultaneously, shortly after the announcement, and they came without warning. In the rioting, millions of dollars' worth of delicate precision instruments were smashed and destroyed before guards could be summoned.

But at Palomar they could not move, they could not act. They could only stand and stare at the telescope through the partition. No one spoke; the silence was like that of a death watch.

Finally a pair of lips in one of the white faces against the glass moved, muttered:

"You big bastard. You big bastard. *What have you done to us?*"

By early afternoon the observatory yard was choked with cars. And still they kept coming up the steep road to Palomar.

They had no valid reason for coming, no real purpose, blindly seeking the oracle, perhaps hoping for a crumb of comfort from the same mighty source that promised them disaster.

The observatory was crowded with newsmen, photographers, Army officials, public officials, and just plain people, dazed by the shock.

Everyone wanted to see Dr. Dawson.

But the Old Man would see no one. He was locked in his study with David, and they had Francis's small radio turned on.

None of the regular programs was being broadcast. There was nothing but music—somber music—funeral music. David twisted the dial to station after station, with the same result.

"You're sure the President is going to make a statement, Dr. Dawson?"

The Old Man nodded. "He assured me he would, when I spoke to him over the phone yesterday, David. Just as soon as we could give him absolute confirmation of this phenomenon, beyond any element of doubt."

The dirgelike music continued.

David remembered something like this a long time ago when he was a boy. It was the day Franklin D. Roosevelt died, fifteen years ago. There was the same interminable music, like this.

And yet it was nothing like this.

Then, back in 1945, the people mourned for one man.

Now, in 1960, they mourned for themselves, and the music was their *own* requiem.

The music occasionally stopped and then resumed jerkily. Sometimes there were long blank spaces of dead air. Sometimes a hesitant voice came in from somewhere and then was cut off in the middle of a sentence. The whole radio frequency dial, from left to right, was uncertain, jittery, frightened. The networks had been caught short. Their organization had broken down. The studios were still there; the microphones, the transmitters, they were intact. It was the people operating them who collapsed.

Like everyone else, they had been stunned by the blow, numbed by the shock; they had lost control.

David and the Old Man listened to one station playing the same transcription over and over. Someone in a studio somewhere seemed to have gone out of his mind. He put the needle on the record, ran it through, began it all over again. It didn't occur to him to turn the record over or put a new one on the turntable. It was enough that something was on the air, anything.

"They've gone crazy out there somewhere," David remarked to the Old Man.

He recalled something Carol had once told him.

Back in New York the networks had prepared and recorded dramatic obituaries of every living great man. When one of them died the studios could almost instantly broadcast his obituary. They'd been making up these transcriptions in advance ever since they got caught short when Roosevelt died.

But this was one obituary they didn't figure on, thought David grimly.

This was *everybody's* obituary.

The music stopped abruptly and a shaky voice broke through:

*"Ladies and gentlemen, we bring you a special message—from the President of the United States. The next voice you hear will be that of the President."*

The announcer's voice broke off. There was a long silence, perhaps a minute of dead air. Then suddenly they heard the President.

His voice trembled with emotion; it was halting, still almost incredulous:

*"This morning, only a few hours ago, a dramatic announcement was flashed to the entire world from the Palomar Observatory in California. By now there are few in this country, and indeed in every other nation of the earth, who do not know that our days are numbered. At this very moment, this cosmic body, this Planet 'Y,' is speeding toward us from somewhere out of the limitless heavens, bent on our complete and final destruction.*

*"In this solemn hour, this hour of tragedy, there is nothing I can say to give you comfort. To those of you who are still skeptical of this coming catastrophe, I bring bad news. I have been reassured that for us on earth, and for the earth itself, there is no possibility, no hope of escape.*

*"No one can doubt that we have been visited with some kind of divine judgment. We must accept it as such and try to face it tranquilly, and with resignation.*

*"I ask you now, the people of the United States, to remain calm in this great crisis. We cannot, we must not, fall prey to violent and destructive hysteria. We cannot, we must not, have anarchy or chaos. As Commander in Chief of the armed forces of this nation, I have already instructed the Army to keep order wherever necessary. I now call upon the governors of every state to alert the National Guard for any local emergency that might occur.*

*"For some months we have faced the threat of terrible war, the prospect of possible destruction. Now—this period of uncertainty is over. Now our destruction has been made certain and complete by a far higher Power than man—perhaps in*

*righteous retribution for our own sins. And we are powerless to avert our terrible destiny.*

*"I ask you now to turn to God Himself for solace and forgiveness. I ask you now to go to your churches and temples and pray."*

The President had finished. There was a moment of silence after his last word had died away. Then a famous clergyman followed with a short prayer. And after him the mournful music again.

And finally a news announcer, the first David and Dr. Dawson had heard, pouring out early fragments of information in an almost hysterical voice:

*"The whole world is stunned and dazed. In the cities throughout the country people have left the factories, the offices, the homes, and swarmed out into the streets, tying up traffic. All transport has been halted, all schools closed as hysterical parents called for their children. The streets are jammed with surging crowds. Authorities fear mass panic.*

*"From China it is reported that soldiers of warring factions have throw down their weapons and embraced each other. . . . The Pope is preparing to address the world from Rome.*

*"A report from Kirensk . . . The Leningrad astronomer, Professor Varanov, is already on his way to Russia by plane to report personally to the Soviet Premier. . . .*

*"Members of both houses of Congress are now meeting in secret and emergency session somewhere in America. . . . Riots, violence, and looting have already begun in many sections. Observatories all over the world have been attacked, valuable instruments destroyed.*

*"At Sing Sing, Dannemora, Leavenworth, and other prisons, inmates have begun to riot, demanding their freedom. The governor of New York State has postponed two executions scheduled for tonight. . . . Thousands of people are beginning to jam airports and railroad stations, moving back to their homes in the evacuated cities. . . . The Secretary of*

*Defense has ordered every man in the armed forces, air, land, and sea, to stay at his post."*

There was a knock on the door of the study.

The Old Man waved his hand, signaling to David to turn off the radio, and then admitted Francis.

"Dr. Dawson," the steward began apologetically, "there's some-one waiting to see you."

"I told you I didn't want to see anyone else right now," interrupted the Old Man.

"Yes, sir. But it's Professor Kellar."

"Kellar? *He's* here at Palomar?"

The steward nodded. He seemed to have aged ten years since the morning; his shoulders sagged under the alpaca coat.

"He drove up from Los Angeles, sir. And he insists on seeing you."

The Old Man hesitated for a moment. Then he said, "Show him in, Francis."

David awaited the appearance of Kellar with more than ordinary interest. Andrew Kellar was a giant in his own field, recognized as the greatest physicist alive. He was reputed to know more about nuclear fission than any other man. It was he who had assembled the first bomb they had ever dropped in New Mexico, he who had been the scientific brain behind the vast Manhattan project of World War II, and more than any other single man, he had been responsible for the bombs dropped on Hiroshima and Nagasaki fifteen years ago.

Since that time, however, Kellar had virtually dropped out of sight, along with many of his colleagues. He had been taken in hand by General Hawthorne, hemmed in and badgered, a virtual prisoner jealously guarded and secluded in a kind of rigid cocoon.

And for fifteen years his genius had become impotent in everything except research for war.

"Dr. Dawson!" The nuclear scientist, a tall spare man, came hurrying into the study. "Thank God, Doctor, for what you've done!"

David stared at Kellar.

His eyes were overbright. They shone behind his thick spectacles; they seemed a little wild, a little mad. Kellar's aged shoulders were straight back, his sunken cheeks unnaturally flushed. His step was springy and buoyant; he almost danced into the room.

He was alternately laughing and sobbing, his voice cracking in falsetto. He grabbed the Old Man's hand, pumped it up and down, wouldn't let go.

He's mad, thought David. He's surely mad.

"I'm free!" babbled Kellar. "Do you understand, Doctor? I'm free now, and so are all of us—Eckert, Davidson, Walker, and the rest of my colleagues on nuclear fission—we're free! *You* set us free! For the first time since Hiroshima, we can sleep nights!"

It was shocking, almost obscene, to watch him, a happy man, delirious with his happiness, mad with it, a lone celebrator in a world of mourners.

"Thank God for that planet you found! Thank God for it, sir, we welcome it. We're out of it now, we're absolved. No one's going to use the bomb now, Doctor, thanks to you. The world may be blown up, yes, but not by *our* hand. Not by our hand, *now!*" He took the Old Man by the shoulders, almost shook him. "Do you realize what it's been like, Doctor, the fifteen years since Hiroshima? We've been *haunted*, living with a stone around our necks. We've seen what we've created desecrated into an instrument of slaughter rather than of new power, of curative medicine. We've been made to feel that *we* were responsible for the destruction of humanity!" He released Dr. Dawson and slumped back into a chair, exhausted. "But now it's out of our hands, thank God. No one can point a finger at us now!"

Dr. Dawson watched Kellar. His face was set and hard, his eyes stern; they showed no sympathy. The physicist quieted down; he stirred uneasily under the Old Man's steady and accusing gaze.

And when the Old Man finally spoke, his voice was as cold and sharp as the edge of a knife.

"If you've suffered, Professor Kellar, you've no one to blame but yourself. You should never have let the atom get away from you."

Kellar spread his hands. "What could we do? You know what happened. There was a war. The Army stepped in. They *took* the atom away from us! We had nothing to say; we had to stand by helplessly." He appealed to the Old Man. "We didn't have a chance. You remember, Doctor, back in the late forties and early fifties, how we tried to warn the world. You remember why we formed the Emergency Committee of Atomic Scientists."

The Old Man nodded.

"We raised a million dollars for propaganda to make the public aware of the destructive nature of the bomb. We told them that it would inevitably lead to war, that there was no particular secret about nuclear fission. We told them, again and again, that the only solution was international control, until the words we were trying to get across simply became clichés." He rose and began to pace the room. "But you can't say we didn't try, Doctor. We went before Congress, talked to a hundred committees—to public meetings— drove our message home over the radio and through the *Bulletin of Atomic Scientists* we issued. And don't forget one thing."

"Yes?"

"We weren't publicity men. We were scientists—amateurs at this business of propaganda. We had to come out of the laboratory."

"Very true," said the Old Man quietly. He lighted one of his small cigars very deliberately. "The trouble was, Professor Kellar, you didn't come out far enough."

"I don't understand, Doctor."

"The point is, Professor, that we scientists have been blind for hundreds of years. We've dealt only in precise things—pounds, feet, degrees, designs, formulas. We've been scientists in everything but the most important of them all—the science of the human mind." The Old Man was emphatic. "But that's wrong, Kellar, *wrong!* It's not enough to be a good scientist any longer."

"Are you suggesting that a scientist become a psychiatrist too, Dr. Dawson?"

"More than that, Professor," snapped the Old Man. "He must

become a sociologist, a philosopher, a humanitarian, a reformer, and yes—even a preacher. Let's look ourselves straight in the eye, Professor. Let's own up to what we've done!"

"Well?" asked Kellar. "What *have* we done?"

"We've been criminally negligent. You and Eckert and Davidson and the others work out nuclear fission. And then instead of weighing the consequences, instead of going slowly and asking, 'What will they do with the atom, and are they ready for it?' you blithely give a fused stick of dynamite and a match to a schoolboy and go back to the comfortable and familiar sanctity of your laboratories."

Kellar did not speak for a moment. Then: "Are you suggesting, Doctor, that we deliberately stop the progress of science?"

"What I am suggesting is that we *control* it and judge whether whatever we create will do more harm than good when it is released."

"I don't think scientists are capable of judging——"

"Then it's about time they started to learn," interrupted the Old Man hotly. "Take myself, Professor. I am an astronomer. My worlds are universes. I use giant telescopes to study them. Should I then condescend to turn to a microscope and study the microbes on my own pitiful planet? The answer is yes. And again, yes! Perhaps I am lacking in nobility, in the pure scientist's approach that the truth is the thing, and damn the consequences. But I believe our first responsibility is to the people with whom we live, not to the things we find!"

David had never heard the Old Man swear before, had never seen him so worked up. His eyes blazed, and he spoke passionately.

"Of course this whole discussion is really academic, Kellar. We haven't much time left. But we've a lot to atone for. We scientists have been responsible for many of the world's ills for a long time. We've failed to understand that science moves fast, it is revolutionary, while the human mind is slow, *evolutionary*. As a result, we have a gap of thousands of years  etween scientific achievement and the human capacity to use it wisely."

"Then we have one of two alternatives," said Kellar. "In order to gain an equilibrium, we must either speed up the growing process of the mind or slow down science."

"Exactly," answered the Old Man. "One or the other. And of the two, the slowing down of our research functions is by far the more feasible. That comes into our province, Professor Kellar. Call it scientific sabotage, if you will. Call it anything you want. We should have put it into practice long ago. Now it's too late."

There was a commotion just outside the study. The door was flung open and two men burst in, sweeping Francis to one side.

One was the Secretary of Defense, and the other was General Matt Hawthorne.

Immediately after the first radio flash had hit their underground headquarters they had conferred briefly with the President. Then they had boarded a jet for San Diego, where an Army helicopter had picked them up and dropped them on Palomar.

General Hawthorne's face was livid.

"Damn it, Doctor, what the hell do you think you've done?" He pounded his fist on Dr. Dawson's desk. "Didn't you ever hear of something we call military security?"

"Yes, General," replied the Old Man quietly, "I have."

"Then why didn't you check with us before you released this information? The press and radio people went crazy on us—rushed the story through before our censors had a chance to stop 'em!"

David saw Kellar's face out of the corner of his eye. It was almost contorted with hate and contempt for Hawthorne. But the Old Man was unruffled as he answered:

"Rather like trying to stop an avalanche with a red pencil, isn't it, General? Besides," he continued calmly, "it was precisely in the interests of security that my colleagues and I released the announcement when we did."

Hawthorne began to retort hotly, but here the Secretary of Defense stepped in. A tall, thin, hawk-faced man, and a former insurance company executive, the Secretary was noted for his brilliant administrative ability and his coolness under pressure.

But now his face was flushed; he chewed his cigar nervously and spoke rapidly, jerkily, as though his mind were busy groping for a solution and had not yet caught up with his tongue.

"Dr. Dawson, we were on the verge of attacking the Soviet Union. As you know, there was a meeting near New York——"

"He knows it all right," interrupted Hawthorne angrily. "His boy here, Hughes, broke my orders and didn't show up. And by God, planet or no planet, I'm going to prefer charges——"

The Secretary looked annoyed, silenced Hawthorne with a wave of his hand.

"Let me finish, General." He turned back to the Old Man. "To repeat, Doctor, we were on the verge of attacking Russia, on the honest premise that it was in our best interests. We were in the process of convincing the President himself that this was the wise course to take, when your bulletin came through. You must realize, you must be aware of the disastrous effect it will have. Our men are at strategic outposts everywhere, ready for action. When they hear about this—this new planet—their morale will break down—their discipline crumble. There's sure to be a wave of hysteria, perhaps some sort of mass panic. Our men may simply throw down their weapons, leave their posts, and head for home, a demoralized mob." His voice rose a little. "And you, Doctor, speak of releasing this bulletin in the interests of security!"

"My colleagues and I, Mr. Secretary, were thinking of *world* security rather than just national security."

Hawthorne stepped in, his face a mottled red, and thrust it close to the Old Man's belligerently. "You say *that*, knowing that our whole military setup, let alone our war industries, may melt away overnight? Christ, man, don't you realize that'll leave us wide open for attack?"

"Attack?" said the Old Man softly. "Attack by whom?"

"By the enemy—by the Reds. Who else?"

For a moment Dr. Dawson did not reply. David watched the Old Man's face closely. He thought he saw a flicker of amusement pass over it for the second time that day. His blue-veined hands toyed with a letter opener, and he tapped it in a kind of rhythmic beat on the desk.

"Gentlemen, apparently you didn't hear the President speak on the air a few minutes ago. He himself has pointed out that the threat of war is over. As for myself, I am an astronomer, not a military man. Believe me, I appreciate your concern for the national safety. But you have mentioned the enemy and it is here I must ask you, General Hawthorne and Mr. Secretary, a pertinent question."

The Secretary's eyes narrowed. "Well?"

"What do you think the men in the *enemy* armies will do, gentlemen, when they hear of the coming catastrophe?"

The red slowly faded from Hawthorne's face. The Secretary, caught off guard, stared at Dr. Dawson.

"As you implied, Mr. Secretary, the men in our armed forces are human and will certainly react by throwing down their arms and going home. But the men in the Soviet armies are human, too, and they will do precisely the same thing. As I see it, this planet is not only scheduled to shatter the earth, but it will shatter some of the primitive notions we have nurtured since history began. Among other things, it will certainly vitiate the will to kill, to destroy each other."

The general and the Secretary listened, hypnotized, as the Old Man continued:

"In short, gentlemen, Planet 'Y' will automatically make a human dream of many centuries come true. It will outlaw war. Men who are threatened with a common disaster do not attack each other. After all, what is there to fight about now? A future? There *is* no future. Territory? Natural resources? Political systems? Ideology?" Dr. Dawson shrugged. "These things are meaningless now."

The Old Man was magnificent, David marveled. He had his two visitors riveted to the spot; they were unable to move, to say anything. David noted that Hawthorne's mouth had sagged open ludicrously and that the Cabinet officer's cigar had gone out.

Finally the Secretary of Defense stirred, fumbled for his hat, and said quietly:

"You'll forgive us, Doctor, if we have to rush off now. The President has instructed us to report back to him immediately." He hesitated and then added hopefully, almost wistfully: "If we could only tell him that there was some possibility, however remote, that this catastrophe may not occur . . ."

The Old Man shook his head patiently. "I'm sorry, Mr. Secretary. But I assure you, my colleagues and I have gone over our calculations, checked and rechecked them numberless times. And there is no escape."

The two men walked slowly out of the study, into the hall of the observatory itself, through the crowd of silent, white-faced onlookers who had come to Palomar.

And David, as he watched General Hawthorne's retreating back, was fascinated by the four stars on each shoulder. When the general had come in the stars had been highly polished; they had glittered brightly in the light.

Now, as he left, the stars seemed suddenly to have become a little dull, as though they had tarnished during the general's brief stay in the room.

It was late afternoon.

Carol and David were still miles away from San Diego when they heard the first faint tolling of the city's bells.

All along the road coming down, at Rincon, Valley Center, Escondido, Rancho Santa Fe, Solana Beach, and Del Mar, they had heard the bells.

Listen to the bells, thought David, listen to the bells. Bells went with wedding days. And this was his wedding day.

But these were funeral bells.

He had intended to postpone this wedding trip to Dago. They were going crazy back at the observatory. There were a thousand things to do, and he had volunteered to stay. But the Old Man would have none of it. He had insisted that David and Carol go through with their plans. And now, thought David, here he was with his bride beside him in the car, and they were racing down the Highway to the Stars to a justice of the peace and a wedding night in Dago. And tomorrow they would return to Palomar.

Listen to the bells. . . .

He was getting married this evening, and it was incongruous, almost ridiculous, on this day of all days. It was just too damned normal to be believable. Getting married was normal, if anything was. You said "I do" and she said "I do" and you went somewhere and had your honeymoon, and after that you settled down and planned for the future.

Or at least that was the way it had been in the old days.

But the old days were yesterday, and yesterday was another age, another era. Yesterday was the day before the Year One. One, two. Christmas Day, 1962.

Now you planned nothing, and there was no future.

Two years and a month. Twenty-five months. It was like walking through twenty-five separate rooms, each smaller and narrower, each with less ventilation and lower ceilings, each progressively colder and darker, each pressing downward and inward, until the last room.

And from this there would be no other escape, no other room.

"David," said Carol. "Listen to the bells."

They sounded nearer now, clearer. They were a great chorus of discordant calamity, wafted through the thin clear air by a hundred bronze mouths. They clashed and clanged and rang; they cried and wailed and sobbed. They welled up from the distant city and rippled across the plain and echoed faintly through the mountain canyons.

Ring out the old, ring in the new.

It was just getting dark when they drove into San Diego.

It was a different kind of darkness from what they had ever known or seen before. It was a darkness deafened and desecrated and made discordant with the awful constant clamor of the tolling bells. It had the feel and the texture and the weight of a great shroud.

It was a darkness of a special quality.

Every house in the city was ablaze with light, as though each held a mourners' wake.

The rooftops were black with people staring up at the sky, staring at something they could not see but knew was there. They seemed to be waiting in a kind of feverish anticipation, as though half expecting that the wildcat planet would somehow appear among the stars and plummet down upon the earth ahead of schedule.

Those who were not on the rooftops swarmed into the streets, thousands upon thousands of them, blocking traffic, moving aimlessly, mechanically, going nowhere.

And they, too, stared up at the sky.

They were close-packed and dense, men, women, and children, like animals huddled together for comfort and protection. They moved and swirled and eddied in an endless crowd, craning their necks upward. They were silent and sullen now, walking like automatons, shuffling along with slow and dragging steps.

But it was there within them, the threat of explosion, of awful hysteria, of terrible violence. It was ugly and alive in their white faces and frightened eyes. It bubbled and seethed and brewed and waited.

The din was deafening. The bells rang, seemed to grow louder by the hour. Horns honked as busses and cars moved by inches through the seething crowd. Newsboys hawked extras shrilly, with screaming headlines: END OF WORLD . . . PLANET HEADED FOR EARTH . . . DOOMSDAY, CHRISTMAS, 1962 . . . READ ALL ABOUT IT!

It was the only story in the newspapers; there was nothing else. There were pictures of Dr. Dawson, of Palomar Observatory, of the great telescope, a blown-up reproduction of the fatal spot of light.

The theater marquees blazed, the stores were brightly illuminated, the neon signs in the bars and taverns blinked reddened invitation.

But they were empty and abandoned. The people were on the rooftops or in the streets, out in the open, where they could look up and see the sky.

Only the churches were full. They were jammed to capacity, and the crowds choked their doorways and spilled out into the streets and waited in long lines. The wailing of prayer and the sound of lamentation came from their interiors, mixing with the din of the bells.

Already there were a few who had begun to make their peace with God.

David and Carol hardly heard what the justice of the peace had said. He mumbled the words in a kind of daze; his hands shook as he held the book.

He married them and signed the papers and took his fee. He was a man in a trance, going through the motions from force of habit. The chances were that he never really saw them, would never really remember them. Nor would they remember him.

Now David edged the car through the crowds, honking his horn. The people were no longer silent and sullen. Their nerves had been stretched taut, tighter than they could stand, and now they had snapped back the other way. They stopped looking at the sky and started looking at each other. They became animated, articulate, shrill.

There was the smell of hysteria in the air.

The streets turned into bedlam. As David and Carol drove toward their hotel they heard the crash of glass, the delighted yells of a great crowd. Someone threw a stone through a shopwindow, and the idea caught on. Soon they were breaking the windows of all the shops up and down the streets, swarming into the stores, ripping the merchandise from the shelves. Sirens sounded; the police fought the crowds. They surged forward and retreated, surged and retreated. Their faces red, their eyes wild and staring, they fought the police tooth and nail.

People who had never taken a drink, respectable people, middle-class people, solid citizens and regular churchgoers, now crowded the bars and taverns, or staggered in the streets, or lay in the gutters, dead drunk. Horns blared in an earsplitting din, women were openly attacked, the looting became general, shots were fired, cars tipped over, and busses turned on their sides.

The planet ended restraint, turning it into release. The pressure was gone, the emotional floodgates spewed wide open, and the people went wild in a kind of ugly ecstasy. They could soar now; they were free and untrammeled spirits; there was no future to face, only a future to forget.

Eat, drink, and be merry . . .

This was the first night of the Year One.

It was almost dawn now.

No one in the city had slept that night.

Carol and David, for the moment, lay quietly in each other's arms and listened to the sounds of the macabre holiday outside. They were still going on, the violent sounds, the honking of unrestrained horns, the distant sirens, the tolling of far bells, the sound of running feet on the pavement.

The hotel was a beehive; it was alive and awake. Its windows, from top to bottom, were ablaze with light, as though it were the hour after sunset instead of the hour before dawn. From them eddied anonymous voices, shrill, high-pitched in drunken laughter, hysterical, babbling, tinged with a kind of madness.

*"To hell with it, Joe. Let it come outa the sky, this goddamn Planet 'Y.' I'll never see it—won't even know it's there. I'll be stiffer than a haddock for two years, Joe, see what I mean? Get myself so blind I won't be able to see it. Yeah. That's the ticket. A two-year bender—starting tonight. Have another drink, Joe!"*

*"Listen, Ann. You wanted that fur coat? Okay, you'll get it. That trip around the world? Sure. We'll go. Anything you want, baby. We're on the merry-go-round, honey. What've we got to lose? Sure, we'll take every dime we've got out of the bank—sell the business. Who cares about money now? Who's saving for the future now? What future? We got two years to have fun in, baby—two years. Let's start now, baby. You know what I mean. It's been a long time. Pull down the shades, baby. We're wasting time."*

*"The funny part of it was, Phil, this insurance agent was up to see me yesterday. Had me sold on a hundred thousand dollars' worth of life insurance. I was going to sign the papers today. Kind of funny, isn't it, when you think of it now? Who in hell would want any life insurance now? For what? Pour me another one, Phil. Make it weak though. I feel a little sick inside."*

*"Darling, listen, I'm calling from San Diego. I'll take the first plane I can get for home. How are the kids? Yes, yes, I'll be home just as soon as I can make it. I don't feel like being alone, either, at a time like this. Please, please, Helen, don't cry. Don't cry like that. Try not to think of it. Try to get some sleep now. Please, Helen, don't cry. Remember what we've always said? If we had to go, we wanted to go together. . . ."*

*"Listen, Frank, it isn't just dying that's hard to take. Everybody's got to die sooner or later. But it's knowing the exact date—that's what's hard, that's what's driving me out of my mind. Christmas Day, 1962, Christmas, 1962. That's all I can think of. Watching the calendar, counting the hours. Frank, for Christ's sake, how are we going to stand it, how are we going to stand it? And watching that Planet 'Y,' that thing up there in the sky, getting bigger and bigger, closer and closer, like an ax coming down on top of your head, and knowing you can't do a thing about it—except let it come. Frank, for God's sake, there isn't any more liquor left. Order up another bottle. I need a drink—I need it bad."*

Finally the voices which had crawled through the blinds became a confused and distant murmur, without meaning and without identity.

And they were alone, the two of them, on their wedding night, clinging and blending, drunk with the desperate having of each other, living a moment of priceless time.

Afterward they lay exhausted, apart, and David thought, God, she was wonderful, wonderful, this wonderful girl who was his wife.

He could never get enough of her, there would never be enough of her, never. There never would be enough time.

From now on Carol and he would live in moments, in desperate moments, each more urgent than the other as the deadline came nearer, each hungrier, each more hopeless. They didn't have long, they didn't have much, only each other. And there would never be the easy anesthesia so mercifully provided by a benevolent Nature, the hope of a natural lifetime, the slowing down by time of youth itself, of passion cooling imperceptibly and painlessly, of "growing old gracefully."

Then finally David whispered:

"Carol."

"Yes, darling?"

"We've got to be careful, very careful. We can't have any children—not now."

She began to cry then, and he took her in his arms and tried to comfort her.

**9.** It was early evening, and the Year One was just two weeks old.

David Hughes sat in his own easy chair, in his own home on Palomar Mountain. There was a scotch and soda at his elbow, and the newspaper he always read was in his lap. He was a bridegroom of two weeks, and upstairs his bride was under the shower, and in a little while they would leave for the Dawsons' house, where they had been invited for dinner. After that the Old Man and himself would go to the observatory, leaving Carol and Emily Dawson and perhaps some of the other staff wives to talk about the little things that women talked about.

It was all very usual and very commonplace, or had been—once. Now the commonplace was a little dreamlike.

He glanced out of the window and stared at the landscape and thought, in a detached kind of way, that the snow was just as white and cold as it always was, it drifted in the same old way, it stuck to the trees in the same patterns. The sun was red on the horizon with its customary redness, and in its customary place, in that gap in the mountains, just to the left of the crimson-tinted dome housing the forty-eight-inch telescope. The kids near the place where the road curved were building a snow man, and it looked as all snow men usually looked, graceless and lumpy, with the same black coals for eyes, the same twig for a nose, the same wide gash for the mouth, the same resigned and patient look.

This was your own personal little picture, he reflected, your own miniature, drawn to accustomed scale, with the same strokes of the brush and the same colors.

Up close, nothing had changed.

But when you backed away from the picture and then looked at it, everything suddenly changed. You saw with a kind of numb horror that the perspective was all wrong, that the colors clashed and shrieked, that everything in it was monstrous and distorted and unbelievable, and that its theme of the commonplace was suddenly hideous.

The sun was too big and, although faceless, it seemed to leer and lean with oppressive weight over the horizon, like a round and overhanging and threatening stone. Its red had now darkened and deepened to the color of blood. The snow suddenly became pock-marked and old and dirty, and the trees, their branches and twigs loaded down with snow, no longer looked like delicate figurines of some frosted fairyland, but rather like white skeletons swaying and rattling hollowly in the wind. The dome of the forty-eight-inch, over the ridge, was no longer round and squat, but long and cylindrical, and its glistening tip was a shining fingernail on the end of a finger pointing straight up to a fiery spot which had suddenly materialized in the clear sky.

Even the kids playing and dancing around the snow man had changed. The red in their cheeks had dissolved away into ashen gray, and their chubby faces had suddenly become wasted and gaunt, and their laughing and yelling became a kind of dismal wailing. The snow man, too, had changed; his lumpy head suddenly seemed to tilt upward, watching the fiery spot in the sky, and there was a leering and malicious smirk on his face.

You'd been too close before to see it. But now that you were a little farther back, you saw that the picture had a black frame around it.

And as you watched, you could almost see the black frame contract and creep inward from all four sides, left and right and top and bottom, and begin to encroach upon the picture. You could almost see it blot out the picture little by little, first the sun, and then the landscape and the trees and the observatory on the ridge, and the snow man and the children playing around it, and the room in which you sat.

And the black frame kept spreading inward, until the picture became a miniature, and finally a tiny square cameo, and finally a pin point of fiery light—the light in the sky. It was like peering through a long black tunnel and seeing nothing at the other end but this blazing bit of light.

And then finally the black closed over the light and there was nothing left.

"David, did you see my nail file?"

Carol's voice came to him from upstairs. He stirred and shook his head, as though to clear it.

"It's in the drawer of the end table, I think," he called back.

It was a little amusing, this, Carol calling for her nail file with the world about to end. It was a little amusing, in a sardonic kind of way. You went through the motions, clung to the commonplace, kept your sanity that way. To go on with the traditional amenities, to hew to the regular routine, was the best defense against the planet, the only real defense. Work eight hours, play eight hours, eat three meals, a drink before dinner, wear blue ties with blue socks, white tie with tails, never trump your partner's ace, kiss your wife when you go out, and kiss her when you come in, remember her birthday and anniversary, and of course Mother's Day, if you had a mother, and see your dentist twice a year.

Otherwise the planet would get you ahead of its ordained time, as it had already gotten a lot of other people. They were running out in the streets, or going mad, or cutting their throats, or jumping off high buildings, or drinking themselves to death.

Already the earth was a kind of revolving madhouse, a spinning apple swarming with maddened ants racing in every direction. It was hard to see close up, but the newspaper on David's knee told him the story. He swallowed the last of his highball, picked up the paper, and let his eye rove over the glaring black headlines.

## RUSSIAN DICTATOR
## ARRIVES IN WASHINGTON

*Goes into Immediate Conference with
President at White House*

That was something for the book. Two weeks ago a visit from the King of the Martians would have caused a lesser sensation.

When the big Soviet plane with the red stars painted on its wings finally taxied to a stop at National Airport, the President and the entire Cabinet were there to meet the Generalissimo, and the United States Marine Band played the "Internationale."

The photographs of the meeting in the newspapers were not flattering. Both the President and the Soviet dictator looked like everyone else, like frightened little men. Their faces were haggard; they seemed dazed as they shook hands . . .

## ARMIES DEMOBILIZED
## ATOM PLANTS CLOSE DOWN

*Experts Mull Problem
Of Bomb Disposal*

The existence of the bombs was almost humorously embarrassing now.

You couldn't just dump them in some junk yard, or store them in some dusty warehouse somewhere, like obsolete merchandise.

You couldn't just bury them in the earth somewhere, or drop them deep on the ocean bed.

The astronomers had pointed out that the other bodies in the solar system had made a slight change in position to compensate for the onrushing planet. Luckily the earth would be spared any violent internal dislocations, but there would still be dangerous stresses and strains on the dry crust and the ocean beds—too dangerous for the deposit of bombs.

Maybe, thought David cynically, they ought to run a contest open to all comers—a million dollars for the best thousand-word statement on what to do with a non-producing atom bomb. Too bad it wasn't a missile like the old-time artillery shells they used a few decades ago. You could always polish up the casings and fill them with dirt and plant flowers in them. Or you could stand them on end and use them as floor ash trays. Whether they held geraniums or cigarette butts, you could get some use out of them, your money wasn't entirely wasted.

But there was nothing more useless than an atom bomb which wasn't working at its trade.

David's eye caught a headline:

## MILITARY DISEASE
## DEPARTMENTS DISBANDED

### *Reveal Plans for Bacteriological Warfare*
### *To Supplement A-Bombs*

Yes, thought David grimly, it would have been a nice little war all around. He read through a list of attack diseases at the bottom of the story:

Botulism, anthrax, pneumatic plague, measles and mumps, glanders, rabbit fever, undulant fever, yellow fever, dengue fever, tick-borne relapsing fever, spotted and "Q" fever, fowl plague, foot and mouth disease, melioidosis, hog cholera, rinderpest.

David shuddered and turned the page.

## RAILS AND AIR LINES JAMMED AS
## THOUSANDS RETURN HOME TO CITIES

### TRAVELERS ON MOVE TO REJOIN FAMILIES

*Food and Utilities Situation
Critical in Urban Centers*

It was like a funeral in the family.

The planet brought everybody home, even relatives who hadn't seen each other in twenty years or who were bitter and quarreling enemies. There was nothing like a tragedy to bring people together in a kind of morbid brotherhood.

But this time it wasn't just somebody else's funeral.

## WAVE OF SUICIDES AS THOUSANDS
## BREAK UNDER STRAIN

### MANY TAKE LIVES BY HANGING, POISON, SLEEPING PILLS

*Heart Attacks Take Toll*

*Insane Asylums Filled to Overflowing*

Ever since the first night it had been like that. The planet pressed down hard on the brain, and its shadow, although still invisible to the eye, already darkened the mind.

Many died before they were born. Thousands of women in the early stages of pregnancy arranged deliberate miscarriages.

## GREAT RELIGIOUS REVIVAL AS
## CHURCHES JAMMED TO OVERFLOWING

*Planet "Y" the Millennium*

In houses of worship all over the world, masses and services were continuous, day and night. People fought to get into churches as they once fought to get into a Hollywood première. The people of radio, the hucksters of Boxtop Boulevard in New York, Chicago, and Los Angeles, looked at their listener-rating reports and stared.

Religious programs, programs of church services and sermons, hit the highest Hooper rating of all time, far above the big-name orchestras and comedians and variety shows.

Right now, radio-wise, prayer was commercial, very commercial indeed.

Give the public what they want. And what the public wanted was comfort, and divine intervention, and deliverance.

What the public suddenly wanted, David concluded, was God.

### GOVERNORS PARDON CONDEMNED MEN
### LIFERS RIOT FOR FREEDOM

*Let Us Live Last Two Years,*
*They Cry*

### INDUSTRIES PARALYZED
### AS WORKERS STAY HOME

*Stores, Offices, Schools Close*

*Wheels Grind to Stop as World*
*Staggers under Shock*

### RUN ON BANKS AS DEPOSITORS RUSH
### TO WITHDRAW LIFE SAVINGS

*Orgy of Spending, Black Markets,*
*Inflation Already a Threat*

### DAWSON DISCOVERY DISPUTED BY
### SELF-STYLED HOLY MAN OF
### HOGBACK MOUNTAIN, ARKANSAS

*I Saw Planet First, Claims Ozark*
*Prophet, and I Didn't Need No*
*Telescope Neither*

*Saw It in a Vision from the Lord*
*Swears Lord Promised World an*
*Extra Two Years for Extra Prayer*
*And Repentance*

David threw the newspaper on the couch and went upstairs. Carol, a vision of loveliness in a long black evening dress, was combing her hair before the mirror.

"Hurry, darling," she said, "or we'll be late for dinner."

It was almost a technique now.

You deliberately and desperately stuck to the commonplace, and it was a kind of pathetic game. You insulated yourself, never mentioned the planet if you could help it—tried not to think of it.

In order to stay sane, you had to make believe that it wasn't up there in the heavens and rushing onward.

But it *was* there.

That was the fact, the inescapable fact, and there was no privacy from it, no escape. Not even in sleep was there any escape any more, for the planet appeared in dreams, everybody's dreams, large and round and menacing and murderous.

As David unbuttoned his shirt he turned on the small television set on the night table.

The video screen focused on a crowd of people, and the camera panned over to a floodlighted entrance to the White House.

An announcer said something about a momentous meeting, and before he finished, the doors swung open and the President appeared with a bushy-haired man in a tight uniform and wearing the star of the Soviet Union.

They posed before the camera. Then, in an unrehearsed impulse, they threw their arms around each other's shoulders.

You had to hand it to the planet, David reflected.

Whatever it did, it was changing things—and changing them in a hell of a hurry.

**10.** In April of the Year One, a dramatic announcement came from Palomar.

Dr. Charles Dawson was preparing to photograph the face of Planet "Y."

He had hooked up a complicated photographic setup, using sensitive infra-red plates, and the apparatus had a special talent. It could ignore what it did not want to see. By scanning the face of Planet "Y" a hundred thousand times and delivering to the camera only the features which appeared on a majority of the pictures it saw, it could eliminate all distortions due to poor seeing or other temporary causes, thus taking full advantage of the light-gathering power of the Big Eye.

Already astronomers knew certain basic facts about the onrushing planet. It had a mass hundreds of times greater than that of the earth, and its period of rotation was eight months. They knew that it was a cold and inert body, surfaced by a frozen layer of methane and carbon dioxide, and that its reflective power was approximately that of sandstone.

It would become visible to the naked eye in September, a mere pin point in the sky, and thereafter would rapidly grow larger. And the catastrophe, the collision, would occur on the far side of the sun in relation to the earth's orbit.

But now the Old Man of Palomar was going to look straight into the face of Death itself. He was getting ready to give the world an advance showing on how the Killer would look when finally it hung in the heavens, clearly visible to the naked eye.

The news from Palomar was an immediate sensation. People all over the world showed a morbid and almost unbearable curiosity to look upon the face of their executioner. Newspapermen, astronomers, and other observers converged on Palomar.

This was the preview.

But whatever face Death wore, it would soon become as familiar to every man, woman, and child as the face of the man in the moon.

The night of the photographing was clear and cold.

David and Carol walked up the road toward the observatory. Carol had been in San Diego all day on a shopping trip, and she had insisted on coming along.

"Everyone's going crazy tonight, David," she had said. "You can cut the excitement with a knife. I've never seen so many newspapermen in one place before—not only from the American papers, but from the foreign ones too. They've been coming in all day. And I want to be in on the fun too."

He had noticed that she seemed pale, nervous, after her return from San Diego.

"It was the ride up," she had explained. "The roads, David, they were terribly icy. I thought we were going to skid right over a precipice a couple of times. And anyway, I kept thinking about tonight and worrying about the seeing. But they've already measured it, and I understand it's going to be good."

David had smiled a little at that. Already Carol was talking like an astronomer's wife. They never asked, like ordinary wives, how things were down at the office. They always asked anxiously how the seeing was. If it was one, that was excellent, the best. Two was good. Three was fair, and so on down the line.

The wind, as they moved up the hill, was like the edge of an ax, cutting deep into the bone, and they half walked, half slithered up the slippery road, huddling close to each other for both support and mutual warmth. The crunch-crunch of their feet as they passed the lighted cottages on each side of the road seemed abnormally loud, the only sound in the night.

Night and silence.

This was the normal state of the universe, thought David. Up there in the night of the sky, the stars and planets, like tiny illuminated vessels, moved slowly and silently across a dark and limpid sea. There were billions of them, pitiful suns lost in eternity, shining by their own light, driven by the breath of God. They were like specks of dust seen in a beam of light, or in the slanting rays of sunshine through a window, worlds and universes, lost in space, gliding, turning, spinning, whirling, drifting, vibrating.

Yet, thought David, so perfectly balanced were these bodies in the universe, so delicate and dependent were they in their rhythm upon each other, that a man, by the mere stretching forth of his hand, could theoretically change the moon on its course.

He thought of the planet, of Planet "Y," and he thought of the death it would bring. And he recalled Dr. Dawson discussing death one morning after the dome had closed and the work night was over.

"After all, David," the Old Man had said, "what is fourscore and ten years compared to the life of the stars and the planets? A lightning flash on a summer day? A drop of rain in a cloudburst?"

David had admitted the comparison, had agreed that it was no more than that when you stood away from a man's life and looked at it in proper perspective.

"But in a sense," he had said to the Old Man, "the whole concept of a man's life is in his own mind. To him a lifetime is forever, the beginning and end of all things."

"True," Dr. Dawson had replied. "But it is pure ego, David, for man to believe that all creation began and ended in his personal segment of infinity. In the heavens an eternity has already passed, and an eternity is yet to come. Up there some stars are being born, some are adolescent, some aged and dying, some dead. In the history of creation, a billion years, a hundred billion years, passes like a day."

But, David reflected, men didn't see it that way. They lived their pitiful era in astronomical time, as though the era would never come to an end. They lived, famously or humbly, making money or dreaming dreams, living in glory and living in sorrow, loving, fighting, sleeping, dying, goaded on by self-indulgence or ambition, believing with an incredible belief that *their* careers, *their* lives, *their* futures were the most serious, the most important, the most weighty in the universe.

Yet if there had been no Planet "Y," the earth, dependent upon the sun for life, would have died a short time later, a mere hundred million years later. The sun would finally lose its warmth and light and roll along through space, a dark and invisible and forgotten star, an icy graveyard.

And when Planet "Y" and the earth finally clashed, there would not be the sound of it in the void, nor even an echo, nor a ripple, to mar the still serenity of the universe.

David suddenly felt Carol tug on his arm, and they stopped walking for a moment.

"David," she said quietly, looking up into the cold and crackling sky, "where will we finally see the planet—up there?"

He bordered the constellation for her, pointed out a star. "That's where it is now, Carol. But when it finally becomes visible its position will have changed."

"Oh." Carol's face was rapt and dreamy. "It's funny, darling. Up to tonight I was afraid of it, of death. But now—now I'm not afraid any more. I keep thinking of life." She turned to him, and her eyes were suddenly wet with tears. "And do you know why?"

He shook his head.

"I was in San Diego today," she said. "But I lied to you, David. It wasn't because I wanted to do any shopping. I—I had to see Dr. Ramsey."

He stared at her. "Dr. Ramsey?"

"You see, David," she said simply, "I'm going to have a baby."

Up ahead on the summit, in the squat, curved white building, in Palomar Observatory, men were feverishly preparing to look at the face of their executioner; they had contrived instruments to do so, trembling in their anticipation.

But David had forgotten it now.

The affair of the heavens had for the moment become relatively unimportant. His mind was confused and whirling with an earthy problem.

His child would be a year old when the end came.

It was wrong, he thought savagely, wrong. When you brought a child into the world, you owed it a lifetime.

But he knew that his concern was partly selfish.

Carol was pregnant, and for the better part of a year she would be denied to him.

God damn it, he thought furiously, helplessly, he was human, as human as anybody. Why did this have to happen?

*Why?*

"Everything set, David?" asked Dr. Dawson.

"Yes, sir." David answered mechanically, almost absently, still preoccupied with his own intimate problem. "I've checked all the apparatus. Wallace had some trouble with the Bowen image-slicer. There was some variance in the temperature of the coudé room, and we were afraid it would distort the image delivered into the high-dispersion spectrograph. But everything's all right now."

"Good." The Old Man crushed his cigar in an ash tray and rose. "You've instructed the newspaper and radio people to stay in the auditorium until the experiment is over?"

"Yes, Doctor. Francis will be there to see that no one wanders out into the observatory."

"Well, David, I guess we're ready to go." The Old Man lifted his phone, dialed two numbers, and said: "All right, Fred, we're ready. You can bring the roof down now."

The Old Man's voice was almost dry in his calm. But David knew he was excited, excited inside. It was a big night, and the world was waiting. It was the biggest night they would ever have from here on in. The face of the planet was something you could not predict or calculate in advance, or even guess at.

Whatever the big telescope showed would be brand new, and it would be just as exciting to astronomers as to laymen.

They walked out into the observatory itself. It was silent now, bathed in the weird glow of soft red and green lights hidden in the cornice. The two men were alone, walking noiselessly on the rubber parquet as they headed toward the elevator.

David forgot his own troubles for the moment. The observatory still affected him, still awed him a little. Walking through it alone, he had always felt a little like an intruder. There was something about it, its hushed and reverent silence, its dim lighting, its echoing and arching vault, that reminded him of a cathedral. He had seen boisterous tourists enter it, and suddenly their voices had dropped to whispers, and they had taken off their hats and walked softly on tiptoes.

Being a little nearer to the stars here at Palomar was, in a sense, being a little nearer to God. The observatory was the last way station to the heavens.

Yet walking through the observatory now with Dr. Dawson, David felt somehow that they and the building itself were already in a kind of celestial motion. It was of course an illusion, you knew it was an illusion, you knew that this building was anchored firmly to the granite body of Palomar Mountain.

Still, here in this place, in the ghostly light and the complete silence, a kind of hypnotic spell stole over you, and already you were moving, soaring through space, as though the great round building had somehow burst from its earthy moorings and was carrying you along with it, a pygmylike passenger, through the starry vault overhead.

As they came out of the elevator on the mezzanine, a motor purred suddenly somewhere deep below. It began to throb and beat, throb and beat, like a great heart. The dome began to open, like an orange slowly unfolding into two perfect halves, and a cold blast of air came straight downward.

After the main floor, the transition to the mezzanine was almost startling. Men of the observatory staff were swarming about the place, running up and down stairways, carrying photographic plates, sheets of calculations, and bound on other errands. They seemed to be moving almost feverishly against a deadline, as though the onrushing planet overhead might decide to veer off and run away before they could catch it in their instruments.

The Old Man smiled. "It's a little like a railroad station around here tonight, isn't it, David?"

"Yes, sir."

"Tell you a little secret," whispered the Old Man. "I'm more excited than anyone else around here. Thank heaven there's only one setting I'll have to take. And I hope I don't fumble it."

The Old Man sounded as though he meant it. He went to his locker, pulled a fur hat fitted with ear muffs down firmly over his head, bundled himself up in a fur coat, and drew on a pair of heavy mittens.

"Well, David," he said, "let's go. And in a short time—if we're lucky—we'll have the answer."

David signaled for lights out and walked toward his desk control station. The lights died, except for one tiny hooded reddish lamp high in the dome. As the members of the staff scurried toward their separate posts, a kind of hush came over the place. But it was a hush that was alive, ecstatic with excitement, and yet filled with dread.

They watched the Old Man silently as he walked with measured stride along the balcony, and then, climbed the short iron stairway to the loading bridge. He looked up into the dome for a moment, as though savoring the drama of what lay in wait up there, far beyond the roof and the earth itself.

Then he pushed a button, and the flying platform swept down from the shadows of the dome, swung in on its curved track, and stopped. He closed the gate, the clang of the steel safety bar shattering the silence like a steely echo. The Old Man pressed another control button, and the platform, with its tiny figure clutching the rail, swept up the track and disappeared.

David stood quietly at his station and waited. His eye swept his control panels, the various switches, the indicators for right ascension and declination, the telescope's zenith angle, wind-screen position, sidereal and standard time clocks, the selsyn transmitters. They were as familiar to him as the dashboard of an automobile is to its driver.

But tonight their phosphorescent faces glowing sickly in the darkness seemed to take on a special and magic and almost human look, as though they, too, were aware that the drama was about to begin.

This was the night. This was the night they had waited for at Palomar for weeks.

Now they were ready, they were all ready to go. And in a few minutes their aching curiosity would be satisfied, theirs and the curiosity of millions of others in every corner of the earth.

The Old Man seemed to be taking a long time getting his call through, thought David. Maybe it was no longer than usual on the clock, but it seemed like an eternity. He pictured Dr. Dawson high in the cage, in the top of the telescope, checking the banks of three selsyn dials for right ascension and declination, as he had so many hundreds of times. The dials indicated rough, intermediate, and fine settings.

The phone buzzed suddenly. David picked up the receiver.

"All right, David," came the voice of the Old Man quietly. "Give me the setting."

David hung up and pressed the "execute" button.

And now the precise mechanical miracle that moved the 200-inch telescope to its appointed place went into action.

The human brain stopped functioning, and an electric brain took over. It was contained in a box twenty feet square, its brain cells were electronic tubes, and it could memorize, add, multiply, and divide billions in a fraction of a second. The name of it was EDVAC—Electronic Discrete Variable Computer—and in an hour it could work out a problem that it would take one human and expert mathematician fifty years to solve.

Now, through its motors, gears, electric circuits, and electronic tubes, it instantly calculated where the big telescope had to point in order to find Planet "Y." In effect, it solved the problem of holding the giant telescope with an accuracy of a single second of arc—a miracle of accuracy comparable to hitting a moving dime two miles away with a high-powered rifle.

It compensated for variable factors all at once—the change in object position caused by atmospheric refraction; the change in refraction owing to the temperature, humidity, barometric pressure, errors in the driving gears, the error owing to the deformation of the telescope itself under its own huge weight.

Then, through a system of cams, clocks, differential gears, and governors, the impulse was passed on to the great telescope drive system. And finally the huge tube swung into position, and the tracking motors took over and kept it aligned—a machine as heavy and as complicated as a locomotive, and yet a delicate instrument as precise as the finest microscope.

And up in a cage a man sat hunched over his instruments, photographing the face of Death itself.

Every seat in the auditorium was filled, and now it buzzed with excited conversation.

The first five rows of seats were taken by members of the Palomar staff, the rest by reporters and radiomen. In the rear a "remote" was set up, and two network men waited with earphones clamped to their heads, with microphones ready to broadcast the news to the world, while the television crews busied themselves with their cameras.

They were waiting for the Old Man now to come out of the photographic lab.

David stood at the projector and watched the faces of the men, listened to what they were saying. He remembered another occasion—the morning the Old Man had broken the news of the planet here in this same auditorium.

It seemed as though it were only the day before yesterday. But actually it was five months ago.

Time moved on wings now, it slipped by fast, it was desperately precious. It was no longer leisurely. Before the planet came, a man could watch the hands of a clock, and they would seem to stand still or barely crawl around the face.

But now you could see them move, you could watch them voraciously eat up the time.

Less than two years more. One, two.

And then the end.

The door opened, and Dr. Dawson came in.

He was holding a slide in his hand. The hum of conversation died suddenly. There was a rustling as the crowd turned to look at the Old Man.

He came in slowly, walking with dragging steps. He looked stunned. His face was blanched; he moved like an automaton.

David stiffened. Something was wrong, he thought. Something had hit the Old Man hard.

But what was it? What had the Old Man seen? What was on that slide?

The men in the room stared at the astronomer stupidly. They sat rigid, fixed in their seats, like men in a trance.

They, too, sensed that the Old Man was suffering from some kind of shock.

Instead of walking down the aisle and going up on the platform to explain what he had seen, he walked straight to David and wordlessly handed him the slide.

With shaking fingers David turned on the projector. Francis turned out the lights, and a funnel of blank white light hit the screen on the platform.

David inserted the slide.

And then they saw the face of Planet "Y."

But it was not really a face at all.

*It was a leering, malevolent, staring EYE!*

As the months went by the world robbed the big telescope of its nickname and gave it to Planet "Y."

After that they called it *THE BIG EYE.*

**11.** Long before it became visible the Big Eye leered malignantly from every rotogravure page and every magazine cover in the country and in the world.

It was a dead kind of eye, with a baleful stare, and it was bloodshot under a puffy eyelid.

And finally, in the late summer of the Year One, it became visible through small telescopes.

In cities all over the world sidewalk entrepreneurs did a bonanza business by mounting telescopes on street corners for a preview of the killer planet. The Big Eye became the biggest show in town.

It was still far off in the void, still remote, but getting nearer and bigger every day. Through the telescope it was about the size of a pea, but remarkably distinct.

And as the planet made its half rotation every four months the Big Eye became distorted and finally turned and looked away, presenting the back of its "eyeball," a nondescript pattern of shadowed ridges and mountains.

But it always reappeared, turning slowly on its revolving eyeball, till it again glared down with a fixed and fishy and knowing stare.

When it was full it always seemed to look directly at you, but, unlike the human eye, it never blinked.

When your turn came for the telescope and you looked through the lens, you saw the Big Eye and you were alone with it.

And when the man who owned the telescope finally touched your arm and said, "Next," it was as though you were coming out of a hypnotic trance. You felt weak and gone inside, and your hands and knees shook, and your clothes were wet with perspiration.

It was all very well for the astronomers to be dryly scientific about it. It was all very well to say that the blood-red color was only the reflection of the sun below the horizon, that the black eyebrow was a huge, curved volcanic mountain range, that the eyeball was a great round crater, that the iris was a darker depression within the crater.

They spoke of the topography of the Big Eye in terms of mountains, craters, rays, rills, crevices, ridges, furrows, walled plains, and shadows. They blandly made comparisons to the friendly and benevolent face of the moon, matched the elevations and contours of the Big Eye with the lunar craters of Tycho, Copernicus, Kepler, Clavius, Grimaldi, Archimedes, and the lunar Apennines.

The astronomers said that what you saw through the sidewalk telescopes was simply a dead planet.

But to you the Big Eye was very much alive.

And it did not deviate. It was right on schedule; it had a date to keep at an appointed time.

The Big Eye, although yet invisible to the naked eye, already had profound effects.

As it plummeted through the solar system it brought about certain natural phenomena. There were high winds, freakish changes of temperature; the tides became erratic; navigation instruments were becoming unreliable. Minor tidal waves were reported, and the number of earthquakes increased, although for the most part they were isolated to those countries already susceptible to subterranean shocks.

Seismologists assured the people who had returned to New York that there was no further danger. What had happened in November was a minor series of tremors, called foreshocks. There had been a small fracture in the bedrock under the city and a subsequent readjustment to a secure and stable base.

But the impact of the new planet was strongest upon the minds of those who lived under it.

In the first few months of the Year One there had been a wave of suicides, an interval of violence and lawlessness, a kind of mass madness. The crime rate had soared; rape and robbery were rampant. Statistics showed, however, that the number of homicides was almost negligible. Under the circumstances, life suddenly became a very precious commodity, and even hardened criminals and murderers showed a certain reluctance to take it.

Alcoholism soared, the demand for liquor far exceeded the supply, and the governments of the various nations all installed rationing systems. The streets swarmed with staggering drunkards and prostitutes. Respectable men and women of sound, churchgoing families, slept in strange beds and each other's beds.

There was so little time.

Yet as time went on the hysteria tapered off. People settled back and accepted the fact that they had to live under the planet, and there was nothing they could do to avert it.

Millions became ardent church- and temple-goers. Some were merely mending their fences for the next world just around the corner. But the vast majority found real comfort and peace in religion. Money became a drug on this kind of temporary market, there were no futures, and rich men gave their wealth away.

There was nothing the Lord loved so much as openhanded charity. It was a good hedge against the hereafter.

In the field of agriculture there was a little trouble at first. Farmers, who were now interested in enjoying the leisure which was the farmers' special dream, saw no reason why they should work from dawn to dusk to supply the needs of others. But the granaries were bulging, and experts calculated that, with only a minor effort on the part of farmers, there would be enough to last through the appointed time. The government buttressed this with emergency edicts, establishing harvest quotas by law.

Poverty began to disappear. At the end of the first few months of the Year One, not a beggar was seen on the streets of any metropolis in the world, not even in Shanghai, Bombay, Cairo, and other cities which had once swarmed with hungry supplicants. The various governments surprisingly discovered that they had all the resources it took to feed and clothe and otherwise take care of its people. It was only a question, to coin an old, old phrase, of proper distribution. Governments had no future to worry about, no more armies and navies to support. The national debt became a figure of speech. And although death was still certain, taxes were canceled.

Everywhere, in business and industry, the wheels began to slow to a stop.

But Government was active, and changing fast.

Politicians, having no re-election to worry about, suddenly became representatives of the people. In Washington the Democrats and Republicans almost immediately merged into a single party. The ordinary issues that had brought forth oratory and filibusters suddenly became obsolete. The Big Eye stared down impartially upon the sunny shores of California as well as the rock-bound coasts of Maine.

And this was only the beginning.

In July a world government came into being.

The Federation of the World, as it was called, took over the old United Nations setup on East River Drive in New York City as its headquarters.

The Secretariat skyscraper bordering Forty-second Street, the Library, the General Assembly Building, the giant office building on Forty-eighth Street once again blazed with light. The hedges on the terrace were clipped, the grass trimmed, the broken windows replaced, and the corridors scrubbed.

There was a tremendous dedication, with hundreds of thousands jamming the area. Batteries of huge searchlights blazed from surrounding skyscrapers, bathing the area in brilliant white light. The East River sparkled with many-colored reflections as one gigantic fireworks display after another boomed in the summer sky and exploded in glittering cascades.

A Supreme Council of the World was elected by the assembled delegates of every nation on earth.

The ex-President of the United States and the ex-dictator of the Soviet Union were elected to serve in alternating chairmanships.

There was no problem as to tenure, and the bylaws of the World Constitution held no provision for any re-election.

On the following morning the New York *Times* devoted its entire editorial page to the event. The lead editorial said in part:

*Today a wistful dream nurtured by mankind for centuries has come true.*

*World government is a fact.*

*It is both wonderful and pitiful. It is wonderful in that we* have lived to see it come. It is pitiful that we shall have it for such a short duration.

Under the glare of the Big Eye, world government had to come. It was inevitable, and natural, and practical. The moment the dramatic announcement broke from Palomar, it was on its way. In the past months we have watched the two great conflicting systems, capitalism and Communism, crumble, disintegrate. We have seen nationalism, isolationism, and all the other isms that separated state from state, man from man, go down into ashes.

And out of the ashes has risen one great universal system— worldism.

After a million years of ignorant infancy, man has finally shed his swaddling clothes. If the Big Eye is a tragic miracle, so, too, is the speed with which it has changed the pattern of our lives. As it swiftly began to shorten the celestial abyss between the earth and itself, it became a powerful catalyst, pushing the reaction forward with dramatic speed. In a few months it did what man in all the centuries of his history had failed to do.

Under the lash of fear, under the baleful glare of the Big Eye, men and nations both suddenly stopped being afraid of each other in their one common fear.

Now they are coming together in universal brotherhood.

The Big Eye will one day bring total darkness, but in the interim it has brought its own light. It has broken up, at one powerful stroke, the false gods invented by man—the legends, the superstitions, the errors and lies and prejudices and hypocrisies accumulated in the human mind for thousands of years.

The overwhelming tragedy is that the new idea has such a short time to live. But there is still another tragedy we cannot fail to note here.

The real tragedy is that we did not begin to create this new world back some fifteen years ago, when the first bomb fell on

*Hiroshima. The tragedy is that all through the late forties and fifties, as the world broke asunder into two worlds, we failed to understand that the bomb was a kind of Planet "Y" itself, in its devastating threat to mankind.*

*Had we recognized the fact then, that the bomb was simply a man-made Big Eye, we might have begun our new Federation of the World in 1945 instead of today.*

*How could we have been so blind?*

*Why did we, beginning from the end of the last war, through the late forties and the early fifties, move apart into hostile and nationalistic and suspicious segments, instead of coming together as we have now?*

*Why did it take a celestial manifestation to bring us to our senses?*

*Why?*

**12.** On the third of September, in the Year One, the Big Eye became visible to the human eye.

It appeared as a tiny pin point high in the heavens, shortly after dusk.

As time went by the pin point thickened into a dime, a penny, a quarter, then a half dollar, varying in color, like the moon. Finally it was a rotting, overripe tangerine hanging in the sky, and the Eye emerged from a shadowy outline to become sharp and clear.

And, like the human eye, it seemed to reflect mood and intent to the viewer.

Sometimes it was dead and expressionless and indifferent. At other times it was bloated and swollen and puffy, as though suffering from some kind of heavenly hang-over. It was capricious, too. It was sly; it flirted and beckoned. It smirked cynically; it leered triumphantly. Sometimes it was hard and threatening, malicious and mischievous, smug and angry.

It was never a shifty eye. It knew what it was about; it was a knowing eye; its purpose was plain and understood.

And the times when it was visible in the day or night sky, whether you saw it in America, or Siberia, or Australia, or Arabia, it never looked at other people elsewhere.

It always looked directly at you.

It was impossible to stare the Big Eye down. It followed you everywhere, like a conscience. And as it grew bigger and bigger it became heavier and heavier, so that your back and shoulders and head seemed to ache with its oppressive weight, and your feet dragged more slowly.

It was particularly vivid when the moon was invisible. Stray dogs howled and bayed at it in the night when it shone alone in the sky. But when the moon appeared with it and the two competed for supremacy, the dogs seemed confused and uncertain. They merely whimpered a little or stopped barking entirely.

At the end of the Year One the moon paled into a sickly white, and the Big Eye dominated the night sky.

It hung high overhead, tinting the night, so that it was never really night at all, but a kind of murky and oppressive sunset from dusk until dawn.

And it kept coming on, hurtling down, nearer and nearer, leering malignantly as it came.

As the calendar shortened, the Big Eye became bigger, bigger, and bigger, rounder and rounder, crueler and crueler, brighter and brighter, redder and redder. . . .

David Hughes and Joe Morgan, the Palomar spectrograph man, came out of the air-line terminal on Forty-second Street.

"Taxi!" yelled Morgan. "Hey, taxi!"

A Yellow Cab stopped short, its brakes squealing. David and his former roommate threw in their luggage, slammed the door, and settled back.

"First the New Weston Hotel on Madison," David told the driver. "We'll check in there—it'll only take a minute. Then you can take us to the Hayden Planetarium on Central Park West."

The driver nodded, and they began to move through a dense wedge of confused traffic.

It was late afternoon in December, and David's first trip to New York since the previous November.

A week ago the Old Man had received an invitation from Dr. Herrick, director of the Planetarium, to lecture on the Big Eye before a Science Council seminar of the world government.

Dr. Dawson had politely declined, for reasons of health, and had offered to send his first assistant and his spectrograph man to substitute for him. Herrick had accepted, and David and Morgan were on their way to confer with the director before lecturing the next morning.

The cabdriver was a small, bull-necked, bald-headed man. His picture framed in the rear of the taxi said he was Frank Leone. And although in the grimy photograph he glared villainously at them from beneath a sinister-looking cap, he turned out to be quite friendly and garrulous.

As he waited for the light at Lexington and Forty-second he turned and asked:

"Been out of town long, gents?"

"About a year," answered David.

"How's the big town look now?"

"Different. It's changed."

"You said it, mister. It's changed plenty."

David noticed that the driver was wearing an expensive overcoat and hand-stitched gloves. He looked more like a prosperous businessman than a taxi driver. A sign of the times, thought David. Only a year to go, what was the use of saving money? Buy the best, live high, eat, drink, and be merry.

Spend every dime, cash in the insurance, go to town, _live_.

He was willing to bet that Frank Leone's wife had a mink coat. He looked out of the window, and as the cab lurched forward with the light he saw that the streets were jammed with what seemed to be hundreds of thousands of people on the Lexington block between Forty-second and Forty-third.

And David noticed that practically every woman in the crowd wore a mink coat.

He turned to Joe Morgan, but Morgan was looking up through the glass roof of the taxi, staring at the towering height of the Chrysler Building. There was awe on his face.

"Look at that, Dave," he said. "Look at that. Not a pane of glass in a window above the first floor."

David had noticed the same thing when they had come out of the terminal. The upper stories of the surrounding skyscrapers were all geometrically lined with open, gaping, rectangular holes. Occasionally the sun glinted on a jagged fragment of glass which still clung to a window frame. They hadn't bothered to replace the windows after the tremor of last November.

"Sure," said the driver, Leone. "All these office buildings are ghost buildings. Most of 'em are shut off above the first floors; the elevators ain't even running. The business sections all over the city are ghost towns."

"Well," said Morgan, "it makes sense. These empty offices, I mean. Accountants, businessmen, they haven't anything to do any more. And take lawyers. No use in lawyers coming down to the office. No one's making any more wills, under the circumstances. There's no more building going on and no titles to work out. And as for contracts——"

"Yeah," interrupted Frank Leone, "who needs a contract now? You make a deal with a guy these days, you don't sign any paper. He takes your word, you take his word, you trust each other. Who wants to kill the other guy, when this damned thing up there in the sky is going to come down and blow us all to hell?" The driver threw on his brakes, bumped a big limousine in front of him. "That's why there ain't a courthouse open today in New York, from Brooklyn to the Bronx. The lawyers and the judges didn't have nothing to do, so they went home."

They inched ahead in the crush of traffic, and David noted that the insurance companies and the banks, too, were closed. The hedges against the future had been clipped at the roots.

But it was the crowd jamming up the sidewalks, barely moving in either direction, that fascinated both David and Morgan. This was a boom town, and the people had a boom look, the look of free spenders. They seemed to be on a holiday. David could see no one hurrying, hustling ahead, as they did in the old days, before the Year One.

But there was more to the crowd than numbers. It was a crowd with a mood.

In the old days, before the Big Eye, the people in a New York crowd looked sullen; they hungered for privacy; they fought and elbowed and resented each other.

Now the faces on the sidewalk looked different.

They looked almost happy, in a taut kind of way. They seemed to say, "Sure, the Big Eye is looking down at me, but it's watching you, buddy, and you, lady, and you and you, and everyone else in this crowd. We're all in the same boat."

David found that he was more relaxed himself, just being here. The tension of the thing in the sky was loosened a little. Palomar was lonely compared to this, and the Big Eye, when its gaze was full, had a trick of picking out its personal target more readily. It was more intimate because you were few in number.

Here, although it was still personal, you could in some measure share the impact with thousands of other people. You could, like cattle huddling together flank to flank under a thunderstorm, find a certain amount of comfort in the nearness of others.

However, David told himself, it was still daylight, and perhaps he had only the illusion of comfort, a temporary feeling of security, here in the bright sunlight.

But the night was coming, and then the Big Eye would hang in the sky, low and leering.

Then David heard Joe Morgan's awed voice.

"I never saw anything like this. The mobs jamming up this sidewalk. Where do they all come from?"

"From everywhere, mister," answered the man at the wheel. "From jerk towns, from the farms, from all over. This town is jammed to the ceiling. You're lucky if you can find a place to sleep. They're sleeping out in the parks, anywhere, no matter where it is. Every train, every plane, and every bus coming in are unloading 'em. I was reading in the paper they got ten million people right here in Manhattan right now, let alone the other boroughs."

"Back a year ago November, this town looked like a morgue," said David.

"Yeah. *Now* look at it!" Frank Leone shook his head. "It's murder just to drive a hack five blocks."

"Why are they all coming to New York?" asked Morgan.

"New York, Chicago, Detroit, it's all the same. People feel better when they're in crowds. The big cities are getting the play. They're all looking to escape, looking for entertainment, for a good time before they die, booze, shows, women. If you got nothing to do tonight, take a walk down Broadway and around Times Square. You'll *see* something there, mister."

As they turned off Lexington and moved west on Forty-ninth toward Park Avenue, Joe Morgan got back to the subject of the crowds.

"Seems to be a lot of foreigners on the streets," he remarked. "Asiatics and Europeans alike."

"Yeah," said Frank Leone. "Only nobody calls 'em foreigners any more. Last summer, when they opened up this here world government over on East River Drive, they let down all the bars of immigration. So they all started to come in—Chinese, Japs, Dutchmen, Russians, everybody. Guess they all figured the U.S. was dreamland, and they wanted to see it before the Big Eye got 'em." The driver grinned. "The first few days it felt kind of funny— like this wasn't the U.S.A. any more."

"And after that?" asked David.

"I dunno," answered Leone. "It was funny, how you got used to it. Nobody gave a damn where anybody came from any more, I guess. Same way in Russia. Me and the wife took a trip over there in September. Blew all our insurance policies in on it."

"How'd you like the Soviet?" asked Morgan.

"It stinks. It's all right to visit, but not to live in. Give me New York any time. But the people are all right, once you get to know 'em. And they don't call it the Soviet any more. Communism is a dead turkey over there. They tore off all the signs and painted over the walls, like they did here. But getting back to the U.S., it's funny how things change. Take the taxi business now."

"Yes?" asked David. "What about it?"

"We got a lot of guys driving hacks that used to be in the Red Army. The doughnut-and-coffee joints near the big hack stands are full of 'em. They drive like they're crazy, and I guess they are. When the big Irish cops around here argue with 'em, *they* go crazy." He grinned back at David and Morgan through the reflector. "Funny how times have changed. Before the Big Eye came I would have murdered any one of these Ivans if I could have got close enough. Now—some of my best friends are Russians."

*"Look out, driver!"* David yelled suddenly.

Frank Leone jammed on his brakes. The cab came within a foot of hitting three children crossing against the light at Park. The youngsters, their faces white and frightened, scurried for safety to the opposite sidewalk.

"Those goddamn kids," sweated Leone. "There ought to be a law to keep 'em off the downtown streets. Ten times a day I almost run 'em down."

"Where do all these kids come from?" asked Morgan. "School out or something?"

"Ain't you heard?" said the driver. "Every school in town closed the week after they found the Big Eye."

"No schools open?" David was surprised.

"Not a one."

"Seems funny," remarked Morgan. "I don't get it."

"Don't you?" The driver began to explain patiently: "Look. Take me, Frank Leone. I got five kids. In the old days, before that damned Big Eye came along, I worked nights, slept days. My kids got on my nerves when they came home from school; sometimes I used to swear at them. Now it's different. Now I can't see enough of 'em. A guy likes to get as much as he can out of his family at a time like this, wants to keep his kids home where he can be with 'em all the time."

As they turned on Madison from Forty-ninth, David thought of Carol, heavy with child, back at Palomar.

And he noted, as they turned, that a long line of people stood on Forty-ninth toward Fifth, waiting patiently to get into St. Patrick's Cathedral.

The cab drew up in front of the New Weston.

"What good is education for kids now?" Frank Leone concluded. "There ain't no future left for them to use it in."

They told Leone to wait. Then David and Morgan went into the lobby of the hotel.

The place was crowded with people looking for accommodations. David was grateful that Dr. Herrick had made reservations for them long in advance.

As the bellboy took their luggage Morgan asked where he could find the nearest drugstore.

"What's the matter, Joe?" David said.

"I don't know. Feel a little under the weather, I guess. Maybe I'm a little airsick or something. I never could take planes."

"Look," said David, "why don't you go upstairs and lie down awhile? I'll talk to Herrick alone and go over the routine for tomorrow morning."

"You're sure you don't mind?"

David shook his head. "No use in both of us going over to the Planetarium. I'll see you here at the hotel in a couple of hours."

At the Hayden Planetarium, David spent two hours with Dr. Herrick. They planned to present an illustrated lecture, with David doing the talking and Morgan showing the plates.

Finally, when David rose to go, the director said:

"David, you can't be very busy at Palomar now, under the circumstances."

"No. Planet 'Y' has made observation pretty difficult. Too much interference from its light. We'll probably close for good in a few months."

As Dr. Herrick escorted David out of the office he said:

"David, I wouldn't want to take you away from Dr. Dawson. But there's a position open to you on the staff here at the Planetarium any time you want it. Of course it'll be routine and unspectacular, but we expect to stay open here"—Dr. Herrick hesitated—"until a month or two before Christmas."

David thanked him and left.

When he got back to his room at the hotel Joe Morgan was just coming out of the shower and whistling.

"Feel much better now, Dave. An hour's nap did it. By the way, what are you doing tonight?"

David shrugged. "Nothing."

"Look, Dave." Joe seemed a little apologetic. "I made a phone call. There's a girl I used to know here in New York. I had some ideas about her at one time, but they never came true. But when I talked to her on the phone she sounded a lot different. I think the planet's changed her, and I'm going to find out." He hesitated. "I can make it for two. Like to come along?"

David shook his head. "Thanks just the same, Joe."

"Okay." Morgan shrugged. "I don't want to corrupt you, or anything like that, and you know how much I think of your wife. But with Carol the way she is, and with just a few months left, I thought you'd——"

"Sure, Joe," said David. "But right now I'm not in the mood. You go ahead. I'll just go out and wander around town."

It was seven o'clock when David left the hotel.

As he walked west down Fiftieth toward Broadway, he saw the Big Eye.

It had taken up its post just as dusk had come, and now it hung directly over the huge RCA sign atop the Rockefeller Plaza sky-scraper.

It was a little bilious now, its color washed and diluted by the great glare of light thrown up from the amusement district beyond.

It followed David as he walked; it stared at him with a fixed and intent look, until mercifully the intervening buildings hid it.

A wind was blowing, a sharp, raw, and incessant wind, and it moaned and wailed through the windowless rectangles in the Rockefeller Center group.

But if the upper floors of the buildings were dead, the streets swarmed with life.

David had barely crossed Fifth Avenue when he ran into the crowds.

They were lined along the sidewalks, waiting to get into the theaters.

The small theater at the Plaza, once a newsreel house, had changed. Now it sported a giant marquee, and although the original sign still spelled "Newsreel Theater," the legend in lights on the blazing marquee told a different story:

HOUSE OF LAUGHS
ONE SOLID HOUR OF LAUGHS
THREE CARTOONS, TWO
FUNNY SHORT SUBJECTS

The signs on the outside lobby indicated the theater ran a continuous performance, twenty-four hours a day. They offered the balm that was box office:

FORGET THE BIG EYE
FOR AN HOUR
COME IN AND LAUGH

The crowd blocked the sidewalk; it lined up snakelike in a continuous line to the Radio City Music Hall just down the block; it spilled over into the street and on the other side of the street, where it was kept in check by ushers and police.

The faces of the people looked chalk-white in the garish light; they chattered incessantly, their voices high-pitched and shrill; they complained bitterly about having to wait so long.

The strange part of it was that David heard no one laugh.

Between Sixth and Seventh, just short of Broadway itself, he noticed a new and unfamiliar group of establishments.

On the second and third stories of the cheap hotels there were neon signs just above discreetly curtained windows.

They bore odd names like "The Careless Hour," "The Green Slipper," "The Mirror," "The Oasis," "Katie's," "Edna's."

And under each sign was a single and discreet word: "Hostesses."

David inched his way through the dense crowds until he came to Broadway.

Broadway was obscene in its incandescent brilliance.

Every marquee was blazing, every electric sign; the dense crowds moved in a great bath of white light. On the corner of Forty-sixth Street a huge spectacular showed an animated clown, laughing and dancing and jumping up and down, advertising a current comedy at one of the big movie houses.

The clown laughed and chuckled; his roars came from his illuminated belly and rolled over the street.

But only the clown laughed.

On the huge television screen, the same one where the old Camel cigarette sign had once been located, a network comedian kept up a fire of running gags, which instantaneously poured into the living rooms of ten million homes, coast to coast.

But on Broadway the gags fell flat.

Nobody laughed.

Yet the marquees indicated that every show was a comedy, every comedy a hit. The producers had learned early that a serious drama, no matter how artistic, would run no longer than a night.

The legitimate theaters were offering performances around the clock instead of just matinee and evening. They accomplished this by the use of rotating stock companies. When one company finished on the stage, there was an hour intermission, and then another company took over.

And everywhere the "Standing Room Only" sign was out.

David managed to travel two blocks. He was mauled, propelled by the thick crowd, crushed, shoved along. He found the experience physically exhausting.

Finally, almost in desperation, he decided on a movie and waited in line. And after a two-hour wait he entered the darkened movie house.

A light domestic comedy, a farce, was on the screen, and once inside the theater, it was different.

The people laughed in waves, they guffawed, they split their sides hysterically, shrilly.

Within the theater they sat under a starry sky devoid of the Big Eye.

The roof of the rococo interior was designed as a romantic heaven, splattered with tiny electric stars; it even sported a dull moon near the second balcony. This heaven was free, wonderfully free, of any foreign invader.

And so the audience laughed, and David laughed with them.

But when he finally came out on the sidewalk again he felt let down, depressed. The real sky was overhead again, and although the Big Eye was temporarily invisible in the wash of Broadway light, he knew it was there.

It was there and coming, closer and closer. . . .

It was midnight.

David came back to his room at the New Weston and found that Joe Morgan had not yet returned.

For a few minutes he puttered around the room aimlessly, restlessly, having no desire to go to bed.

The movie had provided him with a three-hour anesthesia. But now he needed more, something different, something stronger, to take the pressure off.

He thought of Carol and her swollen abdomen and the nights that his whole body had ached for want of her.

It began to ache now. . . .

He thought of the places with the neon signs, the curtained windows, the names, "The Careless Hour," "The Oasis," "Katie's," and the others, licensed and available, and the beckoning signs, "Hostesses" . . .

The phone rang.

The operator asked him to wait a moment, Palomar was calling.

Then suddenly Carol's voice came over the wire. She was hysterical, sobbing.

"David! David! You've got to come back right away!"

"What is it, Carol? What's the matter?"

"It—it's Mrs. Dawson. She had an automobile accident just after you left—died an hour ago. And Dr. Dawson's had a stroke!"

For three agonizing hours David waited in the hotel room until Joe Morgan returned.

Then they took a cab for the airport.

**13.** At San Diego, while Joe Morgan was getting the car, David phoned Carol.

"Mrs. Dawson was driving one of the station wagons, David," Carol explained tearfully. "The roads up here are slippery from the ice—and, well, the car turned over. She lingered for hours, and Dr. Wilk did everything he could. But it was no use."

At the moment David's mind couldn't concentrate on Mrs. Dawson. She was dead; that was gone and done with now. He was thinking of the Old Man.

"How about Dr. Dawson, Carol? How's he taking it?"

"I—David, I'm afraid. When he heard the news he had a heart attack—almost collapsed. Dr. Wilk ordered him to bed, but he wouldn't go. He insisted on staying at Mrs. Dawson's bedside—till —till——"

Carol's voice broke, and she was unable to finish.

David told her that he and Morgan were just starting out in the car, and she said:

"Better come right to Dr. Dawson's house, David. I'll be there—everybody on the staff is there now. And, darling, be careful when you get upon the mountain. It's beginning to snow hard."

The last few miles to Palomar were a nightmare of driving. The snow whipped in horizontally against the windshield, a relentless tattoo propelled by a screaming wind.

Finally, however, they plowed through the observatory road, up the incline, and stopped in front of the "Residence" where the Dawsons lived. The road and driveway were clogged with cars, and the house was brilliantly lit. As David and Joe Morgan slogged through the snow toward the door they saw that the rooms within were crowded with people, their shadows moving restlessly behind the snow-frozen windows.

It was just getting dark before David had a chance to talk to Dr. Wilk.

The colony physician had finally come out of the Old Man's room, and his face was grave as he answered David's anxious question.

"Dr. Dawson's in fairly bad shape at the moment, David. The shock didn't do his heart any good. He'll have to stay in bed—get a complete rest for a few weeks. That's the physical picture. But there's another one—perhaps even more serious."

"You mean—his *mind?*"

Dr. Wilk nodded. "We'll have to wait and see. He acted very strangely near the end."

David gripped the physician by the lapels of his coat. "What do you mean, Dr. Wilk?"

"It's a little early to say anything definite as yet. But I am quite positive, David, that Dr. Dawson has been out of his mind for the past few hours. Just after Mrs. Dawson died he said something very strange."

"Yes? What was it, Dr. Wilk?"

"He kept moaning that he had to stand there and watch his wife die, that he could have saved her, but there was nothing he could do."

He could have saved her, but there was nothing he could do. . . . David tried to analyze that, but it didn't make sense.

"What about Mrs. Dawson? Was she unconscious at the end?" The physician nodded.

"And she never had a chance?"

"On the contrary, David, she did. She was suffering from shock, severe contusions, and internal injuries. But at the beginning she had a fairly good chance. The trouble was that she gave up—she didn't have any will to fight."

"You mean she didn't *want* to live?"

"I'm sure that was the case," said Dr. Wilk. "It's a phenomenon that we in the medical profession have noted recently in an increasing number of borderline cases similar to hers. We've always said that it's instinctive for a human being to fight for his life, to want to live." The physician hesitated. "But now I don't know——"

"You think the planet affected her somehow, Doctor?"

"Yes. My theory is that Mrs. Dawson knew, deep in her subconscious mind, that she had little time left, even if she did recover. And this militated against her fight to survive, broke her will to resist. Perhaps it's wrong to rationalize, but it's the only explanation I can offer. And as I said, our medical associations have several reports of the same thing happening elsewhere in the country. Patients who could have won through simply gave up."

"And you explained this theory to Dr. Dawson, sir?"

The physician nodded, then put on his hat and coat. "It's a great loss to Palomar, David. Emily Dawson was a fine woman. I don't know how Dr. Dawson is going to get along without her—for the remainder of the time we have left."

"Perhaps I'd better stay here with him tonight," said David mechanically.

"No," answered the physician. "That won't be necessary. I've already asked Francis to sit up with Dr. Dawson for the rest of the night. And in the morning I'll arrange for a day and night nurse."

When David and Carol went out they found it impossible to move the car in the deepening and drifting snow. And so, with heads down against the fierce, battering smash of the snow-needled wind, they plodded through the snow toward their cottage.

As he stumbled along, David thought bitterly, Why did Emily Dawson, why did *anyone* have to die now? Why wasn't there a moratorium on death under the Big Eye? To die now was a tragedy far deeper, more profound, than ever before.

Emily Dawson was near sixty; she was an old woman by calendar years. Under normal standards she was almost ready to go. But there were no longer any normal standards, and the calendar was different and brand new.

By the new calendar, in this, the Year Two, Emily Dawson had died a young woman, with almost half a lifetime left to live.

"David! David!"

David woke suddenly out of an uneasy slumber to find Carol shaking him. He opened his eyes to look up uncomprehendingly into her frightened face. Then, half drugged with sleep, he realized that the doorbell was ringing insistently.

"Someone's at the door, David," Carol whispered. "The doorbell's been ringing for over a minute. I can't imagine who it could be out in this storm now. It's almost one o'clock."

David, lying warm in bed, lingered a moment, hoping the ringing would stop. But it continued, became more insistent, more urgent than ever. Finally he cursed softly, got out of bed, put on a robe, and went downstairs. The storm literally shook the house, and he could hear the windowpanes rattle.

He wondered savagely what damned fool was out there in the blizzard at this time of night, pumping his doorbell.

He fumbled with the latch, flung open the door. The cold wind blasted a barrage of snow into the living room. David blinked at the impact, tried to make out the snow-coated face of the muffled figure in the doorway.

"Dr. Hughes! Dr. Hughes, sir!"

It was Francis, the steward. He came in, and David slammed the door behind him.

"Francis, for God's sake, what are you doing out in——"

"Dr. Hughes, it's Dr. Dawson. He's—*disappeared!*"

"*What?*"

Francis began to stammer piteously. "Dr. Hughes, it's my fault —it's all my fault. I'm afraid I dozed off for a little while in Dr. Dawson's library. When I awoke I went upstairs and looked into his room. He—he was gone!"

David seized the steward by the shoulders, shook him savagely. "Francis, are you sure?"

"Yes, sir. I went all through the house. I looked into—I looked into Mrs. Dawson's room—in the attic—in the cellar—everywhere. He's out in this blizzard somewhere, Dr. Hughes. My God, he's out in this terrible storm."

"Where? Where'd he go?"

"I don't know, sir. I don't know. But his clothes are still in his room. He must be in his pajamas—his robe. He's unprotected, Dr. Hughes. He'll freeze to death unless we find him. Lord, lord, he'll freeze to death! I didn't know what to do—where to look. I came straight here—straight to you. I was so upset—I even forgot to phone. Dr. Hughes, he's out in this blizzard. He ———— out the back way. I don't know, I didn't hear a th———— began running down Francis's cheeks; he was o———— hysteria. "It's my fault, sir. I'm to blame. If we car———— fore——"

"Stop it, Francis!" yelled David. "For God's sak———— went to a decanter, poured out a stiff shot of whisky———— this!"

The steward took the glass with a shaking hand, s———— drink, managed to swallow the rest.

"Now wait for me here," David said to him. "I'll ge———— on and be right with you."

He drew on his trousers over his pajamas, then————

mackinaw, rapidly telling Carol what had happened as he dressed.

"David," said Carol, "where on earth could he have gone—in this snow?"

"Not very far," grunted David. "But I've got a hunch he's gone to the observatory."

"The observatory? On a night like this? Why?"

"Don't ask me why. I don't know. It's just a hunch, and I may be wrong."

He raced downstairs, and together with Francis he plunged out into the storm.

The wind slashed at them, hammered them as they floundered through the drifts. They could see nothing before them; the murky white wall slanted in at them, blotted out their vision ten feet ahead. They saw no tracks in the snow, but that proved nothing. If Dr. Dawson had come this way ten minutes before, the snow would have already buried his footprints.

As David plowed along, his head bent against the screaming wind and his arm interlocked with Francis's, a nagging doubt began to seep through him. Perhaps the Old Man hadn't gone to the observatory at all. There would be no one there now, no work in progress, not on a night like this. Maybe he'd gone the other way, thought David desperately, down the road. There was no way of telling. They were just guessing.

The Old Man didn't know what he was doing; the loss of his wife, as Dr. Wilk had pointed out, must have driven him out of his mind. It was suicide to walk out in this damned blizzard with just pajamas and a robe. Even through his heavy mackinaw and mittens David could feel the numbing cut of the wind. If the Old Man had walked out just before Francis had awakened, if he had gone to the observatory, there was still a chance. If not . . .

He yelled at Francis to hurry, but Francis was unable to hear him over the banshee yell of the wind. The steward was gasping for breath, staggering through the snow like a drunken man, exhausted. David released his arm and stumbled forward, fighting the drifts. Like feathery straight jackets, they tried to hold him, they clung and wrapped themselves around his legs, they tried to trip him and tie him down.

And then David was in the observatory yard. The squat building loomed suddenly in front of him, like a fat gray ghost leaping up from the drifts. He scraped his hands against the rough wall, moving slowly, trying to find the door. He cursed as his fingers encountered nothing but wall. Finally, after a long minute of exploration, he found the door just as Francis came up.

The door was open. They went in, slammed the door shut against the storm, and stood gasping in the foyer, swaying in their exhaustion.

The lights were on in the foyer.

"Come on, Francis!"

David plunged ahead up the wide, curving staircase, out into the circular corridor, raced past staff quarters, the computing rooms, the darkrooms. The breath sobbed from his tortured lungs as he ran up the stairs to the mezzanine.

Finally a last short flight of rubber-covered steps and he plunged out into the main rotunda of the observatory.

Then he stopped short and stared.

The dome was open!

Stupefied, he pointed upward as Francis came panting up the steps. The wind was howling down through the open dome in an icy blast. The snow was coming in; it was snowing inside the observatory itself. The white particles slammed down gustily, as though propelled by a high-powered gun, filtering down on the floor itself, and feathering the upper part of the telescope so that a faint lace of white on the shell was already visible.

"He's here!" yelled David to Francis. "The Old Man's here, somewhere. He's opened the dome to the blizzard. It couldn't have been anyone else. He's mad, Francis, stark raving mad. But even so, he wouldn't do that unless——"

The echo of David's voice ricocheted through the dome for a moment and then clipped short. Numbly he stared into Francis's chalk-white face, and in the steward's eyes saw the same dawning suspicion, the same awful horror.

With a single accord they broke and ran for the automatic elevator leading to the upper deck and the loading bridge.

The elevator seemed to whine up and up forever. Finally it stopped, its door slid noiselessly open, and they burst through and onto the wide ring-shaped deck.

The aerial platform running to the top of the telescope was gone! That could mean only one thing.

The Old Man was up there.

He was up there at the top of the telescope, perched in the cistern of the observer's cage, exposed to the icy blast of the blizzard slamming down through the open dome.

Somewhere in the shock-twisted depths of the Old Man's mind he had chosen this fantastic way to commit suicide. Fantastic to everyone else, perhaps, but quite logical to Dr. Dawson. He had built the telescope, it was his life. He had spent many years of his life up there in that dizzy place, bundled in heavy furs. He knew how cold it could get up there.

David ran over to the panel where the push-button control for the aerial platform was located. As he yanked open the metal door the thought throbbed through his mind, *How long?*

*How long had the Old Man been sitting up there, waiting to die?*

He pressed the control button, peered up at the four slender rails arching up and curving into the darkness of the dome. But nothing happened. The monel-metal platform stayed at the top of the telescope.

The Old Man had locked the controls at the top.

David slammed the panel door shut, went back to where Francis was standing.

"What are we going to do now, sir?"

"You'd better go down and phone Dr. Wilk, Francis."

"Yes. But you——"

"I'm going up to the top by way of the handrails and get Dr. Dawson."

The steward paled. "Be careful, sir. It's dangerous now. Those rails might be slippery and——"

."I'll make it all right, Francis. You go ahead."

Outside of the flying platform, this was the only method of getting to the top of the big reflector. The handrails and narrow steps went straight up, like the ladders in the engine room of an ocean-going vessel. Finally they led to a steep iron platform on the back of the girder carrying the flying platform. It was a dizzy ascent, and with the rails wet, as they were now, it was dangerous.

David gripped the handrails, climbed gingerly, carefully, conscious of the hazard. As he went up, higher and higher, he found that he could not raise his face upward toward the dome. The storm coming straight down through the dome blinded him by its fury, slashed his face in a pin-point attack, forced him to lower his head.

He remembered stupidly, now, that neither he nor Francis in their excitement had thought of the obvious thing—to close the dome before he began his climb. The blizzard came straight down, sucking through the open dome in a powerful downdraft, and once or twice he swayed under its force and hung on desperately.

But finally the precarious steps began to level off. He was high up in the soaring steelwork now, running over the abyss, almost blinded by flying snow.

Then David was looking down into the cistern of the observer's cage.

The Old Man was sitting there in his usual place, in the little revolving seat before the instrument board.

He was sitting there, stiff and rigid, like a grotesque snow man.

The snow whipping down upon him from the open dome had covered his bowed head with a white fez. It stuck to his face, powdered his robe and pajamas, and had already drifted up above his slippered feet on the steel floor.

Looking down from his dizzy, wind-swept perch above, David Hughes knew that he had come too late.

The Old Man of the Mountain was dead.


Two weeks later, California Tech, the university administering Palomar, closed the observatory.

David wired Dr. Herrick at the Hayden Planetarium, accepting his offer to work in New York.

And then Carol's baby was born.

It was a girl, and they named her Emily.

**14.** In the last four months the Big Eye was visible both by day and night.

It did not seem to get any larger now; its approach seemed to slow. It seemed simply to hang in the sky, waiting. Now the planet was pursuing the earth, moving in the same direction, as the earth swung around its orbit to the other side of the sun.

In September the astronomers, after extensive calculations, announced that the catastrophe would occur at exactly 8 P.M., Greenwich time.

In New York and on the Atlantic seaboard, zero hour would be 3 o'clock in the afternoon.

The Eye would be in full glare upon the earth, and the end would come out of a daytime sky.

On the first of October, the Hayden Planetarium closed for the duration.

At dusk David closed his desk and gathered together the few personal effects he wanted to take back to the apartment.

He found it difficult to concentrate on what he was doing; his eye kept straying toward the window.

The Big Eye swam in a red bath high over an apartment building across the park. It would stay that way until the sun sank deep enough behind the western horizon so that the first stars would just begin to twinkle.

Then it would emerge from its bath, huge and heavy and frightening, and dominate the sky, and the stars would disappear.

For a full minute David stared at the Big Eye, unable to turn his head away.

It looked particularly malevolent at the moment. Its leer was confident and assured; its message to David was familiar and personal and intimate.

"Damn you," David suddenly blurted out hysterically. "You big red bastard, you'd like to end it right now, wouldn't you? If you had *your* way, you wouldn't wait until Christmas!"

He went to the window and viciously yanked down the blinds. The room darkened in semi-gloom, and for a moment he experienced overwhelming relief, the throbbing cleared in his head.

But then he fancied that even now, with the blinds shut, the Big Eye was still looking into his office. The reddish light was seeping in through the blinds, through the cracks and crevices, through the solid wall itself. And now the office was tinged with a weird reddish light; it reflected from the glass top of his desk, from the framed pictures, from the paneled walls.

In a kind of feverish desperation he took his hat from the rack, flung open his office door, and hurried down the corridor, through the adjacent Museum of Natural History, and finally out of the door and onto Central Park West.

The Big Eye hit down on him like a blow of a hammer. Now, in the dying light, it was beginning to take shape. He could already see the familiar leer pushing through the reddish haze.

It etched the sky line of the east side in sharp relief, and the trees in the park stood black and stark against the light. It slanted down on the road and sidewalk and ricocheted up into the eyes of the pedestrians. It glinted from automobile windshields and the glistening chrome on the radiators.

There was nothing soft about it, like the set of the sun. It was harsh and brutal and direct and unfiltered.

David hunched his shoulders in his topcoat, put his head down, and got into his car at the curb.

At Eighty-third Street he stopped at a newspaper stand. The man in the small booth was smiling broadly under the peak of his frayed cap.

"Paper, mister?"

The owner of the newsstand drew a dirty finger across the head-lines of the stacked newspapers.

"Good news for a change," he said. "Me—I can't wait for to-morrow night."

The headlines were the same in all the evening newspapers—the *Journal-American,* the *Post,* the *World-Telegram,* the *Sun.*

They were big and black and bold across the front page, and they said simply:

## CLOUDY, RAIN TOMORROW NIGHT!

Cloudy and rain. That *was* big news, front-page news. Cloudy and rain meant that the Big Eye would be blotted out for a merciful evening. It meant that the nightly pressure would be off for a few precious hours, that they would not feel the direct visual and phys-ical lash of its stare, even though they would still sense it.

Tomorrow night the streets would be crowded with people, drenched with rain, maybe, but laughing, exhilarated, buoyant in their relief.

Cloudy and rain. An eyelid closing over the Big Eye for just a little while, a little wonderful while, as it slowly revolved toward its full phase.

Cloudy and rain.

David grinned back at the man in the newsstand, bought a paper, and scanned the lead story. The weather forecasters were almost positive of overcast weather and even held out hope for an extra day of clouds or rain.

David reached his apartment building and walked into the lobby. Tom, the parchment-faced elevator man, greeted him with a grin as he opened the elevator door.

"You heard the news, Dr. Hughes?"

"Just a few minutes ago."

"I hope they're right," said Tom anxiously. "I sure hope they haven't made a mistake this time. They've been wrong before, Dr. Hughes, these weathermen."

"They'd better be right, Tom," answered David grimly. "They'd better be right."

When he came into the apartment Carol was in the kitchen, feeding the baby. Emily's curls were still wet from her bath; there was a smear of gelatin dessert on her mouth.

She gurgled and held up her arms to David.

He picked her up, swung her high in the air, and she laughed and squealed.

"Piggyback!" he said, grinning. "Piggyback!"

He held her arms around his neck, so that she hung like a sack of flour down his back, and ran into the living room. Then he lifted her clear over his head, and his daughter laughed delightedly, wriggling like a bug in his upstretched hands.

"Airplane," he told her next. "Airplane ride!"

He carried her through the living room, pressed her tiny nose against the cold windowpane, carried her into the bedroom, ran around the crib, flew her into the bathroom, dipped her deep toward the bathtub in mock ferocity.

"Dear," he heard Carol call from the kitchen, "please bring the baby back. She hasn't finished her supper."

Then as she laughed and squealed he carried her back into the kitchen. . . .

The same old wonderful ritual.

Later, when their daughter was ready for bed, he brought forth the pièce de résistance.

He picked her up and swung her back and forth, back and forth, across the bed. There was a spark of fear in the baby's eyes as he dropped her on the soft bed so that she bounced.

And then the child laughed and laughed and held up her tiny arms to David to do it again.

Finally he kissed her good night and gave her to Carol to tuck in. And there were tears in his eyes.

The same old wonderful ritual, until Christmas.

Later David Hughes lay on his back, sleepless.

The Big Eye stared through the window like a great round Peeping Tom. It was like living with your own hangman, he thought, month after month. You saw your death before you; it followed you, peered over your shoulder, hung over your head, shone through your window, like this.

Men had been executed before, he thought, but the execution had been reasonable, civilized, merciful. The condemned man never saw the chair or the noose till he was ready for it.

David turned toward his wife.

"Carol," he whispered. "Awake?"

Her hand fumbled for his in the darkness. "What is it, darling?"

"I can't sleep."

"Neither can I."

"Carol, can't we do something about that damned window? The way that thing shines in here every night, it's enough to drive anyone crazy. It's like having a third party in our bedroom every night. Why can't we get those blackout curtains that everyone else seems to have?"

"I've already ordered them, David. But they're hard to get. There's been a run on them—everybody wants them—and there are so few stores open any more. I've almost finished making drapes."

He reached over on the night table, picked up a cigarette, lighted it. They shared drags for a minute and then he said:

"Carol, are you afraid of what's coming? Are you *really* afraid?"

She was silent for a moment. Then she answered:

"I don't know, David. I was for the longest time, but now I don't know. I've thought a lot about death, and I keep wondering what it'll be like. A flash of flame? A whirling in darkness? And after that, what? How long will death be?" She hesitated. "I don't know. I guess we're like children, David, asking how long the night will be when we go to bed, because we love the daylight in which we play." Her hand tightened about his. "Darling, I think if I feel anything at all now, it's regret. Not so much for you, not for me, but for the baby."

He said nothing, and Carol went on:

"I keep thinking, David, our baby sleeping there in the crib, she'll never have a birthday party of her own, or go to school or a movie, or eat a sundae, or wear an evening gown, or have a boy friend and fall in love, and have a husband and children of her own. She'll never even have a Christmas, David, not really."

The baby whimpered in the crib.

"Oh, David!" Carol began to cry.

He rose and padded over to the crib in his bare feet and picked up his daughter. She clung to him sleepily as he took her to the bathroom. Then he carried her over to the big bed and placed her between himself and Carol.

And so they finally slept, the three of them, close to each other.

But the Big Eye, looking at them through the window, was wide awake.


In the fall of the last year the Big Eye appeared nightly as a great flaming, coppery-red sphere in the sky.

The effects of the new planet's intrusion into the solar system were gradual and cumulative.

Japan suffered tremendous earthquakes, so that its entire remaining population was evacuated to the mainland of China. Much of California was abandoned for the most part, although the shocks were not as serious. Seismologists listed earthquakes in Alaska, Lisbon, Calabria, Chile, and many other places already susceptible to disturbances in the earth's surface.

The tides were erratic and no longer could be charted. There were tidal waves in the Philippines and in the Caribbean. Acapulco, Mexico, as well as Cape Lopatka, on the southern tip of Kamchatka Peninsula, were completely inundated. The sea level rose in some coastal areas, fell in others. In the islands of Polynesia and the Coral Sea there were spectacular volcanic eruptions.

Landslides were a daily occurrence in the Swiss Alps, in the Himalayas, the Rockies, and many other mountainous areas.

All over the world the temperature dropped progressively, degree by degree, and the Big Eye loomed bigger.

In New York there had been no summer. June, July, and August became early spring or late fall, thermometer-wise.

But the most significant changes were man-made.

In the last year, goaded by the driving and demanding leer of the Big Eye, men had made some long-time dreams come true.

They had stopped making atomic bombs and instead were making atomic bullets, as tracer detectives and interbody projectiles. From the Oak Ridge laboratories, which once gave the world the most painful problem of the age, came a steady stream of radioactive isotopes.

And in August of the last year they had discovered a cure for cancer.

This was only one of the many other great achievements in the field of medicine.

By using radioactive isotopes as a means of prying open the once bolted door to the inner processes of life itself, by probing deep into the inner mysteries of the human body, they had found quick and positive cures for most of the myriad diseases of the bones, heart, tissues, nerves, and other organs, diseases which once had taken a great toll of human life.

This, the golden age of atomic medicine, was not without irony.

In the last year the *Journal* of the American Medical Association calculated that the life span of man had increased twenty years and that new medical techniques had progressed to a point where man could normally expect to live a hundred years.

The article was interesting in a wistful kind of way.

The final year had also ushered in another golden age—the age of practical atomic power.

At the Hanford laboratories in the state of Washington, which, in another era, had made plutonium for atomic bombs, the nuclear scientists had released a seething storm of neutrons from spontaneous fission in a huge atomic pile. Later they had applied this power to run ocean-going vessels, locomotives, and other great fuel-consuming machinery. The heat which was generated as a by-product from the pile was piped to great cities and used in huge central heating systems. Coal, gas, and oil became unwieldy and expensive, antique fuels to be laboriously torn from the earth. City planners drew up blueprints for generating plants whereby the householder would receive all the power he needed for a fraction of the cost he had heretofore borne.

The blueprints were pretty to look at and breath-taking in their concept. But no one thought of translating them into the practical phase. Under the circumstances, file and forget.

The Year Two was a year of peculiar phenomena in a hundred different ways.

The death rate hit a rock-bottom low.

To be sure, some people died by accident. Some were drowned, or killed by falls, or hit by vehicles, or struck by lightning. Some died in the now frequent earthquakes or tidal waves. And some still died of natural causes, despite the great advances of medicine.

But not a man, woman, or child died through war. And no man died in violence by the hand of his neighbor. Not a Jew was murdered, not a Negro lynched. Not a single person died of hunger, not even in India or China. Neither did any man, woman, or child suffer death because of exposure, or lack of medicine or medical attention.

There were no strangers left in the last year. No man held himself aloof from his neighbor on grounds of religion, caste, color, or environment. The Big Eye was blind to these differences; it was not socially selective; it was completely impartial.

Its clientele was not restricted.

In the fall of the final year, in the cities and towns and on the farms, men waited to die.

A special commission of the Federation of the World, called the World Conservation Commission, planned and enforced just enough productive activity to maintain economic life until midnight on Christmas.

Not a hammer or saw was heard anywhere, and only a few wheels turned, of necessity. The spindles and machine shafts of the factories became quiet gray forests of steel, and cobwebs grew in the gears and belting of drill presses, lathes, milling machines, and shapers.

Farmers sat on their porches at the time of the autumn harvest and looked idly across their weed-grown fields, unplanted in the spring.

There were no longer any profits to be calculated, any reserves to be accumulated, any investments to be made, any new business to anticipate. There were no bills to be sent, no debts to be collected nor credits advanced, no taxes to pay for next year, no accounts receivable.

There was simply one big Account Payable.

The world still spun on its axis, but the surface was almost motionless.

And the only sound heard upon it was the sound of prayer.

The Big Eye fattened to a great luminous globe and filled the heavens day and night and kept coming on and on. . . .

And at last Christmas came.


**15.** For some deep and illogical reason people everywhere observed Christmas in the usual fashion.

It was the last day of their lives.

Yet they were stubborn, they were perverse, they insisted on following the traditional ritual step by step.

They played at life up to the very end, desperately going through the motions as though the future were forever, finding a kind of comfort in it, in these, their last few hours.

Everything in the apartment looked the same, as it might have on any other Christmas morning.

The wreaths were on the windows, the stockings hung over the fireplace. The tree was in the corner, glittering with many-colored lights, topped by a star, speckled with silver tinsel. And beneath the tree the gaily wrapped presents.

A silk robe for David, a new wallet, a solid-gold tie clasp, an initialed cigarette lighter, a half dozen ties, a pair of fleece-lined slippers, a new electric shaver.

A jeweled wrist watch for Carol, a new handbag, a Paul Revere sterling silver bowl for the whist table, three handmade nightgowns, a new fur coat. A huge fluffy rabbit for Emily, a pair of golden-haired twin dolls.

It was warm and cozy in the room, and the snow was falling outside and piling on the sills against the frost-fingered window-panes. The last Christmas was a white Christmas.

There was the opening of the presents, the warm kisses, the embraces, the tears. There was the last breakfast, and the last careful ritual of dressing, and the last walk to church. There were the last hymns, and the sober faces, and the heads bowed in prayer, and the last sonorous sermon, the last story of Bethlehem.

It was the final day of their lives, but it was still Christmas.

There was the last dinner, turkey and stuffing and mince pie and coffee and brandy and all the fixings.

They went through all the motions with a kind of hysterical intensity, even to the salutations of "Merry Christmas . . ."

But the other part of the traditional greeting, the rest of the salutation, the "Happy New Year," was conspicuously missing.

And the clock ticked on toward three, as on any other Christmas.

It was very much the same as it had always been, yet so very different: the carols they would never sing again, the sermon they would never hear again, the tree they would never adorn again, the stockings they would never hang again, the good wishes they would never give again, the presents they gave but would never use.

It was not a Merry Christmas, and there would be no Happy New Year.

It was a pathetic kind of Christmas.

And yet it was comforting too.

At two o'clock the bells began to ring.

Slowly they rose in volume, opened their brassy mouths, swelled the cold night air with a somber and mournful symphony.

It was very near the end.

Carol stirred in David's arms.

"David."

"Yes?"

"It's time to go."

They had decided to go outside, out in the street, to die. They were going out into the open, under the sky, where they could watch the Big Eye. Already from their apartment they could hear the hum of a crowd below, like the buzz of a great swarm of bees far away.

It was easier to die outside, where they could see their executioner. Waiting for the end in the apartment was too much like dying alone. It was easier out in the street among other people, thousands of others, millions of others, packed close for warmth, for courage, for comfort, for anonymity.

It had always been easier to die en masse than alone.

They were silent for a moment there in the bedroom. They heard Emily whimper once in her nap, and then it was still again.

Still, except for the ticking of the clock on the dressing table.

And David thought: This is the last time, this is the last time I'll hold my wife in my arms like this. Soon, the last kiss, the last warm embrace, the last touch of her hand and the thrill of her skin, the last sound of her voice, the last scent of her hair, the last long look in her eyes. The last, the last of everything. This is how it is to wait to die. A poignant, rending, unbearable awareness of the last in everything, because it *is* the last. Funny, he thought, I have no fear. Only regret. Regret for what I have now, and what I shall soon lose. I haven't had enough of what I have. Yes, that's it. That's what I want and can't have. More daylight. More life, more living. More Carol, more Emily, not the last, the absolute, final last, but more, more, more. . . .

*Tick-tock, tick-tock, tick-tock, tick-tock . . .*

And Carol thought: In an hour it'll be over. And I'm not afraid, I'm not afraid, I'm not afraid. As long as David is close to me, and the baby is in my arms, I'm not afraid. I don't know. Maybe it's just because I don't believe it. In an hour I'm going to die, and I don't believe it. Maybe death is unbelievable, even to the dying. Something that happens to everyone else but not to you. Funny, about the way it feels, about going out to die. It's like leaving on a long trip. Yesterday I cleaned and scrubbed the apartment from top to bottom. Crazy-clean for the hereafter. Can't die with an untidy house. And this morning I made the beds. Can't die with the beds unmade. And I washed the dishes. Can't die with dirty dishes in the sink, even if there'll be no one around to eat from the clean ones. And I drew the blinds and fluffed the cushions in the living room and turned off the electric stove and defrosted the refrigerator. Just as though I were going away on a long trip with David and the baby and would return someday. Everything but pack the bags. But we'll never be back, we'll never be back again. I won't be back, and David won't be back, and the baby won't. The baby. Emily. I hope she sleeps in my arms, that she's asleep when it comes, when the Big Eye comes, in an hour. I wonder what she would have been like, what she would have grown up to be? Would she have grown to be sweet, and generous, and lovely, and beautiful? And the husband she'd never have, who would he have been, and what? Rich and handsome and intelligent? And the children she might have had, the grandchildren I might have had, David and I. What would they have been like? I'll never know, we'll never know. Still, I'm lucky, I'm lucky. I've had something out of life. Daughter, lover, wife, and mother. But I want more, more, more. This is the last, the very last, the last hour. And I want more, more, more. . . .

*Tick-tock, tick-tock, tick-tock, tick-tock . . .*

"It's time to go," she whispered to David. "It's time to go out there with the others. David, David, David, it's time to go."

"All right, darling."

They kissed, and embraced, and wept. Then they rose and went into the other room, where Emily was sleeping.

She was lying there, her face buried in her own curls, resting on her elbows and her knees, her buttocks arched up, as she had lain in the womb. The blankets were half off, and she clutched a doll in her two tiny fists, and the huge bunny rabbit was at the foot of the crib.

For a long time the two of them stood by the crib, looking down, watching their sleeping child by the reddish light of the Big Eye filtering through the blinds.

And then David said: "Carol, let her stay here. Let her sleep."

"No, David." Carol's eyes were wet, and the tears were in her throat. "No, David, no, no!"

"She'll never know," he whispered. "She'll be sleeping and she'll never know. Maybe it'd be better for her that way."

"No, David, no. Not alone. Not like this. Not away from me. I'll hold her close in my arms. She'll sleep. She'll go with us, David. All together. You couldn't leave her here alone. You *know* you couldn't."

"No," he said. "I guess I couldn't. It was—just that she looks so warm and happy and wonderful now—here—in the crib." He spoke brokenly now. "I—you're right, Carol. If we walked out of the door without her I'd have come back for her."

They watched her for a moment more. And the clock sounded loud in the silence:

Tick-tock, tick-tock, tick-tock, tick-tock . . .

*Hurry-hurry, hurry-hurry, hurry-hurry, hurry-hurry* . . .

"Wake her up, David," whispered Carol. "Wake her up now."

He reached out his hand, touched the child's cheek. She whimpered and then turned on her back and lifted her arms toward David. He snatched her up and pressed her close, so that she was warm and sweet against him, so that his tears stained her sleep-blushed cheek.

Carol dressed the baby warmly in a long-sleeved shirt, sweater, overalls, and snow suit.

Finally they were ready. As they opened the door they heard the insistent sound of the clock:

*Tick-tock, tick-tock, tick-tock, tick-tock . . .*

David hesitated on the threshold, stopped, and gave the baby to Carol.

Then he walked into the bedroom, and the clock stopped ticking.

After that he returned and closed the door behind him, and they went down into the red afternoon.

It had stopped snowing, and now the Big Eye shone down balefully upon the frozen city.

It was low and directly overhead, and it seemed to hang like a heavy stone on an invisible thread, filling the winter sky.

It reddened the snow and the faces of the people as they turned upward, and glared back at itself in the waters of the rivers and the sea and in the darkened windows of the cold skyscrapers.

It had a gaunt and hungry look as it waited voraciously to spring upon and devour its prey.

It was fifteen minutes to three and almost time.

There was no sound but the mournful, funereal ringing of the bells.

No vehicles moved, no horns blew, no trains roared in the paralyzed city.

There were the bells and the people, thousands upon thousands of them, thronging the sidewalks, jamming the streets, choking the park in a solid mass of silent and waiting humanity.

From the churches and temples, illuminated by the pale flicker of candles, came the wail and lamentation of prayer.

Every face was turned upward toward the Big Eye, the faces of men, women, and children, and the stamp of death was upon every one of them. There was no fear, no hysteria, only silence and resignation.

The glow became redder, the Big Eye bigger, the bells louder.

And then it was three o'clock.

The people, with a single accord, dropped to their knees in the snow and bowed their heads and prayed and waited.

The bells stopped ringing, and it was still.

A minute passed.

The Big Eye hung suspended in the sky and looked down, as though delaying a little to savor the moment.

Five minutes passed—and then ten—and fifteen.

And still the Big Eye hung in the sky.

At last a great sigh spread through the kneeling crowd, a kind of convulsive shudder. Heads that were bowed turned upward with a kind of wild, unbelieving hope.

The people started to whisper, and the whisper spread and rustled through the mob and went from one to the other, like a rippling electric shock.

Then someone shouted hysterically:

"Look at it! Look at the Big Eye!"

The shout traveled like wildfire; it was contagious, almost instantaneous; it became a wild roar, a bedlam; it possessed the crowd and gripped them and shook them, and a sea of faces turned up to look into the sky.

It seemed to them, and they swore to it afterward, that the Big Eye had stopped leering, that it had for the moment smiled.

The people knew that it would not strike, that God had stayed His hand and deflected the Big Eye and given them life again. And the people cried and wept and shouted:

"*A miracle! A miracle!*"

It was Christmas, and they had been given a miracle.

They stayed on their knees and prayed.

An hour later the flash came from the Harvard Observatory, the official clearing center for all astronomical data.

The planet, Planet "Y," the Big Eye, was passing on into the eternity of space, away from the earth. The astronomers professed bewilderment. They could not account for it: the Big Eye had betrayed their calculations and their charts. In time, perhaps, they might have a logical explanation for this extraordinary phenomenon.

But the people knew that it was Christmas and that God had given them a miracle.

They knew He had been pleased with what they had wrought in the last two years, the new and better world they had made.

As the crowds began to dissolve and move homeward, as the bells rang in deafening clamor, as the people laughed and shouted and prayed and wept and embraced each other, amid the roar and clamor and the wild hysteria, David Hughes heard the calm voice of Dr. Dawson on that night in the Old Man's study, when he had first known about the Big Eye:

*"I can only say this, try to console you with this, David. You must have faith—faith in a miracle—another miracle—a miracle of redemption."*

**16.** The world had been caught short by the miracle. It had not expected any future and had not prepared for it. Only by the most drastic measures and by strict rationing of food supplies was it able narrowly to avert a global famine.

As the months passed into the year 1963 the Big Eye grew smaller and smaller.

As it spun off into the void its circumference shrank, and the Eye itself began to blur in its outline.

It no longer hovered directly overhead and followed people about, bowing them down with its weight and paralyzing them with its baleful stare.

Yet people knew that it was still watching them, that it would be watching them long after it had disappeared into the sky.

They had seen the miracle, and they knew that the Big Eye, wherever it was or would be, would always be watching them.

And the effect of this knowledge upon them was profound.

There were pessimists who predicted a return to the old patterns, the old folkways and mores, the old way of life. It was all over now, they said; the predatory instincts of men would come to the surface again; they would rebound from their idealistic stupor and be themselves again.

It was bound to come again, they said. The world government would slowly disintegrate, and nations would build up the fences they had torn down. There was profit to gain now, and power, and prestige. Men would go back to the luxury of hating each other again, indulging in their pet prejudices, reviving their favorite whipping boys again.

A Jew would become a dirty Jew again, and different-from-us; a Negro, a lousy nigger again, and different-from-us; a capitalist, a fat, blood-sucking son of a bitch again, and different-from-us; a Communist, a goddamn atheistic Red, and different-from-us. There would be wops and spicks and greaseballs and squareheads and Chinks, and all of them different-from-us.

It had to happen that way, the pessimists said. The Big Eye was going away, and now the sky was the limit again.

There'd be customs again, and passports, and tariffs and identification cards, and classifications, race, color, creed. There'd be restricted areas and selected clienteles, and they'd build new railroad tracks where they had torn up the old ones, with a right side and a wrong side. There'd be cliques and cartels and monopolies and black marketeers and labor racketeers and profiteers all over again. The rich would get richer and the poor poorer, as they did in the good old days.

The instincts of men ran pretty deep, and they were very tenacious, the pessimists said. In time they would again rise and assert themselves. And one day, they even predicted, men would contrive to go to war again.

But somehow the people did not listen to the pessimists.

They had seen the miracle, and they remembered, and they were grateful.

And they started up the machinery again and went right on living in the same old new world they had fashioned, after the Big Eye had first been seen at Palomar.

It was October of 1963, and David sat in the Old Man's study at Palomar.

Three months before, California Tech had reopened the Observatory. They began negotiations for a new director and in the interim offered David the post of chief research astronomer until the permanent appointment was made.

David had accepted the offer and moved back to Palomar with his family.

Now he turned to the task of sifting through Dr. Dawson's voluminous papers and personal memoranda.

David had spent a few hours each day opening the bulky manila envelopes in the files, sifting out the notes and correspondence, and segregating material for the observatory library.

He went through folder after folder, reading, fascinated. The correspondence was, in effect, a biography of the Old Man's life. His student life at Harvard, then as a young professor, his career on the *Astrophysical Journal*, his invasion of the National Academy of Science when still a young man, a brilliant child in a learned and aged society.

There was much of his trips abroad and his awe at viewing Galileo's telescope in the museum at Florence. He had written in a letter to his wife how he had wanted to look through Galileo's little telescope, and the authorities had flatly refused him the privilege. Then an Italian astronomer, Abetti, had interceded and persuaded the museum people to go along. An so the Old Man had carried the telescope, like a priceless diamond, to the Arcetri Observatory. And there he had fixed it to the equatorial mount.

"I waited for the night to come, Emily," wrote the Old Man. "It seemed years—centuries—before the sun went down. But then at last the stars came out one by one. If I ever lived for any moment, my dear, this was the moment. I cannot describe my sensations when I grasped the same tube that Galileo had grasped. My hands rested where his hands had rested—my eye was against his eyepiece, where his eye had been. And then I saw what he had seen —three hundred years ago.

"There it was, Emily, high in the south, the same Jupiter the old master had seen on that first voyage of man through the void of astronomical space. And the four moons, a string of bright diamonds, hugging the mother planet close, just as Galileo had seen them. Clear—and wondrous—and beautiful—and mystic. I have seen Jupiter a hundred times, Emily darling, through every kind of telescope, but just then I felt the same awe that Galileo must have felt. I felt that I had seen Jupiter for the first time. I felt uplifted and humble at the same time, and I think I even wept."

There was more. The Old Man's battle with industrial tycoons and wealthy patrons of the sciences to put up money for Palomar. The skeptics, the critics, the men who said the 200-inch reflector couldn't be done and called it a crazy dream. The faith that turned the dream into the biggest telescope in the world. The heart-breaking technical problems—the eternal grinding of the great lens, interrupted by the war in the forties; the problems of the mount and the supports.

And finally the dedication in 1948.

As David took up the last big folder, marked "Current," a slip of paper fell from it and dropped on the floor of the office.

He leaned over, picked it up, and was about to insert it back into the folder. But something about it caught his eye. It was a piece of scrap paper, and on it were rough drawings and notations.

Probably something the Old Man forgot to throw away, thought David. It didn't seem to belong with these letters, these documents.

Then he stared at it, and his mouth dropped open and the room began to spin around.

He read it again and again.

The discovery began like a whisper, then swelled up and burgeoned out through his brain and mushroomed through his nerve centers and grew and grew, louder and louder, until it was like the beat of a hammer inside his skull, until he trembled uncontrollably.

After a long time, in the haze of his reeling mind, he thought of Dr. Ellender. Ellender, his old professor, Ellender at the Harvard Observatory, *he* would know!

Ellender had been one of the astronomers the Old Man had called in on that fateful conference before they had announced the coming of the Big Eye.

*Ellender would know the truth.*

He stuffed the scrap of paper into his pocket, got Carol on the phone.

"Pack my bag, Carol," he said. "I've got to take a plane to Boston right away!"

Dr. Ellender looked at the scrap of paper on his desk for a long time.

It was a diagram in pencil of the Big Eye—of Planet "Y"—and the earth.

And underneath the Old Man had written in crooked lines, almost as though he had been doodling:

*Planet "Y" and earth. Closest Christmas, 1962.*

*Cosmic clash close—close, but not quite.*

*Lie—hoax—hoax—will it work? Must work—world at stake —must work—must. . . .*

Ellender sank heavily back in his chair.

"Then you know, David," he said finally. "Then you know."

David nodded.

"Where did you find this piece of paper?"

"In a file of Dr. Dawson's correspondence, sir. It must have been put there by mistake."

"Yes," said Ellender slowly. "We were sure we destroyed all data. In fact, we burned all our notations and diagrams—the true ones—that night."

There was silence for a while. Ellender's gray eyes searched

David's, his eyes probing deep. He saw the demand in the younger man's eyes, the burning desire to *know*.

"Sit down, David," he said finally.

Ellender lit a cigar very deliberately, waved out the match, and dropped it in an ash tray. Then he leaned back in his chair, fingering the piece of paper on his desk, as though searching for a way to begin.

"I'll have to tell you, David," he said. "I'll have to tell you the whole story now. You know something now, but not enough. In this case—a little knowledge is a dangerous thing." Ellender paused a moment. "Later on, when I've finished, you'll know why."

"Yes?"

"Back in the beginning, back in November of 1960, I received a phone call at the observatory at Harvard. It was Dr. Dawson calling from Palomar. He told me of his new discovery and asked me to come to Palomar at once. Naturally, this was sensational news. I dropped everything else and took the first plane out that I could get."

"Then you didn't know about the path of Planet 'Y' when he phoned, Dr. Ellender?"

"No. Not then. It was only when we gathered at the conference that night that Dr. Dawson broke the news. It was then we learned that Planet 'Y' would just miss crashing into the earth on its heavenly journey. Dr. Dawson insisted on our checking his calculations to make sure that he was right, that it *would* miss."

Dr. Ellender fell silent for a moment. Then he put down his cigar and said quietly:

"It was then, David, that Dr. Dawson asked for our collaboration in a gigantic hoax."

David leaned forward, his eyes riveted on Ellender's immobile face.

"You mean, to misinform the world—to tell people that Planet 'Y' and the earth *would* meet?"

"Yes. I'll never forget Dr. Dawson then, David, as he stood up and began to speak. His eyes blazed, and there was the look in them

—well, of a prophet. He told us that this was our chance, the only chance to save the world from destroying itself. It was a heaven-made opportunity, he said, to save men from their own folly, from blowing themselves up with atomic bombs." Ellender's face was rapt. "We listened. We sat there without stirring, and listened. Dr. Dawson went on. He pointed out that this, this objective, was worth everything, the complete sacrifice of our scientific integrity, everything. Our duty now was not to truth, but to humanity. We who sat there, we astronomers, knowing what we knew, had the power to save the world. It meant that we had to lie to the world and deceive it. It meant that we had to enter into a great conspiracy."

"I see."

"Of course the proposal stunned us. In effect, we were being asked to participate in a great and colossal lie. But then Dr. Dawson pointed out that we, as scientists, could not afford to let things slip out of our hands this time. We could not afford to make the same mistake as the nuclear scientists who had failed to weigh the social consequences of their discovery and had given the atom over into irresponsible hands. War was imminent. The first bombs might drop at any moment. We had to act fast. And we did."

Now, out of the mist of David's memory, came something Dr. Dawson had said to Professor Kellar that night at the Big House. Now it was clear, now it added up. He heard the voice of the Old Man again:

*"Professor Kellar, I am an astronomer. My worlds are universes. I use giant telescopes to study them. Should I then condescend to turn to a microscope and study the microbes on my own pitiful planet? The answer is yes. And again, yes. Perhaps I am lacking in nobility, in the pure scientist's approach that the truth is the thing, and damn the consequences. But I believe our first responsibility is to the people with whom we live."*

David heard Ellender as he went on:

"And so we released the joint announcement that there would be a cosmic clash on Christmas Day of 1962 the date when the two planets would be nearest each other. We knew the consequences of such an announcement would be staggering, its effect shattering. We knew that there would be suicides, that few if any children would be born. But on the scales, the cost in human life was trivial compared to that of an atomic war."

David stirred. "How did you know some research astronomer— some man who wasn't present there that night—would not rise to dispute your calculations on the basis of his own?"

"We took a chance on that, David," answered Ellender. "And it was a desperate gamble. But the margin of difference was so small —almost infinitesimal—that even a crack research astronomer might have doubted his own figures. And we counted on Dr. Dawson's prestige and our own to add weight to our conclusion. As it turned out, we were lucky."

"And so you kept the secret within the group? You didn't extend the conspiracy to anyone else?"

"No. We entered a solemn pact, David, that we would tell no one, not even those close to us, not even our immediate colleagues, not even our own wives. That is why Dr. Dawson did not tell his wife of the lie we had created, and that is why he did not tell you. We knew that if the truth of our hoax ever got beyond our own small circle it would somehow leak out and spread, and that would be the end. A secret like this, we reasoned, was too big, too important, to hide for very long. Its possession, under the pressure of the Big Eye, under the stresses and strains it would bring about, would be almost unbearable. Only we would know it, we decided that night, only we would live with it. And when we died, it would die with us."

Now David remembered the Old Man on the night Emily Dawson had died. Dr. Dawson knew, and he might have saved his wife by assuring her that there was a future to fight for, and live for, but he had kept silent. He had kept silent and watched her die, and it had been too much for him. And so he had gone to the top of the telescope to die. But even when his mind had gone, he had kept the secret and died with it.

Dr. Ellender was watching David steadily. Finally he rose and began to pace the floor.

"Well, David, now you know. Now—you know everything. You discovered our hoax by accident, and now you are one of us."

"Yes."

"Now," continued Ellender, "we have seen an exciting new world come to pass in the last two years. Now that the Big Eye is passing away, almost every second woman on the street is bearing a child; a new generation will be born. Our hope is that as the elders die out the old concepts of greed and power will die with them, while they are still under the influence of the miracle. Then the new generation, trained in the concepts of this new world, and never knowing any other, will take it on from there."

Ellender turned to the desk, picked up the slip of paper, and handed it to David.

"Well, David, that's all," said Ellender quietly. "I ask only this of you. Say nothing of our conspiracy to anyone—not even your own wife. Take what you know to the graveyard, as we will. Let the people go on believing that they have seen a miracle. If they ever find out the truth they will be disillusioned. They will go back to building atom bombs, to their prejudices and ancient fears, to wars and the same old destructive insanity. Let them believe that they were saved from the Big Eye only by divine will. Let them believe that they have been given a last chance—to make good. Let them have their miracle."

David nodded. He shook hands with the shaggy, gray-eyed man and then walked out along the corridor to the observatory door.

As he stood on the threshold his eye strayed up toward the heavens.

The Big Eye was still there, but it was a pin point now, and very far away.

Slowly David Hughes reached into his pocket, took out the piece of paper, tore it into shreds, and threw the fragments into the wind.

Then he walked out into the night.